BERNARD RAFFA

SECRETS
OF THE
LOUVRE

A NOVEL

LEGACY
POND
PRESS

ISBN 13: 978-1-64343-860-3
Library of Congress Catalog Number: 2021922875
Printed in the United States of America
First Printing: 2022
26 25 24 23 22   5 4 3 2 1

Book design and typesetting by Dan Pitts

Legacy Pond Press
939 Seventh Street West
Saint Paul, MN 55102
(952) 829-8818

PREFACE

I WROTE THIS BOOK because I was enchanted with the great and majestic Louvre Museum in Paris, having visited it on a number of occasions during my lifetime. The Louvre, with its old building and new additions, invokes one's imagination about who has occupied it since it was first built in the year 1200. Without a doubt, there are thousands of stories to be told about what took place within those walls—not just about the people and events, but about the beautiful antiquities, sculptures, and master art treasures that have passed through the thresholds of those buildings over the generations. One can only imagine if those walls could talk and share with us the intrigues, the tragedies, and, of course, the historical decisions that have taken place there. It is worth one's time to research and visit the Louvre. The number of exhibitions and periods of art will stimulate your desire to broaden your knowledge of the great master works of the world and the people who created them.

The characters of this book are fictional, but the story is based on historical events and real people. Some of these people are infamous, well-documented criminals who lived during World War II. I have integrated into my story many historical facts to pique your curiosity and intensify your desire to read this historical mystery.

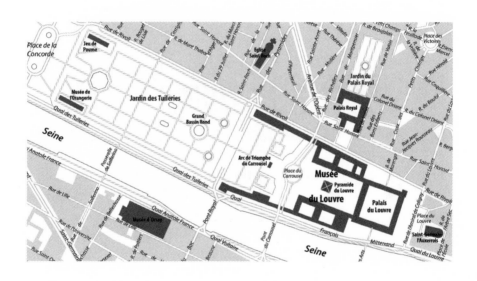

CHAPTER 1

PARIS HIT-AND-RUN

He felt the weight of his body pressing down into a bed as he slowly drifted in and out, riding the crest of a dream. He could hear, but he couldn't see. Nor could he move a muscle. *Am I alive*, he thought, *or in limbo*? Whatever limbo was.

He heard voices whispering in the darkness, but he couldn't understand them. They sounded faint and scratchy, as though stuck between radio stations. He smelled something sweet and stinging. *Maybe disinfectant*? As he began to doze off again, he thought, *I can hear. I can smell. I can think. I must be alive, but where*?

His mind was a void.

"Can you hear me, Antone . . . ?" A gentle voice stirred him awake and he felt pain, lots of it, all over his body. It was excruciating. "Antone? Can you hear me?"

He tried to speak, but nothing came out. His throat was sore as hell. *Why can't I move*? It felt like his body was in a straitjacket. He could breathe, but his breath was shallow. His chest hurt. His head hurt. Every damn part of him hurt.

Who is Antone? he thought, dozing off again.

The same scene kept repeating itself, adding more and more questions but offering no answers, only the same soothing voice, gently urging him to respond. "Antone, try to stay with me."

He stirred awake and knew time had passed. He had no idea how long. Something was slowly sliding, being removed from his throat. It felt like a piece of sandpaper, coarse and rough and harsh. His throat was too dry to swallow. It seemed impossible. He nearly gagged and tried again. He couldn't remember the last time he'd swallowed. His throat seemed so dry it would crack.

"Be careful, his jaw is broken," said the soft, pleasant voice. "We had to pin it in several places." With the sandpaper gone, he felt relief.

"He tries to talk," said someone else, "but his voice is so garbled it just sounds like a tired frog."

"Please stop trying to speak," interjected the woman with the beautiful voice—perhaps a nurse? "You have been making great progress. I'm not sure you can hear me or even understand what I am saying, but we need a way to communicate. It will help us to speed your recovery."

He heard the intermittent beeps and the steady drone of machines.

"I've given this problem some thought," said the woman. "Your injuries were so severe, you've been immobilized. To heal your head and eye requires absolute stillness. Your left leg is also broken in two places. It's in a cast. Can you wiggle the toes of your right foot? Move your foot up and down twice to answer yes. I know it's simple, but it's all we've got . . . "

Antone was slow to react. He'd been lying still so long it took a concerted effort to command his muscles to act. He moved his right foot up and down twice, indicating *yes*.

She spoke to him softly and slowly. "You've heard me? You understand?" He moved his foot again and he heard a squeal of delight. He felt a soft, warm touch on his foot. It was the gentle squeeze of her hand.

"Okay," said the soft voice, "to answer no, move your foot side to side." He did so and she clapped. "Oh, how wonderful!" she exclaimed. "Now, we must bring you up to speed on your physical condition." He heard the rustle of papers and imagined a clipboard. "I only want you to listen," she said.

"My name is Alana Muller and I'm the trauma nurse who's been by your side since the moment you arrived. Everyone here in the hospital has been cheering for you. Honestly, no one thought you had a chance. It was a daily battle to keep you alive. You've made tremendous progress, but you're not out of the woods."

Alana sighed and continued. "Your head injuries have been the most difficult to diagnose. Your doctors will give you more details next week, after your brain scans have been completed. For now, the most important part of your healing process is rest. Do you understand?"

He "nodded" his right foot twice.

"You don't know how wonderful it is for us to see this progress," said Alana. "God has most certainly been by your side."

CHAPTER 2

THE GIFTED CONSERVATOR

Hans Muller was a quiet, introverted fellow who owned a small, but prosperous, art shop in a Jewish neighborhood in the 19th arrondissement of Paris. He'd never been a large man, but after five decades spent hunched over canvases, his frame now seemed even smaller. Perhaps it was the way his back never fully straightened when he finally stood up or the way he seemed to make himself shrink deferentially when he admired a beloved masterpiece.

He specialized in the Old Masters, the highly skilled European painters who worked between the Renaissance and about 1800. Hans was highly regarded for his discriminating eye and the superior quality of his meticulous work. Though he'd never attended art school, over the years he had honed his skills to perfection. He'd mastered the art and science of mixing traditional pigments, commanding the forces of light and shadow, and rendering 3D perspective on a two-dimensional surface. With this knowledge and his skill, he was able to copy, repair, and bring antique paintings back to life.

This he attributed to his early studies as a young apprentice, working for his father and grandfather who were also both master restorers. With their endless patience and careful guidance, Hans had learned the various brushstrokes and other nuanced techniques used by certain artists, at certain times and places, throughout the fifteenth, sixteenth, and seventeenth centuries.

Shortly after World War II, he'd come to realize *the real money* wasn't in selling his own humble paintings, but in repairing the highly prized pieces of rich collectors and museums. For three generations now the Muller family had done this kind of painstaking work, establishing a long list of clients from all over Europe.

Over the decades, Hans's father and grandfather had amassed quite a collection of their own and discreetly become quite wealthy. Unfortunately, much of that collection was either destroyed or looted by the Nazis during the war. Even so, Hans had been known over the years as an intuitive, gifted conservator who could always be trusted to keep his clients' identities secret—an invaluable skill in the tightly knit art world where discretion was a must. Though he'd never advertised or gone out of his way to find work, his backlog kept growing and growing, eventually helping Hans to gain back much of the family wealth.

Prior to their displacement, the Muller family had lived on the outskirts of Berlin, not far from Charlottenburg. Somehow, most of the family survived *Kristallnacht,* the nights of terror when Nazi forces looted and burned Jewish shops, and—thanks to Hans's exceptional skill—managed to avoid being sent to a concentration camp. Eventually, Hans managed to escape his Nazi captors in 1944, when the Allied air force conducted their massive bombing raids on major German cities.

Hans and his wife Elsa had been living and working in the Berlin train station, essentially under house arrest, their children sent abroad. Elsa was killed in the bloody chaos when the nearby railyard was bombed. During the fire and confusion, Hans managed to escape, but his wife did not. Eventually, he made his way to France with a handful of art supplies and his grandfather's prized black ledger.

Now in his mid-seventies, Hans rarely, if ever, worked on typical art restoration projects. Instead, he sold the works of younger, contemporary artists on consignment at his shop. Luckily, his grand-daughter was a nurse who worked irregular hours in the hospital trauma unit, so she helped out whenever she could. She was there most Saturdays and intermittently throughout the week.

Occasionally, Hans still conducted assessments that required his discerning eye and peerless expertise. These were for higher profile, extremely wealthy collectors, museum directors and important curators throughout Paris. With over half a century of experience and firsthand knowledge of numerous masterpieces, Hans was able to identify with remarkable precision the specific time period in which a painting was made. He intuitively understood the various practices and techniques that artists had used in different geographic regions over the past three hundred years. Given this astonishing talent, he was often asked to assess a piece's authenticity or perform difficult repairs. Since the mid-1950s, reputable museums and private collectors demanded their own independent assessment of any historical piece before they would buy it at auction or even directly from another collector.

Over the years, Hans had attended countless gallery openings in both a professional and personal capacity. Often, he was paid to provide advice on a work's authenticity, condition, previous restorations, and recommendations for preservation. Many of his closest friends and clients currently worked as directors or curators at prominent Paris museums and other world-renowned museums in Europe.

In his old age, however, Hans's desire to travel and attend art exhibitions had dwindled. Consequently, he only traveled elsewhere in Europe a few times each year. Instead, he confined himself to his favorite Paris museums: the Louvre, the Musée d'Orsay, and occasionally, the Musée Picasso. His passion and interest lay with specific mid-century artists like Renoir, Cézanne, and Le Douanier. Most of the time, his curiosity only roused when one of these artists' works was displayed or a museum unveiled an Old World painting previously believed to have been lost or destroyed during the war.

CHAPTER 3

THE PATIENT SURVIVES MAJOR TRAUMA

Antone awoke to a flurry of activity around him. His mind was clear today and he had been slowly gaining some of his memory back. Still unable to speak coherently, however, he forced himself to raise his right arm to get someone's attention. Having done so, he was greeted by the angelic voice that been watching over him.

"I have good news today," said the nurse, moving closer to his bed. "Your MRI and CAT scan results have been reviewed by your doctors. They are here to remove the bandages from your head and eyes to give you a prognosis." He felt her soft, reassuring hand gently touch his shoulder. "Be calm and try to be patient," she said. "Your right eye has sustained minor damage. They will look at that one first. We've kept it covered mainly to eliminate any strain you might have put on your left eye. I'm sorry to say, that one had significant trauma."

He heard the scuffle of shoes on the floor.

"Antone, I am Dr. Juan LaPlaint," said an authoritative male voice. "I'm a brain surgeon. With me is Dr. Louis Rouen, a well-known and highly skilled ophthalmologist."

"Hello, Antone," said another male voice.

"We've been attending to your injuries since the first day you arrived," said Dr. LaPlaint. "Your case has been quite complicated due to the type and location of injuries you sustained. These injuries required back-to-back surgeries on your brain and left eye." The doctor sighed. "Along with internal bleeding and some small punctures in your lungs, well, quite frankly, no one thought you'd survive. Alana, please remove the patient's head bandages."

Alana, he thought, *what a beautiful name for this angel who has been attending to all my needs.* He tried to say it out loud, but his lips barely moved.

"We've dimmed the lights," she said, soothingly, "but it's still going to be quite a shock. Try to breathe deeply and slowly and let your eyes adjust."

Alana slowly began to remove his bandages. All he could think about was the nurse's soothing, melodic voice and how well she'd cared for him throughout this terrible ordeal. Her gentleness, her concern... *Who is she?* he wondered.

She unwound the last layer of gauze and he scanned the room, slowly acclimating himself to the light. He'd half expected to see a real angel. After all, this incredible woman had nursed him through life-threatening trauma these past several . . . days? Weeks? Months? "Are you okay?" asked the nurse.

Antone's voice warbled and cracked, but he heard himself answer, "Yes."

The shades were drawn and the lights were dim, but he could see her facial form slowly take shape. Their eyes met and Antone smiled, his eyes welling with tears.

"This is a very positive sign," she said, with confidence. Antone tried to speak, if nothing else, just to thank her, but the words stuck in his throat. Suddenly he was aware that his jaw was wired shut. *How can I respond to her kindness?* Frustrated, he wondered how a ventriloquist speaks and projects his voice without moving his mouth. If only he had those talents. How badly he wished to thank this earthly angel—and everyone in the room—for the precious gift of life.

"Good morning," said Dr. Rouen, "I performed surgery on your left eye. Before we get into your physical exam, I'm sure you must have dozens of questions. Nurse Muller has been coordinating your care from the start, so she will walk you through everything we know. Alana?"

"Antone, do you remember anything from the accident . . . ?"

Antone signaled *no*.

"Very well," said Alana, "I will tell you all that I know. Most importantly, the impact on your car was so severe that the side airbag only provided minimal protection." She glanced down at the floor to regather herself. "As a result, your eye was dislodged from its socket. The swelling in your brain also put enormous pressure on your skull. We had no choice but to induce a coma. Dr. LaPlaint and I faced these compounding problems and decided which to tackle first."

"Your life was at stake," said Dr. LaPlaint. Antone could see how much Alana was struggling to continue, but she persisted.

"Forsaking the possibility that you could lose your left eye," she said, haltingly, "the operation on your skull was done first. Thankfully, this released the pressure on your brain and probably saved your life."

"Needless to say, the brain is a very delicate organ," said Dr. LaPlaint in his deep, authoritative voice. "It was our first order of business and it turned out to be the right decision," he said, gently putting his hand on Antone's shoulder. "Tragic as it may be, your life—indeed, the quality of your life—is more important than eyesight. Your brain is damaged," the doctor continued, "but we believe it's minor. Your memory may be affected, and you will need to relearn many of even the simplest tasks. Do you understand what I have said, Antone?"

He managed to get out a garbled "*Yes*."

"Good, then let's proceed, nurse," said Dr. LaPlaint.

Alana stepped forward and began to unwind the last remaining bandage.

"Before the nurse removes your final bandage," said Dr. Rouen, "I need you to close your other eye. Slowly now . . . " Antone did as told and the world went black. "Okay," Rouen continued. "I want you to slowly open your eyelids, keeping them partially closed. Can you tell me what you are seeing and experiencing visually? Is it blurriness? Open both of your eyes fully now. Do you feel dizzy?"

Antone signaled *yes.*

"Your left eye is still very bloodshot," said Dr. Rouen. "That's completely normal at this point, considering what you've gone through." The doctor leaned in and examined his eye. "The cornea, iris, pupil, and lens look like they've not been damaged," he said. "This is very good news. The arteries and veins also look okay. Nonetheless, I strongly recommend you wear an eyepatch or sleep mask at night and when you nap. No reading either, for now. Avoid any kind of eye strain and quick or jerky head movements. Based on what I see, however, you should have no visual impairment. I'll continue to monitor your progress for the next couple of weeks and then we'll further examine your inferior rectus muscles, which control eye movements, as well as your optic nerve. This will require some special equipment to look behind your eyes. We'll have to move you to do that, but we'll do it as soon as we can."

Finished with his exam, Dr. Rouen instructed Alana to rebandage Antone's left eye. "You can start mild physical therapy tomorrow on your right arm and leg to prevent atrophy," said Dr. Rouen, "but absolutely no vigorous exercise. You need to rest and heal. Those nerves and muscles are delicate. We need to prevent further trauma."

I am now half of a man, thought Antone. *Will I ever be able to make myself whole again?*

CHAPTER 4

INVITATION TO THE LOUVRE'S SPECIAL ART

Dear Mr. Muller,

You are cordially invited to the Louvre for a new presenting of paintings, sculptures, and other works from the 15th - 17th centuries. This exhibition includes several items from France's National Collection and others formerly scattered in private collections, as well as the Musée Rodin and the Musée d'Orsay. There will be private viewing of the newly discovered works, some of which have never been on public display until now. A selection of sculptures, paintings, and tapestries will be auctioned off at a later date.

Handwritten at the bottom was a personalized postscript:

Dear Hans,

I hope you can find time to attend this gathering. There will be a special viewing the day before the one noted on the invitation. I will

*be hosting this event for major donors, local artists, and VIPs. Please
be my guest.*

Cordially,
Louvre Director Jean Pierre Rolland

Hans was delighted to receive this invitation. He hadn't been to a new
exhibition for some time. He was nearly overcome by a wave of exhilaration, in fact. He wondered how old the paintings were. From
which countries? From which artists? Most importantly, from whose
collections? He thought of the hundreds of pieces he and his father
had restored for museums and private owners. *Might some of these
paintings bear the hallmarks of my father's work? Or perhaps, even my own?
Have they stood the test of time, or have they aged even further?*

Hans was so excited he knew he must respond right away.

To my friend Jean Pierre,

*I received your wonderful invitation. I would be thrilled to attend. If
possible, I have but one request. My beautiful granddaughter Alana
is a trauma nurse at a renowned Paris hospital. She is very special to
me. I have been pleading with her since she was a little girl to attend
the university and study art. As a young girl, she exhibited a great
deal of natural talent. She also won numerous awards for her cre-
ativity and expert techniques, which seemed well beyond her years.
I believe she has all the innate skills of a world-class artist: visual
perception, steadiness of hand, a wonderful sense of color, and the
ability to capture the essence of the subject matter. She only lacks the
passion. Perhaps all the tragedies that have occurred in the Muller
family over the past three generations have dissuaded her from making a career in this field.*

*At the moment, art restoration and painting are definitely not part
of her agenda. However, she does share the love of art with me and
has studied many of the great masters. She even works for me at the
shop part time. My intention has always been to leave the bulk of my
art collection to her, as well as pass on my business. She is my only*

biological heir. Perhaps attending this new and exciting exhibition will nudge her to reexamine her future in the art world. Hopefully, these new works will excite her and move her towards carrying on the legacy of the Muller family business.

Very truly yours,
Hans Muller

CHAPTER 5

THE AGREEMENT

The Louvre was first built as a fortress in the twelfth century by King Philip II, its architecture similar to many European fortresses of that era. Subsequent wings and rooms were added over the years, along with countless art treasures from the many kings and monarchs who used it as a palace. The final major design was completed in 1850.

The result was a huge, sprawling complex shaped like tuning fork with additional wings on both sides. The building stood four stories high, with basements and sub-basements below. With millions of art treasures from all over the world, it remained one of the most popular tourist destinations not only in France, but all of Europe.

The Louvre's unrivalled collection contained some of the world's most famous and beautiful works of art. Among them were the paintings *Mona Lisa*, by Leonardo da Vinci, and *The Lacemaker*, by Johannes Vermeer, which Renoir dubbed a masterpiece. The sculpture collection included the world-famous *Venus de Milo* and *The Winged Victory of Samothrace*, both over two thousand years old.

It had rained the night before the special gallery opening and the streets were still wet. It was spring and early in the morning of a midweek day. A curious blend of odors that had been trapped in winter's icy grip for months were drifting up from the pavement as the morning sun worked its magic of evaporation. The car- and people-traffic was light, so Hans and Alana decided to stop and have an espresso at a small coffee shop near the Louvre.

At a table outside, invigorated by the spring sun, their discussion reverted to the topic of Alana taking over the shop. Like always, Alana told her grandfather about her schedule at the hospital, especially busy recently; she'd been attending to a patient transferred from her trauma ward to the rehabilitation center. The man had barely survived a horrible truck accident. She helped save his life and was determined to keep working with him until he'd fully recovered.

"He is a bit of a mystery man," she told her grandfather. She paused and sipped her espresso. "Aside from his passport, all his identification papers, computer, cell phone—everything—were lost when his car caught fire." Then she told her grandfather what he least wanted to hear. "The poor man is all alone. He doesn't have anyone who can help him." She glanced away for a moment, then looked at Hans. "I'll have to give up working in the shop for a while." Naturally, Hans was quite disappointed.

They came to an agreement that once they got inside the museum, they would go their separate ways. Alana would wander around the permanent collection and Hans would go straight to the special exhibition.

Of course, Alana was very familiar with the Louvre, having been there numerous times with her grandfather. As she wandered its cavernous halls, her mind returned to the hospital and her mysterious patient, Antone. Physically, he'd made good improvements. His leg cast had been removed and he was progressing well with his muscle therapy.

His left eye was on the mend, but he still felt dizzy much of the time. This was very apparent when they took short walks. With only one eye functioning, his perception and balance caused him to walk erratically and he was prone to falling. A broken hip would not be good at this point, so he required her full attention throughout his workouts.

Thankfully, Antone's speech was much more discernible. Recently, he'd figured out how to talk without moving his jaw. "I'm a ventriloquist," he joked. With improved communication, Alana found herself developing a strong bond with her patient. She was now determined to stay by his side until he fully recovered.

The strange, disconcerting thing was his lack of long-term memory. He asked her daily about who he was. She had shown him his French passport repeatedly. He acknowledged the information but looked quite confused. The brain surgeon who attended him ran additional tests to further diagnose his condition, but as of this week the results were still inconclusive.

CHAPTER 6

PHYSICAL, BUT NO MENTAL RECOVERY

Over the weeks of his recovery, Antone's most frequent thoughts centered on how to thank all the people who had saved his life, from the person who dragged him out of his demolished truck before it started on fire, to the medics who rushed him to the hospital by ambulance—not to mention the numerous doctors who had attended to the myriad mental and physical issues he'd faced throughout his ordeal.

And of course, his angel, Alana.

There was something so beautiful and special about all these unselfish, dedicated people. He could never repay them, but how could he thank them . . . ?

Other times he tried to remember his past—his youth, his schooling, his teen years and early adulthood, but there was nothing. All he recalled were the events that had taken place since he'd come out of his coma weeks ago.

He wanted to believe he was truly Antone La Rue, but something didn't feel right. He'd seen his passport. His address was verified by the local police. The building manager had seen him many times, coming and going from "his" apartment. All of his other belongings, however, had been burned to ash in the fire; his phone, his laptop, his briefcase—everything. All he had was an address.

Alana had followed up with the police to gather any other information they might have about the accident, but there wasn't much. She was told it was a hit-and-run, with no witnesses and no leads. The police gave her the distinct impression they had better things to do.

If only I could remember something, anything, thought Antone. *Even the smallest scrap of information might trigger my memory.* The doctors said he would get better, but when? He wasn't well enough to leave the rehabilitation center on his own, but when that day finally came, who would be there to help him?

CHAPTER 7

OLD MASTER, WHERE HAVE YOU BEEN?

The gallery space was quite large. Hans remembered what Jean Pierre said before they parted the day before: "Be sure to locate the new paintings, which were thought to be lost or destroyed during the war. I would like to get your opinion about their authenticity, condition, and value."

This feels good, Hans thought to himself. *This is my domain, my field of expertise. This will be an interesting challenge.* Excited, he focused on the work, made careful notes to review later with Jean Pierre, and the rest of the world melted away.

Suddenly, he found himself standing in a secluded area near the last exhibition room. Even from a distance, one of the exhibit's major paintings caught his eye. He drew closer.

Ah yes, he thought, *this must be the painting Jean Pierre specifically wanted me to evaluate.* He took half a step closer and was stunned by what he saw. The painting was by Hans Holbein the Younger, an undisputed master of the Northern Renaissance style. Seeing it here on display conjured up strong feelings of tragedy and heartbreak, horrible destruction, and the Holocaust.

The color drained from his face. He could feel his heart pounding and pounding, as though ready to leap from his chest. After a moment, Hans regained his composure and took a step back to view the entire piece. *This is* impossible, he thought. *It must be a forgery. There's no conceivable way. Unless . . . No! It can't be. I must examine it further, of course—I must view it much closer before I can make my judgement. But it must be a forgery . . .*

Most paintings from the Old Masters displayed the telltale signs of various restorations over the years. Naturally, at over four hundred years old, this painting had been retouched and repaired multiple times. Hans admired the work. The inpainting was outstanding, a nearly perfect match indistinguishable to anyone but an expert. He also admired the way the conservator had resolved a problematic blind cleavage in the lower left corner. In fact, it looked like the same technique he often used himself.

Suddenly it hit him like an avalanche. *My God, this is my work!*

The more he examined the painting, the more he recognized his own techniques. There was no question about it. There were several obvious signs of his meticulous workmanship. *Had they been copied too*?

He felt a jolt as it all flooded back. It was early 1938. The war hadn't yet begun. He remembered his father's shop overwhelmed with customers. Every day there were more. Collectors and gallery owners from across the city urgently wanted their artwork to be preserved, packaged, and stored in a secret location, if not shipped away to a mysterious address. Where they went, Hans never knew—until 1941, when he was told to repair and ship this very painting for Nazi Reichsmarschall Hermann Goering. He had the documentation to prove it in his battered black ledger.

His hands began to shake and he felt a chill. With its copious notes and detailed documentation, his humble ledger could affect the provenance and subsequent ownership of many art pieces now circulating throughout museums all over Europe, not to mention the art purchased and shipped to the Americas.

The ledger had been passed down from his grandfather to his father and finally to Hans. The information it contained spanned the three generations of repairs and restoration. The information inside could prove the origins and sources of hundreds of looted pieces that had been stolen by the Nazis during World War II.

During and after the war, many of these treasures were sold illegally and shipped all over the world. Hans's mind was a whirlpool of thoughts and emotions, each with consequences more horrible than those that came before. The information he possessed could disrupt the art industry throughout the world. No one in the community would ever want this information to see the light of day. The fights and legal battles that would ensue over the rightful ownership of the pieces could ripple for years.

"If I only knew what you were thinking," said Jean Pierre, standing behind Hans. Hans hadn't heard him approach. He was startled by Jean Pierre's voice. He quickly tried to gather himself together. "If I could peer into that head of yours and see your thoughts, I'm sure it would properly be worth many francs and a good bottle of wine. I've watched you from a distance. You've been staring at this piece for some time."

Hans needed to refocus. He'd barely understood a word the director just said. With a deep breath he turned and said, "Yes, yes. Sorry. You have. You've given me quite a challenge. Prior to the tour you asked me to analyze some of these works. I fear my passion for the Old Masters has gotten the best of me. I've been scanning every detail and I was lost in my own world."

"Are you familiar with this particular portrait?" asked Jean Pierre. "Do you happen to know the artist and the time period it was commissioned?"

The question felt menacing and heavy with subtext. Clearly, it wasn't nearly as straightforward as it seemed on the surface. If Jean Pierre knew about Hans's involvement with this particular painting and the hundreds more like it, there was no telling what might happen. Hans would need to be silent and destroy the book. Fear momentarily consumed him—not only for himself but for his precious granddaughter. Hans tried to deflect and appear completely calm.

"It's in remarkably good condition," he said. "Did one of your people work on it? Has it been recently cleaned or repaired?"

"Not to my knowledge," said Jean Pierre. "In fact, we received explicit instructions *not* to touch it. The note said it could be displayed, but not retouched or restored. Why do you ask?"

"I couldn't help but notice the pigments," he said. "The colors are resplendent, without the characteristic dullness we see on many centuries-old paintings hanging on gallery walls. My guess is that it hasn't been on display."

Jean Pierre's head cocked slightly, as though hearing a faint noise in the distance. *Does the director know something?* Hans continued: "The brush work looks to be from the original artist. The few places it has been restored are remarkably well done. It's also in stunning condition for this period, almost as if it had been painted within the past few years, not centuries ago."

"Unfortunately, we have very little information," said Jean Pierre. "It came to us from an anonymous collector with instructions to show it in our next exhibit and make known it will be auctioned off at a later date. I suppose they wanted to see what kind of interest it generated."

"I see," responded Hans. "I wonder, with your permission, if I might examine it further, under controlled lighting conditions before I give you a true quantified assessment."

"Yes, of course," said Jean Pierre. "I'm sure that would be quite helpful. I think the owner, whomever they are, would welcome the input from a man of your background and experience."

"Do you happen to have the shipping container it arrived in?" asked Hans.

"Yes, I believe we do," said Jean Pierre. "I was told it was built for shipping and long-term storage. It looks to be quite old. I will arrange for you to perform your assessment Monday, if that fits in your schedule. We are closed to the public then, as you know. That would be the best time to let you take a much closer look."

Hans was both relieved and overcome with emotions. He fought to conceal any outward signs of distress. He was certain he had worked on this painting. After a closer look, there would be no doubt. The two men set the date and time and Jean Pierre disappeared down the hall. Watching him walk away, Hans once again drifted back to Berlin and the railroad yard where he'd seen this masterpiece loaded onto a Nazi freight car. *Had it been hidden all these years? And where are the hundreds of other pieces I worked on and crated during the war, pieces that were shipped out from that same railyard? Are they hidden somewhere? Right here at the Louvre, perhaps? How many of Goering's treasures are still out there somewhere? Where have they been sold, and to whom?*

"Are you ready to go home, Grandfather?" Alana asked, gently taking his hand. As he turned to her, she said, "Oh my. You look very tired and worried. Did something happen?"

Hans silently shook his head. "It's been a long day for me," he said, overcome by the weight of it all.

On their way out of the Louvre, Hans's mind churned with terrible thoughts and images of his past. Some reputable sources said that thousands of artworks were plundered by the Nazis. The history attached to each piece nearly overwhelmed him. Most of the original owners had probably been sent to the death camps. Hans and his wife, Elsa, had witnessed train loads of men, women, and children packed into windowless box cars to be sent who knows where, all their worldly possessions stolen, even their gold fillings. The thoughts and horrible images tucked away in the back of his memory had suddenly returned and they seemed all too present. He had witnessed so much himself. Others had documented these horrible tragedies for the world to see.

Later, at home in bed, he lay awake consumed by anxiety. Memories continuously flooded back, like an endless, tragic newsreel of what he'd seen during the war. He felt the weight of it all pressing down. The day the Allied bombing raid killed Elsa . . . He'd been the lucky one, or had he? He'd managed to escape but was riddled with the guilt of his involvement in the preservation of Goering's treasures. It had haunted him most of his life. Now, this painting brought back vivid horrible thoughts of his past.

Not wanting to admit what he realized that day was real, Hans kept repeating to himself, *You have jumped to a conclusion too quickly. You need to examine the painting in more detail. It could be a fake. You may be wrong; your eyes are old; you may not have seen what you thought you saw.*

He dozed off for a moment, but the cacophony of images and train whistles would not let him rest. He thought of his beautiful and beloved wife, Elsa. *Where are you, my love? I am lost without you. I need your love and support. You were my rock.*

He remembered that fateful day in the railyard. They'd watched Hans's mother and their own two children board the train for Switzerland. Hans had made a bargain with the Nazi devil Goering. "I will work for you," Hans had told him, "but first you must make sure my family gets out of Germany safely." Elsa's strong and reassuring words echoed in his head: "You've made the right decision, my love. There's nothing else we could do. We will do their bidding to get our loved ones out of Nazi Germany."

Hans finally fell asleep, despite the overwhelming memories and the crush of emotion.

CHAPTER 8

IN SEARCH OF MEMORY

Alana worked two jobs, her normal nursing rounds and the task of attending Antone on weekends. She went to the rehabilitation center where he stayed almost every day, reading to him and suggesting historic events that everybody knew, famous dates, childhood experiences, anything that might trigger his memory. She knew he'd recently undergone another round of brain scans and an MRI test. With minimal lasting damage and no serious trauma, the doctors reiterated how very fortunate he was. His memory would come back in time. He just needed to be patient.

"Bed rest is best," they'd told him. "The healing process is slow when it comes to this most complicated, vital organ in the human body. Moderate physical therapy will help, as well as walking, conversing, and reading, all of the normal things we often do without thinking. Attention to these will help you get back to your old self."

Antone knew he would be discharged soon. One afternoon he asked Alana if she could help him move back to his apartment. She happily agreed and they made preparations.

It was a warm, sunny Tuesday when he finally went home, over two and a half months since he'd been pulled from his truck by heroic strangers. A part of him still couldn't believe it. He was filled with a turbulent mixture of happiness and apprehension as the taxi slowed to a stop in front of his building.

His apartment key had been lost or destroyed in the fiery crash, so they went to the manager's office to get the spare. As they entered his office, Antone realized, *Yes, I have been here before. But not as Antone La Rue! I was known by another name.*

He racked his brain. He remembered leaving the apartment and knowing he would be gone for an extended time, but for what purpose? Further back, he remembered being at the airport with minimal luggage. Two men had met him there. They'd given him a key and this address, which they'd called *strategically located*. Before disappearing into the crowd, they'd also given him a large envelope, containing cash and various documents. He'd been hired to *do something* by the two men, but he couldn't conjure up what it was.

"Good morning, Monsieur Antone," said the proprietor. "It is so good to see you at last. What can I do for you?"

Without getting into the details of his dramatic accident, Antone politely requested a replacement key and asked if he could get a copy of his lease agreement. He said he'd misplaced both, somehow, during his extensive travels.

As Alana and Antone entered the apartment, they were immediately met by the smell of recently applied disinfectant. He recalled his lease included bimonthly cleaning, but with no one living there, what was there to clean?

Like so many urban apartments, the place was definitely small. Thankfully, it was large enough not to give one the feeling of claustrophobia. There was a large window facing the street and a cozy kitchen nook. The bedroom was also small, with a queen-size bed and nightstand nearly filling the room. All things considered, it seemed like a typical Parisian apartment: compact, clean, and expensive, especially for this part of the city.

A small closet stood near the entrance. Antone searched the contents for any kind of clue as Alana searched the kitchen cabinets and drawers. There wasn't much to look through, so it didn't take very long.

"Alana, did you find anything?" asked Antone from the closet.

"Nothing," she answered, dejected. "Did you really live here? There's not a thing to eat. Your cupboards are all bare and your refrigerator is empty except for beer, some very fermented milk, and a container of mysterious leftovers that were once *who knows what*." With a note of optimism she asked, "What about you? What did you find?"

He placed a small wad of money and a key on the table. "Not much," he said. "These items were hidden in my jacket in the closet. A very clever design, I might add. The first time I searched I found nothing, but then I noticed a very small bulge near the jacket's armpits. They were concealed in there."

"Very curious," said Alana. "I wonder what it means."

"I have no idea," he said. "Let's have a look at that lease. Perhaps there's something there that will give us a clue."

"Does any of this make sense to you, Antone?" asked Alana, picking up the key. "This is a pretty expensive apartment to lease for nine months and have literally *nothing* in it but a few changes of clothes and a mysterious key with—" She squinted down at the key. "A series of small numbers on it? There are no bills or other mail, even after all this time. Did you move here for a new job? And how do you explain that special tailored jacket with hidden pockets? You are definitely a mystery man!"

Antone laughed. "I'm sure it's nothing like that," he said, but something in the back of his mind told him it might not be that far-fetched.

"I'm sorry," said Alana, "it's late and I have to work the early shift tomorrow. Can I call you when I'm finished?"

Antone glanced up from the lease. "Oh, I guess I thought . . ." he started. "Well, honestly, I don't know what I thought, but you've already gone above and beyond the call of duty."

"Well," said Alana, sheepishly, "I was thinking, this year the first day of Hanukkah is Thursday, December 12. I'm sure that you know it's a special day for Jewish families and I guess—well, I was wondering—my grandfather and I would like to invite you to dinner." She took a quick half-step forward. "I mean, if you feel up to it, of course. You can decide tomorrow. In the meantime," she said, moving right next to him, "see if you can make sense of these mystery objects we found." She leaned forward and kissed him lightly on the cheek, turned, and left the apartment.

For the first time in many weeks, Antone was alone. He sat in a chair and closed his eyes. Fleeting thoughts and images were scrolling through his mind, but nothing clicked into place. He got up and went to the kitchen, where he found a pen and some paper in the door. Standing at the corner he started to write everything he knew.

First, he was bilingual. He knew this because he'd overheard two physical therapists at the center speaking English. Walking with Alana through the Paris streets to get his legs in shape, he'd also understood the British and American tourists.

Next, he wrote down *key*. It looked like the kind of key that went with a storage locker, but where? The bus depot, the train station, the airport? The city was full of such lockers.

He wrote down *jacket with hidden pockets*. It was hanging in the front closet, but clearly custom made. Other than a key and some cash, what were the pockets for? His wallet, his passport, a *gun*?

Suddenly, he was exhausted and decided to go to bed. There was no way to solve things tonight. Instead of answers, he'd found *more questions*. He would have to think when his head was clear. Maybe in the morning it would all make more sense.

Antone woke up in a cold sweat, his heart beating rapidly. His mind had gone back to his boyhood in a small town in Minnesota. He was on a tractor plowing a cornfield for his father. The images were palpable as he fell back to sleep, trying to rationalize and piece together the small bits of memory he'd unexpectedly retrieved.

In the morning, Antone remembered the flashback he'd had. In his bones he knew it was true. He remembered helping his dad all summer on the farm throughout his high school years. *How strange*, he thought to himself. *What is a farm boy from southern Minnesota doing in Paris in a leased apartment? Why am I here? Why do I have a special jacket with secret pockets? Do I normally carry a gun? What does the key unlock and what might be in the locker?*

He decided to do something normal, like shop for food and cleaning supplies. His refrigerator was a smelly, unusable mess. It obviously hadn't been opened the entire time he'd been gone. The few things that were in there had turned into a completely unrecognizable greenish slime that smelled terrible.

He decided to shave before leaving. The beard he'd acquired during his long hospital stay needed to go. Maybe a clean-shaven Antone La Rue would stir up more images of his past. As he studied his face in the mirror, he surmised he was in his early thirties. No major wrinkles, dark black hair with deep-set eyes. His face was drawn, showing recent weight loss, as if he he'd been on a diet.

All of that made sense, of course, considering he'd been recuperating for months from a nearly fatal accident. His olive skin gave the impression of Mediterranean heritage. It occurred to him that Alana may have been attracted and devoted to him while he was in the hospital because she thought he was Jewish.

Is that why she invited me to their Hanukkah celebration? he wondered. He would accept her offer. His feelings toward her went well beyond those of patient and nurse. She was still his angel, and there was also a deep feeling in his heart that he would never let her go. He tried to conjure up feelings about other women he may have known but ran into dead ends. *If I am indeed in my thirties,* he thought, *I certainly must have dated. It's likely I've even had a few special women in my life.*

It was all speculation, of course. For all he knew, he was married with kids. Every day he had more questions, but very few answers.

CHAPTER 9

A MEETING WITH THE DEVIL

Hans was suffering through another sleepless night, his mind a swirling vortex of memories. It was late 1938. He was at work in his father's shop, learning the restoration trade. His grandfather had recently passed. The official cause was pneumonia, but like thousands of other soldiers who had fought for the Germans in World War I, he'd been exposed to mustard gas. He'd had intermittent breathing problems even before he returned from the front.

Unlikely as it may seem, Hans's grandfather, Manfred, had first opened his shop during the depression that followed the Great War, as World War I was sometimes called. Under the Treaty of Versailles that ended the conflict, Germany lost all its colonies outside Europe and many of its European territories. The country was essentially bankrupt, and yet it was forced to make reparations payments to the Allies for the death and destruction they'd caused. Only the rich were able to avoid Germany's deep depression.

With his unique talent for restoring artworks, Manfred opened a modest shop in Berlin where the wealthy went to have their precious art collections cleaned and restored. Through the years, the eldest Muller became very prosperous, thanks to his special talents. His shop was the place to go to for the repair and restoration of valuable works of art, as well as objective appraisals.

Over time, he also began to buy, sell, and trade pieces of art. As Germany slowly recovered from the devastating effects of the war, he was able to build a very impressive and valuable collection.

When Hans's grandfather passed, Hans's father, Otto, took over. Even as a young boy, Hans knew deep in his bones one day the shop would be his. Otto worked with him closely, helping him to not only learn the business but the various techniques and tricks of the trade passed down through the generations.

"This kind of information, you cannot find in books," Otto often told him. "It can only be learned at the side of a great restorationist like your grandfather. This is the core of the business. People who own fine paintings and other antiques will pay dearly to preserve and protect their investments. Your grandfather was able to use these skills after the war to earn the trust of wealthy patrons."

How clearly Hans remembered that day so many years ago. He could smell the turpentine and mineral spirits. He remembered the stickiness of the pigments and various cleaning solutions . . .

Suddenly, the image came of two German soldiers bursting through the door. One of them held the door open as a broad-shoul-dered man in an expensive but gaudy military uniform strode into the shop, his heavy boots thundering across the wooden floor.

"Is your father in, Hans?" asked the man. Hans was startled by the man's deep, commanding voice. He'd never met this stranger and yet, the man addressed him by his first name.

"Y-yes," responded Hans, haltingly.

"Tell him Reichsmarschall Goering is here," said the man, the words hanging heavy in the still shop. "It's time to pick up my painting. Be quick about it now. I'm a very busy man. I don't have time for formalities."

Hans would never forget the man's stern, stony face and authori-tarian posture. *He is definitely not someone we could afford to keep waiting.*

Hans went to get his father, who immediately put down his brush and darted out from the back. He whisked a carefully packaged painting from its spot and presented it to the stranger. A short conversation ensued, then Goering left the shop as briskly as he'd entered, followed by the two silent soldiers. Hans breathed a sigh of relief as he heard the Reichsmarschall's Mercedes start up and drive away.

Hans didn't say a word about the mysterious visitor until Otto finally locked the door for the day and they began putting everything away. "How did that man know my name?" he asked. "I've never seen him before or even heard you talk about him . . ."

"Hush now," said Otto. "He rarely ever comes here and he only deals with me." Hans's father held his son by the shoulders and looked deeply into his eyes. "Listen, that man is pure evil. He's been bringing his stolen art here for years for repair and restoration. Have you heard of the Gestapo, the secret police? That is the man who created it. He's also commander in chief of the powerful Luftwaffe. He is one of Hitler's closest confidants. Other than the Führer, I'm not sure there's anyone more powerful in the whole country."

Hans felt his father's hands shaking. He'd never seen the man so upset. It was like he had seen a ghost.

"My father . . . your grandfather," he continued with a great deal of effort, "and eventually . . . *myself* . . . we've been doing work for him for years. He's been a collector for quite some time and now his collection grows every day. Some of his early pieces were ordinary. Nothing of great value. Some of it was quite good, but it was all from lesser-known artists. Now, because of his position and authority, he *acquires* old masterpieces as *gifts*—or bribes—to gain his favor. These pieces were most likely plundered from the countries the Nazis have invaded . . ."

Otto looked despondent as he stared at the floor, silent for a moment.

"Almost all of them have required cleaning and repair because they were not handled properly as they were stripped off walls to be shipped to Berlin. Most, if not all of these works, were stolen from the Jewish collectors they've killed or sent off to the work camps or from museums that the Nazis deem *degenerate*."

Hans felt the urge to hug his father, but the horrible things he was hearing literally paralyzed him. He didn't think he could even lift his arms. He tried to close his eyes, but that was worse. In the darkness it was easier to picture the atrocities.

"Now, he comes here to the shop only if a painting is highly valuable," said Otto, "something he plans to keep for his private collection. He gives me specific instructions to do *exactly* what he wants. I . . . can only do as he says."

Otto looked defeated. The boy could see the man was trapped.

"In the past," his father continued, "I was instructed to send some of the restored works to Carinhall, Goering's large hunting estate northeast of Berlin, in the Schorfheide forest. Over the years Goering has amassed a personal fortune in stolen paintings, sculptures and rugs, furniture, and jewelry. There's nothing he won't steal from private collections and museums throughout Europe. Recently, he said a *new arrangement is coming,* and I don't like the sound of that, even if I don't know what it means. He's a very dangerous man who will stop at *nothing* to get what he wants."

Otto could barely continue.

"People who disagree with Goering—even the lowest-ranking Nazi—well, they wind up missing or dead."

CHAPTER 10

THE SECRETS OF THE BLACK BOOK

"Hans, please follow me," said his father, leading the boy to the small storage room at the back of the shop. "Come in, come in," he said, motioning with his hand. "Close the door now. Be quiet."

With all the old easels and canvas stretchers, the two of them barely fit into the small, cramped space. Sitting on top of the cabinet was a small case with multiple drawers, each filled with special paints, brushes, and palette knives of unsurpassed quality, some of which were irreplaceable. They were designed to match the paint strokes of the Old Masters, to replicate their work on their priceless pieces.

"Listen to me now," said Otto, holding the boy's shoulders squarely, "the time has come for you to know the Muller family secrets. Believe me, I don't take this lightly. What I am going to show you could put our family's lives in danger for years to come. I was hoping to protect you, but I fear my own life is now in danger. You know of my work with—Goering," said Otto, choking on the man's name. "You know about my . . . involvement in restoration and how it ties me to much of the stolen art now under Nazi control. I am what you might call a little millstone around their necks. I know some of their secrets, the original owners of dozens of pieces that have illegally passed through our shop."

Otto reached for the case and slid it towards himself. He pulled open one of the drawers and spun the case to face Hans. They were standing quite close together, even before they'd bent down to look. Now, Hans could feel his father's warm breath tickling his face. It smelled like cardamom from the tea he constantly drank.

"For now, Goering will use us for his personal gain," said Otto, "but we will be discarded as soon as we're no longer convenient." He reached under the two back corners of the case and pressed upward, releasing two hidden latches showing the case's back. He gently slid it upward, revealing a hidden compartment.

"With what I'm going to show you," he said, "perhaps someday in the future, we—*you*—will be able to make things right for some of the victims of this Nazi regime."

The first thing Otto showed him was a small wad of money. It was rolled very tightly and had a slight metallic scent. "This is the rainy-day fund," he said. "It's a mix of German, French, and Swiss bills. It's not a lot, but enough to get you started. You must sew it into your clothes, or the guards will find it."

Next, Otto showed him a small black leather book. It was about half an inch thick, four inches wide, and six inches tall, wrapped in a velvety fabric that was also jet black. "Do not open this until it's absolutely vital," he said. "It may buy your freedom someday. Years ago, your grandfather began recording all the details he did on the rare, old masterpieces that were brought to him by powerful people. His notations in this small journal include the titles, the name of the artists, the name of the original owners, and the approximate values at the time of repair. His original purpose was purely business. Often, pieces of art are used as investments. Detailed records of his work enabled him to make better appraisals on art prices for clients."

Otto sighed deeply, feeling the gravity of what he was going to say.

"At the time, your grandfather had no way of knowing that this inconspicuous business ledger would someday become an irreplaceable record of provenance. Many of the entries from the past ten to fifteen years . . . you'd be heartsick knowing who some of the original owners were. Tragically, since the war started, the vast majority of the works' owners have become the Nazi elite, including Hitler himself."

Otto held the book gently, as though it would break if he wasn't careful. The fingers of his right hand rested on the worn black cover.

"It began as book of transactions," he said, "now it's a book of victims. Certainly, some of these entries are honest business dealings, but many are stained with blood. This book will help to identify precious pieces that were seized or looted from Jewish collectors. We can only hope someday they will be returned to their rightful owners. Hans, you are now just the second living person who knows of its existence."

Hans was startled by this revelation. He'd worked for his dad and grandfather for years, totally unaware of this ledger. He felt a wave of fear wash over his body.

"Father, we must leave Berlin," he said.

His father was silent a moment, mustering the courage to continue. "It's too late for me, my son. The Nazis know me too well. Already I am followed wherever I go. It's the Gestapo, I'm sure of it. There's still a chance for you, Elsa, and the children to flee to Switzerland. Your mother's sister lives there. Switzerland is neutral. Your mother and your aunt are not of Jewish decent. I'm hoping that will help. It's going to be me that they're after."

Otto removed one of the drawers and flipped it over. A thick envelope was affixed to the drawer's underside. He gently worked it loose and set it flat on the table.

"I've been preparing for quite some time," he said. "As you must know, this past March, the Nazis annexed Austria. In September, the United Kingdom, France, and Italy signed the Munich Agreement, fully believing Hitler controlling the Sudetenland would be enough to appease the Fürher. Instead, he's stepped up his preparations for war. It is clear to me there is no stopping him. He has convinced our countrymen that the so-called Aryan race is superior. He's goaded them into believing *only they* should dictate how society is structured, throughout Europe and all over the world. He and Reichsmarschall Goering are vile and evil men who are destroying our country, the Jewish way of life, our faith and our history. The world is under siege by a great cancer called the Third Reich."

Otto ran a thin palette knife under the flap of the envelope and opened it carefully. He reached inside and pulled out the contents.

"I have prepared new passports for the whole family under your mother's maiden name, Wyss. Using her Swiss surname should get you across the border to her sister's home in Basel. I must remain behind and try to come later. With your aunt's help, your mother and I have opened bank accounts in Switzerland. We did it years ago, also under her maiden name. There should be enough money there for you to get by. Hopefully, once the war is over and this tragic chapter for the Jewish people concludes, you might be able to start a small business and carry on the family trade. We must make plans now to get you and your family out. Quickly. Before it is too late."

CHAPTER 11

THE CARETAKER OF THE LOUVRE'S TREASURES

The day had finally arrived. Hans was back at the Louvre to analyze the painting he'd seen at the preview exhibition, his mind fraught with the emotional memories that still lingered from his encounter with Goering decades ago. The discussion he'd had with his father was still imprinted on his brain, as were his fears that his grandfather's black ledger, if discovered, would jeopardize his family's safety. Would examining the mysterious painting confirm his suspicions? What did he hope to discover? More importantly, what did it mean?

First things first, he thought, as his friend Jean Pierre arrived. They'd agreed to meet at one of the Louvre's private entrances. It was still quite early, but Hans required nothing less. It would take the entire day to make a proper examination.

"Prompt as usual, I see," said Jean Pierre, extending his hand. "I like a man who is that way," he said as they shook hands. "It means he is dedicated, ambitious, and ready to work. So, let's get to it, shall we?"

As they proceeded down to the lower levels, Hans couldn't help noticing the myriad rooms and walkways that wound through the various wings. It was impossible to know if they were under the original fortress, or one of the many additions.

"A person could get lost down here," he observed.

"Oh yes," said Jean Pierre. "It's certainly been known to happen. Until we installed phones and put maps on the walls, it tended to happen *quite often*."

"How many sub-floors are there?" wondered Hans.

"Ahh," said Jean Pierre, "that's a very good question."

For a moment there was silence, nothing but their feet on the stony floor and the distant low hum of the museum's special heating and cooling system, designed to keep the paintings and other art treasures environmentally safe.

"As you know," he finally continued, "the main entrance for visitors and guests is on the second sub-level. There are galleries and exhibitions on the next level, minus one, but the top three levels are devoted to the bulk of the museum's holdings. Underneath it all are basements and sub-basements extending in seemingly all directions, like a spider's web. There are storage rooms, tunnels, and workspaces that even I haven't seen."

Hans thought he detected a slight smirk on the museum director's face. *What are you hiding?* thought Hans. *What is it you don't want to tell me?*

"This place is quite historical," said Jean Pierre as they turned down yet another long corridor. "It began as a medieval fortress in the twelfth century. After that it became a palace and finally, the museum. Throughout this period of nearly eight hundred years, there have been many additions and improvements. You'll notice, as we proceed from one building to the next, different construction techniques, methods, and materials. The many occupants have also left their unique legacies in the form of vast collections of artifacts and antiques from all over the world. From the outside, you might never know. The architecture is quite consistent and looks to be uniform. Inside, the story is different, a twisting maze of mystery that holds many unexpected surprises.

"The man you're about to meet has spent a lifetime working here. I would guess he must be at least five years older than you and yet, he has a mind like a trap. I've never known him to forget *anything*. His knowledge of the Louvre and the location of tens of thousands of artifacts is beyond belief. At any given moment, he knows where things are stored or displayed, if they've been given on loan to another museum or taken down for restoration."

Jean Pierre suddenly chuckled to himself. He turned and smiled at Hans. "There is a word for these gifted people who have photographic memories and the uncanny ability to retrieve facts at will. I keep telling myself I will have to look it up someday."

Hans had indeed noticed the changes in the building's styles as they'd been walking, but with all the twisting and turning, he had no idea if they'd been going in circles or were a kilometer from where they started. To say the Louvre is massive barely begins to convey its size.

"His name is Maurice Devenue," said Jean Pierre. "There are probably fewer than ten people in the entire world with his ability. We are very lucky to have him. Through the years he has held many different positions. Among his other duties, he currently manages shipping and receiving, logging every piece as it arrives or is sent to exhibitions elsewhere. He's like a walking encyclopedia. Presently I'm having him build our first computerized master inventory list—a database, I suppose I should say—with a building by building, gallery by gallery breakdown of the entire museum. You will enjoy working with him. I am anxious to hear your findings and learn what you've discovered. I will set up a lunch meeting soon; then we will have a chance to discuss everything in greater detail."

After a series of brief introductions, Jean Pierre excused himself to attend to his numerous daily duties and responsibilities.

"Well, Mr. Muller," said Maurice, "I've been instructed *personally* by the director to assist you in your evaluation. Where would you like to start?"

"Do you happen to have the original shipping container?" asked Hans.

Maurice looked a bit surprised. He hesitated a moment before answering. "Yes . . . I believe we do," he said. "I've taken the liberty of having the painting brought here, to our in-house restoration and cleaning department. Perhaps you'd like to start with the painting itself? That way you don't have to wait while we, um, track down the shipping container."

A man with world class memory needing time to track down *the shipping* container? *How can that be?* "They should have the tools you need to do a thorough assessment of this painting."

After a short walk, Maurice led Hans into a brightly lit but private work area. He surveyed the workspace to be sure he had everything needed to do his assessment.

"Thank you, Maurice," said Hans, "this is perfect." He inhaled slowly and deeply. "This is my domain. All I need now is time."

"I will leave you then, monsieur, and return in, say, three hours?" said Maurice. "If you need me, that phone on the wall is a direct line to my office."

Hans wasted no time, swiftly removing the backboard and frame.

There it is! he thought, nearly exclaiming out loud.

When a reputable restorer or conservationist works on any cultural heritage artifact, he leaves an identification mark somewhere out of view on the piece. He does this for a number of reasons but most importantly, the unique mark, or signature, identifies the restorer, holding him accountable for the quality of his work. There's also a notation, of course, of when the work was done. This also helps curators and collectors track the item's provenance, tracing an artifact's history and ownership.

When Hans saw the piece hanging in the gallery, he instinctively knew it was his. Still, he wanted to be doubly sure. He put the painting gently on a special, padded easel and slowly lifted a small portion of canvas with a long, thin metal blade. He inhaled sharply and felt his heart skip a beat. Indeed, there it was, in the lower left-hand corner where he typically left his mark.

As he jotted down the string of numbers that identified who, when, and where the piece had been restored, he was overcome by the emotions and flickering memories he'd experienced the previous night.

It was November 9, 1938, the night his father's shop was broken into and ransacked by Brownshirts and Nazi sympathizers. Hans had left early that evening to spend time with his wife. His father, however, stayed late to work alone, as he often did.

Hans's father heard the front window shatter, followed by the sounds of someone breaking down the front door. He put down his brush, took off his apron, and walked calmly to the front of the store. He'd hoped to surrender himself in order to save the art.

Instead, two large men grabbed him and dragged him outside, where he was beaten and kicked by multiple people. He heard himself begging for mercy, but the vicious assault continued until a new victim caught their attention.

There were people everywhere, breaking glass and lighting fires or swinging sledgehammers, knocking down doors and walls. Years later the riot would be known as Kristallnacht, the Night of Broken Glass. Over seven thousand Jewish stores and businesses damaged and looted, if not completely destroyed. The rioters also leveled 267 synagogues throughout Germany, Austria, and the Sudetenland. Thirty thousand Jewish men were arrested on flimsy false charges and taken to Dachau and other concentration camps. Jews and historians considered that horrible night to be the beginning of the Holocaust.

When Hans arrived after most of the chaos had subsided, he found a figure gasping on the street. His father! Blood was streaming out of his nose and mouth. Hans fell to his knees on the pavement as his father whispered what had happened. Then he let out one last breath and was gone. Han felt his guts had been ripped right out of his body as he struggled to breathe himself, a flood of tears running down his face.

Later, Hans returned to his father's store to see if he could salvage any of the paint and special brushes required to continue his trade.

As he was boarding up the door and windows, a well-built man in his early thirties approached.

"I work for Reichsmarschall Goering," the man said. "He wishes to speak to you about this . . . *incident* and the death of your father. You must come with me now. I will see that your shop is protected."

Goering began the meeting by disavowing responsibility for everything that had happened. "I am . . . *sorry* for this incident," he said, "especially the death of your father. We played no part in what happened. Nor did the Gestapo. In fact, as I'm sure you must know, our security force intervened and finally got things under control. I also dispatched a squad to make sure your father's store wasn't burned down."

Hans was stunned by Goering's statement. As he listened carefully to every word, he didn't believe any of it. There was zero empathy or sincerity in Goering's voice when he described his twisted version of the event. Hans knew the truth was much different. He uttered not a word in response, waiting to hear the man's true motives.

Why did you bring me here? Hans wondered. *What do you need done? What is it you want from me?*

"Your father was a very gifted and talented man," said Goering, snapping Hans from his reverie. "He restored and cared for many of the paintings in my collection over the years. He will be greatly . . . *missed* for his talents and skills."

The Reichsmarschall leaned back in his chair, the seat back groaning beneath his weight. "I propose an *arrangement*," he said. "I am in constant need of a man with your skills and aptitude for restoration and repair. I know the quality of your work and compare it quite favorably with your father's. In fact, you've already worked on some of my lesser-valued paintings. You possess the same skills and techniques your father did. The quality of your work is extremely good."

Goering leaned in closer. The buttons on his gaudy uniform, from who knows what time period, were strained almost to the point of popping. "This is what I propose," he said. "Your father's shop will cease to exist. In fact, I believe it's unlikely that *any* Jewish business will survive the coming year. As you must know, the Führer now prevents Jewish ownership of any kind. You must accept my offer and when the war is over, you will be given passage to the country of your choice, along with a modest stipend to set up a new shop. Until we are victorious and win the war, however, you will work for me. You will receive no pay, but live and work under my protection. If you choose to reject my offer, well, truth be told there is nothing I will be able to do. You will be sent to the camps. I hope you know it's the greatest honor to be given this opportunity."

Hans knew it wasn't a choice. Turning Goering down would be a death sentence for his family. *My family*, he thought, *their safety is paramount. I have to try to save them.*

Hans's lips were bone dry. His stomach was churning like a small cyclone. He swallowed hard and slowly began. "I will agree," he said, haltingly, "but I must ask that you spare my mother, my children, and my wife. If they could get the proper papers, you could send them to Switzerland . . . My wife has relatives there. Please, Herr Goering, I—"

"It's Reichsmarschall," snapped Goering. "You will address me properly."

"Yes, yes, of course," said Hans. "I meant nothing by it. I am sorry, Reichsmarschall. Please forgive me."

"Your mother and children can go. Your wife will stay here," he said. "If you try to escape, I assure you—*you can't imagine the consequences it will bring for you and your wife.*"

Hans reluctantly agreed, knowing that he was now under the thumb of a very dangerous, evil man. A man who had likely broken dozens of promises over these last few years. Trusting him to fulfill his pledge would be a fool's errand.

"You have two days to prepare your mother and children," he said. "They will each take only one suitcase, containing nothing of value. Your brushes and equipment will be moved to your new workshop immediately. This will also be where you live."

Hans mustered the courage to meet Goering's eyes with his own. "Until I see my family loaded onto the train, I'm not going anywhere," said Hans. "I need proof that they'll be on the train. You can shoot me here if you like, but I must insist."

Hans saw a wave of anger wash over the Reichsmarschall's face. "You will be handcuffed," he said. "You will watch from a troop transport truck."

Hans knew he was taking a risk, but he also knew, after this, he'd have no leverage and no hope of escape. He was surrendering his life to save his mother and children.

"We are done here," Goering thundered. Two soldiers rushed forward and grabbed Hans roughly by the shoulders. Hans didn't put up a fight, but one of the soldiers hit him regardless. They dragged him to the front door and flung him into the street.

CHAPTER 12

GOERING'S MASTER PAINTING

Maurice returned, followed by a worker who was transporting the packing crate on a special padded dolly.

"It took a bit of digging, but we finally found it," said Maurice. The worker gently tipped the crate from the dolly, setting it on the floor. "Well . . . I'll leave you to it then," Maurice continued awkwardly. "You will . . . Please let me know if there's anything else."

"Yes, of course," said Hans. "Thank you for your assistance."

Maurice nodded and the two men left.

Staring at the crate, Hans remembered the orders he'd been given the day he'd last seen the painting, one of Goering's personal favorites. It required impeccable care and needed to be packed securely for a long trip by rail. A special millwright had been assigned to build the packing crate while Hans completed his restoration. Once the repairs were through, Hans was told he would oversee its packing and protection. Above everyone else, he would be responsible for its safety in transport.

All these decades later, as Hans inspected the shipping crate in a work room beneath the Louvre, he noted that all of the shipping labels had been carefully removed. The only identification marks that remained were the small swastikas burned into the wood and the unique embossing that signified the crate and its contents were the work of Hans and the millwright. Without a doubt, this was the original shipping container.

Suddenly, Hans noticed a label etched in permanent ink on the lower left back corner of the shipping container. It must have been added sometime later. It had been partially sanded off, but some of the marks remained. Even with his keen eyes, however, Hans was unable to decipher the container's final destination. He discreetly copied the remaining information as best he could without being detected.

Throughout the war, hundreds of the paintings Hans had been forced to restore were then shipped to Hitler's and Goering's various residences. Other than knowing they all went by rail to southern Germany, Hans had no clear idea what their final destinations were. Nonetheless, he was certain this painting had not been displayed in any museum in all this time. It had been stored somewhere in a carefully controlled environment. The wood shipping container almost looked like it was new and there were very few signs of aging or repeated openings. In fact, the painting itself showed no degradation from exposure to light. It had remained nearly untouched since the day it left the railyard in Berlin.

Where has it been all these years? Hans wondered. *What happened to the hundreds of other paintings I worked on that were shipped from that same railyard? Did someone find a cache of paintings that had been hidden for decades? Are they now trying to sell them off, one at a time?*

The paintings were worth millions of dollars on the "gray market" where unscrupulous curators, gallerists, and collectors bought and sold artwork and antiques without fully vetting their true origins. Their scheme was almost flawless, except for one simple fact: Hans had in his possession a small black ledger full of hundreds of records and proof of provenance.

"Have you completed your analysis, Hans?" Maurice had slipped into the room quietly, without detection. Hans was momentarily startled but managed to conceal it.

"Why yes, I have, for now," said Hans plainly. "I think I may need to do some more precise testing later, if Jean Pierre wishes that I give a more accurate accounting of its value."

"So, what are your conclusions?" asked Maurice.

"I am sorry, Maurice," Hans said diplomatically, "but I need to inform the director of my findings first. I'm sure you must understand. It wouldn't be proper protocol for me to share anything with you at this time."

"Yes, but of course. Please forgive me. I am also anxious to know," said Maurice.

You appear a little too curious, thought Hans. "Yes. The director tells me you've been working here ever since you were a young boy," said Hans, changing the subject. "During that time, I believe you've held many different positions. Would it be all right if I asked you some questions?"

"Of course, just don't ask me my age," joked Maurice. "I am happy to answer all of your other questions objectively and honestly."

A good, friendly start, Hans thought. Some of the questions he was about to ask could put his life in danger. Hans knew he must find out who was behind this scheme to release stolen art treasures that had been hidden since World War II back into the world market.

"I'm curious to know more about your special gift for remembering and retrieving information related to virtually everything you read, hear, see, or do," said Hans.

"Yes," said Maurice with a chuckle, "everyone wants to know more about the gift I was born with. Some have called it total recall. At my age, I must admit, it's now beginning to fade. I believe this is why the director has asked me to put together a database for all the Louvre's artifacts, identifying where these art treasures came from, what buildings they are housed in, and in which room they're displayed. Of course, all of this information exists, but it is contained in numerous filing cabinets throughout this maze of buildings. I have the ability to retrieve that data without ever leaving my office." Maurice gave another chuckle. "With these databases all in my head, I guess that's why I'm still here. I am their cheap human computer."

"So, when did you start working for the museum?" asked Hans. "How did you get a job?"

"My father was killed in the first world war," said Maurice. "As the older of two sons, I was expected to help support the family. Even though I was still in my teens, I had to quit school and get a job. Of course, school was quite easy for me due to my ability. One of my instructors learned I was quitting to help support my family, so he helped me find a job. You might say he was my mentor. He knew my gift was being squandered, so together we searched for a vocation that could utilize my special abilities. I must thank him for my first position here at the Louvre.

"During that time," Maurice continued, "France was recovering from World War I. Every industry was in need of qualified workers. The Louvre lost a large number of its employees to the war effort. Some of its most skilled people were killed or wounded in the war."

Maurice paused mournfully, remembering that terrible time. He regathered himself and pressed on.

"France had lost over one million men. I was sixteen at the time. I didn't have any sort of trade skill. My instructor went to the Louvre and managed to talk them into hiring a sixteen-year-old boy. Funny as it may sound, my first job here was in the shipping and receiving department. It didn't require much skill, but I was quickly noticed for my incomparable memory. I checked all the documents of what came and went from the Louvre. It was a clumsy and inefficient paper system. Because I could remember every piece we received, every piece we shipped out on loan, they expanded my role and eventually I supervised and managed all the museum's logistic functions.

"Through the years I've held many positions; purchasing, personnel—you name it. I worked in every department, yet I never fully left shipping and receiving. My personal knowledge of where everything is located made me indispensable. Everyone comes to me for the quickest answer with regard to the location of antiques, paintings, sculptures, even pieces of equipment. I was only one person, but I performed multiple jobs. Of course, I am grateful they took a chance on me at the start, but I'm not really sure they've ever truly appreciated my value to them," Maurice squinted his eyes, as though he were trying to see someone far in the distance. "I've definitely never been properly compensated for the unique skills that I've brought to my many jobs I held here."

Maurice's face slowly softened.

"During the second war, I became the director's assistant. You can only imagine what happened to this museum when the Nazis invaded and went on to occupy France. By then they'd established military units known as the *Kunstschutz*. They were ordered to take anything of value to help finance their war effort. The invasion began in May 1940 and France capitulated in June." He shook his head in disbelief. "Can you even believe the fighting only lasted six weeks? What's even more amazing is that the Nazis took Belgium, Luxembourg, and the Netherlands at the same time.

"In the beginning we scrambled to find safe storage and hiding places for our most valuable national treasures. It was an impossible task, of course. All of our government's money was going towards the war effort. It all happened so quickly that there was very little time for us to ship our most valuable pieces out of the country. Even after the armistice, we didn't have the skill, resources, and manpower we needed to pack and ship even a fraction of our collection. The sheer size of the Louvre and lack of help led to a complete failure to protect the Louvre's precious contents from the Nazis.

"Even on the first day they occupied France, the Nazis began to plunder our churches and our museums. They established squads and networks with the sole purpose of taking cultural property from every country they occupied. With all of its world-class museums, France became their number-one target. It's a well-established fact that hundreds of train cars loaded with our treasures were sent to Germany, not to mention the stolen goods they took from the other countries."

Maurice stopped and breathed deeply. His voice had cracked a few times as he recounted the terrible memories.

"It was during this time that I first met Reichmarshall Hermann Goering. Of course, he'd been to the Louvre many times, before the fall of France, meeting with Jean Pierre's predecessor, Louis Dequire. As you probably know, Goering had amassed a huge collection of stolen art before and during the war, especially works held by Jewish people. Perhaps some of the artwork you repaired long ago has even found its way into his collection . . ."

Hans gave no indication that this was indeed true but shrugged to acknowledge the possibility. By then, Hans was starting to piece some things together and he didn't want to give Maurice the slightest indication of his indirect involvement. He knew he must remain silent for now.

"Please go on," said Hans. "Did you have other occasions to meet with Goering during the German occupation?"

"Many times," said Maurice, "and here is the strangest, most interesting part about those encounters. During each visit he came with a list of specific art pieces he was looking for.

"Hitler had also visited the Louvre before the war. His dream was to build a bigger, more spectacular museum in Germany that would house the most important art pieces in the whole of Western Europe. Goering was directed to take specific items for the Führer's museum. Of course, Goering also had special art pieces he wanted for his various homes. Their appetite for art was insatiable.

"I believe that somewhere a logbook exists containing records of where all our treasures went, but I have never seen such a book, let alone had access to it. When the Allies retook Paris, the Nazis destroyed countless documents before they left. It took many years to track down the whereabouts of our treasures and there are still many more missing."

Afraid his fact-finding mission with Maurice may begin to draw too much attention to himself, Hans decided to carefully end the conversation. The information about Goering began to percolate through his thoughts. He knew that Jeu de Paume, another famous Paris museum, was relatively close to the Louvre. In fact, the two museums were separated by less than one thousand meters. *Did Goering and his men dig secret tunnels that connected the two buildings? There's no telling what they could have hidden below the sidewalks and flower beds of the Jardin des Tuileries. Are many of the missing artworks buried beneath one of the most popular destinations in all of Paris?*

Maurice escorted Hans back to the visitor center, cordial all the while. Hans said very little, not wanting to reveal even the slightest hint of what he knew. Both men parted ways with many more questions to be asked. Perhaps another time.

CHAPTER 13

MEMORY RECALL TRIGGERED

It was the day before Hanukkah. Antone was excited about celebrating this important Jewish holiday with Alana and her grandfather. He had discovered some new information about himself as he remembered more details from his youth. He was anxious to share all of it with Alana.

The memories had presented themselves in the form of dreams so detailed and realistic he knew they must be true. These movie-like visions had also triggered a cascade of memories and facts.

Antone had grown up in small-town America, somewhere in Minnesota. He wasn't yet sure which town, but he vividly remembered going to a John Deere implement store. His father was thinking of buying a new tractor for their farm. He remembered bits and pieces of the conversation that took place between his father and the dealership owner. The two of them were very good friends.

Antone also remembered that as soon as he'd gotten his driver's license, his father often took him to the implement store to get various replacement parts. He'd been there dozens of times. The owner greeted him by name. *Chris*, the man had called him.

Chris, he thought to himself, *I'm not Antone, I am Chris. I am the middle child. The third boy in a family of five boys.*

Chris remembered how the John Deere dealer often kidded him about when he was going take over his father's farm. None of his brothers had any interest in farming after their father retired.

Chris remembered his dad's quick response. "Not until he finishes college," he'd said. "It's imperative that all my boys attend a university before making career decisions. Farming requires a strong back, a lot of patience, and faith in the weather. Chris certainly has all of that, but he's also quite intelligent. He can use those smarts to make an easier and better life for himself and his family. As you know, farming is damn hard work and the rewards can be minimal. Besides, Chris will graduate number one in his class and can pick whatever college he wants in the fall."

The movie in Chris's mind shifted to his graduation from high school. He'd actually graduated second in his class, not first, as his father predicted, but he was *magna cum laude* with honors. He recalled some of the speech he'd given on that commencement day. He'd been commended in the local paper, the *Austin Daily Herald*.

That was it!

Austin was the nearest town to their farm. He'd gone to Austin High School in southern Minnesota.

Knowing his first name and the high school he'd attended, Chris went to the local library to see if he could learn more. Scanning numerous yearbooks on his high school's website, he finally found his senior class picture. *Christopher Da Vita*, it said, beneath a picture of his younger self. He breathed a deep sigh of relief. With his memory and some research, he'd finally been able to track down his name and true identity. He could hardly wait to share this information with Alana at dinner.

Obviously, there was still much more to be done to uncover the mystery of who he really was and why he'd been living in Paris under an assumed name. Nonetheless, for now, he was elated by his discovery.

He slept that night intermittently with frequent dreams of his past, interrupted by a seemingly endless string of questions. *How did I acquire two names? What was I doing in France using a forged passport?* Once again there were many more questions than answers. Unlocking the mystery that surrounded him would not be an easy task.

Hanukkah would be a big day. He would spend most of it with Alana. Over the past two months, their nurse-patient relationship had slowly transformed into something more complex and beautiful. She was gentle and kind and their relationship had blossomed into a deep connection, a bond one might call *real love.*

This was new for Chris. He couldn't remember ever feeling like this before. He and Alana understood each other intuitively and had a wonderful commonality of ideas and values. Emotions stirred within him whenever they were together. His heart and mind felt like a swirling kaleidoscope—changing, shifting, moving so many directions at once—but always pulling him toward spending his life with her. With so much mystery and uncertainty, Alana helped to keep him grounded.

Learning more about who he really was had become the paramount question, for him, for his future, for his life. *How can I express all my feelings and boundless love for her when I don't really know my past and understand the situation I'm in?* he wondered. For all he knew, he was married and had a family back in the United States. His heart began to ache with the feeling that he could lose Alana. Overwhelmed by these thoughts, he focused on finding a way to uncover the answers he needed.

Alana picked him up at his apartment after she'd finished her shift at the hospital. As they drove to her father's house, Chris began to share his new discoveries with her.

"If only I had a newer, faster computer at my disposal," he told her. "I know that I could speed up my personal history investigation, which could help jog my memory. The computers in the local library are old and slow, but I don't seem to have the money to purchase a new one for myself. I need to find a job. The lease on my apartment has only six weeks left. I'm not sure what I'm going to do."

Alana listened intently to him as they drove to her grandfather's home. "Well, Antone . . . or should I call you Chris? We'll figure that out. But today, and especially tonight, is a very special time for my family. We celebrate Hanukkah, known as the Festival of Lights and the Feast of Dedication, for eight days. During this time we give gifts, make contributions to the needy, and sing special songs. Each evening, we also light a candle in our menorah—a special candelabra—until all eight candles are lit. The story of Hanukkah dates back to 165 BC. Please enjoy our special night with us, and then we will work on solving your problems. I promise."

Alana smiled and glanced at Chris. "Of course, you're going to hear all of this again," she said. "My grandfather *loves* to tell the story of Hanukkah. He tells it like his father, and his grandfather before him, told it to their families. It is a tradition in its finest form. As we celebrate, you will hear many stories of our family's past. Most are about our happy times together, but some are quite sad. I'm sure you'll enjoy this evening and our celebration. Afterwards, we can discuss your situation with my grandfather. He's not only a good listener, but also a great problem solver. You're going to love him."

Chris's introduction to Hans Muller wasn't formal at all, but warm and friendly.

"I've been looking forward to meeting you, Antone," said Hans. "My granddaughter speaks of you often. One would think you're part of our family. All that special attention you've been getting used to go towards me. I am quite jealous, you know."

Antone didn't quite know how he should respond to Hans's remarks. Having never met him before, he couldn't tell if Hans was joking or actually irritated, though he seemed happy to be meeting him. Thankfully, before Chris could respond, Alana jumped in.

"But you, Grandfather, are not in need of a nurse," she said. "You're very self-sufficient and in great health. You have more energy than people half your age."

"Yes," Hans responded, "I suppose all of that's true, but I'm still envious!"

Hans led Chris and Alana into the living room. "Alana has kept me well informed with regard to your recovery and the progress you've been making," he said as they sat down. "From what I've been told, there have been some very difficult moments for you, but I see you've survived them all with the exception of some memory loss."

"Yes," Chris responded. "From what I understand, I'm very lucky to be alive and the fact that I am can be attributed to Alana. Through the darkest hours and days, as I was completely unable to communicate, she gave me the will to live. She is my angel. I have no idea how I could ever repay her for the hundreds of caring moments and healing words of comfort. I have so much to be thankful for."

"Indeed, we all have," said Hans. "That's why I asked Alana to invite you to our celebration. For us, the Muller family, it goes back many generations. It is a time for reflection and healing, a time for rededication to God and the values of our faith."

As Hans told the Hanukkah story of the Second Temple of Jerusalem and began the lighting of the menorah, Chris was overcome with emotion. Hans's powerful words and stories brought him to tears—not tears of sorrow, but of joy. He thought of his own family, his brothers, his parents, happy times from his past, but he couldn't remember the last time he'd seen them or how long it had been. The Christmas holiday was a very special time for his family as well. If he only knew more about himself and the life he'd lived. *I must be patient,* he thought. *The doctors keep telling me it takes a lot of time with these kinds of head injuries.*

Chris felt a very strong connection with this family forming in his heart. He was no longer alone. Listening to this powerful and emotional story truly felt like a transformative religious experience. He could feel the physical tension that had built up in his body through the long recovery process releasing and draining away. It was almost as if a huge rock had been lifted from his shoulders.

His thinking was clearer now and he was more determined than ever to get his memory back. Again, he felt his subconscious pulling him back to his youth in Minnesota and his family, as though it, too, was searching for hints and clues about his identity. His mind was overtaken with a desire to find out who the hell Chris Da Vita really was.

"Are you all right?" Alana asked him. "Are you lost deep in thought?"

"There's my angel again," Chris said aloud. The altruism of her actions was always there, never ceasing to answer any of his needs. "Yes, Alana, it's true. I am so anxious to discover my real identity."

"It's customary now for us to share food and gifts and sing songs," Hans interjected to lighten the mood of the serious moment taking place.

"It's time to share gifts!" Alana shouted out.

"But I have no gifts to share," Chris said apologetically.

"Ah, but you do," Hans interjected. "Gifts are not necessarily *material things*, as you shall see. Alana and I have been discussing your memory problems and I wish to help. She told me that you've been using the local library's computers to search for clues about your identity. Believe me, I'm well aware of the library's equipment deficiencies. I've tried to use them myself. Even at my age, because of my type of business, computers have become a necessary part of life. Some time ago," he said with a gentle smile, emphasizing the part that came next, "*with the help of my granddaughter*, I purchased and installed two computer systems for my business, one for my office at my shop and one for our home. With these modern devices, I'm now able to manage my business from both locations and do it much more efficiently. More importantly," he said, looking at Alana, "my assistant and I can communicate with customers all over the world, in the office and at home. My computers have been extremely useful in managing and conducting sales transactions for the type of business I'm in.

"Now that I'm getting older," he said with a sigh, "my desire to restore master paintings has come to an end. My time in the shop is now confined to cleaning, appraising, and estimating the values of paintings and art objects. I also do occasional work for some of the museums in Paris and other parts of Europe, but this is as much as I can handle at my age.

Hans now looked at Chris. "I have a double proposal for you," he said. "Of course, you don't have to accept any of what I'm about to propose, but please do give it some thought. We can discuss it in more detail if you have any questions.

"I know you are in need of money and a computer. So, this is what I can offer. I've been asked by the director of the Louvre to do some special appraisals and assessments for their master artworks. These are rare works of art only recently put on public display. This job will require me to spend quite a bit of my time at the Louvre throughout the coming days to complete my investigations and assessments.

"So, here is my offer. I am now in need of someone to attend to my shop and customers while I work on site at the Louvre. The job is eight hours a day, five days a week and a half-day on Saturday. You will have full access to my computer at the shop. I will pay you for the time you work and—if you choose—you can use part of the money to buy one of my computers. At this point, I really don't need both for my business any longer. You should also know," he said, with a twinkle in his eye, "Alana works for me when she can, in the evenings and on weekends. So, she can help you learn the business and how we do things. In your free time you can pursue your quest of discovering your identity."

Chris couldn't believe what he was hearing. The two most pressing problems he faced were solved: money and the tools to continue his research. On top of that, he would be with Alana. As he thought of how to respond, he looked at Alana. With a radiant smile on her face, Chris understood they were together on his decision.

"I do not know how to respond properly other than by saying yes," he said. "Yes, *yes*, of course. I don't know how to thank you."

"Good!" responded Hans. "Then you will start immediately. I have a lunch meeting tomorrow with the Louvre's director, Jean Pierre Rolland, to discuss his projects."

CHAPTER 14

THE SCHEME STARTS TO UNWIND

"We need to meet," said Jean Pierre into the phone. "Yes, the usual place . . . Yes, I will arrange it . . . Ten p.m. on Sunday . . . "

Their meeting place was in one of the many sub-basements of the Louvre. It was just a small room, more like a storage area, with two chairs and a table and a lockable storage cabinet. A number of shipping documents were scattered across the table.

"Do you think he knows?" asked Jean Pierre.

"I do not think so," Maurice responded, "but he is doing more than just *evaluating* the painting. He spent almost as much time inspecting the shipping container as he did on the artwork. What could be so important about the crate it was shipped in? How does that affect the painting's value in any way?"

"It doesn't," Jean Pierre responded. "I'm having lunch with Hans tomorrow. Let's see what he's discovered and where all this is going. What questions did he ask you? And what did you tell him, Maurice?"

The way Jean Pierre said his name was almost accusatory. Maurice shifted in his seat. The room felt warm and stuffy

"Nothing of importance, I assure you," he said. "Just the usual stuff: the history of the Louvre, when I started working here, what was happening here during World War II. And *nothing* about my involvement with Hermann Goering during that time. Not a word was spoken that could connect either you or me to this painting. Hans is curious for some reason, but I don't know why."

"As I've tried to tell you, Maurice, he's not some commonplace craftsman who restores the occasional painting," said Jean Pierre. "He has skills that cannot be taught, especially when it comes to works of the Old Masters. We need him for now. If we're going to sell these paintings for what they're truly worth, we need his expert assessment. We've already come this far. This is the last of it."

"Is he going to evaluate any of the paintings that we've sent to other museums?" asked Maurice. "Maybe we should bring him in as a partner. There's plenty of money to go around. It's enough for all of us."

"I've considered that in the past, but ruled it out because of his faith," said Jean Pierre. "He is a man with strong convictions, from an old Jewish family that goes back for generations. I'm sure he is well aware of all the atrocities that occurred during the war. In fact, I've been told that he escaped from Nazi Germany near the end of the war. Before his escape, I am sure he witnessed a lot of hardship and death among his people. He lost his wife during one of the major Allied bombing raids. I've known him for years, but he's never spoken about it or told me what he was doing there or how he escaped.

"I have a strong sense that he has a deep connection to some of the stolen art that was taken from Europe before and during the war. I believe he is *very familiar* with the art piece that I've asked him to evaluate. Given his reaction, I think there's a strong likelihood it was restored by him. You should have seen the look on his face when he first viewed the painting. He couldn't conceal his excitement. He tried to portray an air of objectivity and detachment, but I could see how much it moved him.

"Let's see if I can get him to open up about his past on Monday and get some answers. We must also not forget that his father and his grandfather were both doing this work for years. There may be a connection there. He once told me they'd taught him the special restoration skills to do this kind of work. I imagine he and his family worked on hundreds of master art works over the years. We need to know more about him and his past history before we can consider recruiting him into our scheme.

"Time is running out for us, Maurice. We need to get rid of as many of these antiques from Goering's hidden chamber as we can before our plan is discovered. Let's not get too impatient or reckless now. Or greedy for that matter. I was successful in depositing the money from our previous transactions into various Swiss bank accounts without raising any red flags. We aren't on anyone's radar and we've accumulated quite a large sum of money. It's more than I ever imagined. Our families will live in comfort for the rest of our lives."

Jean Pierre's joy turned to frustration as the fantasy faded. "What about our other problem, Maurice, the snooping investigator? Your son tells me the man somehow survived the accident."

"Yes, I'm afraid he did," said Maurice. "A passing stranger saw the collision and pulled the driver out of the car before it exploded in flames. The driver was rushed to the hospital with what we thought were fatal injuries, but somehow he survived. I am told he's still convalescing and that his brain injuries have severely impaired his memory. He doesn't know who he is, much less what he was doing, and it could be years before he gets his entire memory back. *If that even happens.* Nobody really knows. It's a day-to-day thing with the guy. If he does recover, however, we will be long finished with this whole operation.

"My son has an undercover contact in the police department. As far as they're concerned, it was a hit-and-run case. The car was totally destroyed by the fire. All the man's documents, his briefcase, and his computer were incinerated. The man driving the truck that hit him ran off and the police don't have any leads. There was only one witness, and he was the man who saved the driver's life. The city truck that we used was stolen and there were no fingerprints to be found. The case was closed indefinitely due to a lack of evidence. Based on this information, I believe we've totally eliminated any possible connection or involvement with this affair."

"I hope you're right," said Jean Pierre. "The next big question is, will the man ever regain his full memory? And if he does, will he remember what he discovered at the Louvre, the Musée d'Orsay, and the other museum he had under surveillance? And then, will he even have the mental ability to put all the pieces back together? Will he even remember what he was investigating? He will have to retrace his steps, regather his documentation, and present his findings once more to whoever he's working for?"

Jean Pierre leaned back his chair, projecting an air of confidence.

"Even if he does, Maurice, as I've said, a very short time from now, there will be no traceable evidence to tie us back to this painting or any of the other works we have taken from the hidden chamber.

"I have to admit, Maurice, establishing a private security company with your son has proven to be *very beneficial* to the success of our plan. With all my Parisian museum contacts and my recommendations about the benefits of his security system, your son was easily able to get contracts with most of the museums in the city. Don't you find it ironic that even as your son's company collects the imagery data from various security tapes—a system designed to compare the images of attendees who visit museums to identify and track potential art thieves—we've used that system to help protect our scheme from being detected?" Jean Pierre laughed. "Even with all of the new identification software available today, and a comprehensive database of potential thieves and scammers—we have molded that very system to our advantage.

"We were very fortunate that your son identified this man due to the frequency of his visits reviewing the security tapes. I believe he was getting close to identifying many of the missing art pieces exhibited at the other museums. He must have sensed we were selling artworks and antiques stolen during World War II. He may have been close to understanding our methods. Perhaps he was getting ready to disclose our plan to the authorities. Or perhaps he was hired by *someone else* with a strong desire to find precious artworks that have never been found.

"Yes, I believe that is more likely. There is a great deal of money to be made selling these artifacts in the underground market. We have certainly proven that! I'm sure we're not the only ones doing this type of *business*. There are multiple lists of the works the Nazis plundered from *every country they occupied*. Hundreds of those works are still missing.

"More questions remain, however. Did this nosy investigator have an accomplice? Was he working alone? Or had he been hired to recover lost antiques for a private party, some unknown person or firm? Was it a Jewish organization, perhaps, seeking to repatriate looted treasures?

"It could be any number of countries who established repatriation teams after the war. There are hundreds of people all over the world working to recover and return confiscated and stolen art. Some of these organizations are still very active and are trying to return these missing treasures to their original owners. Or possibly it could be a private individual or cartel looking to gain access to the millions of dollars of art. In any case, the removal of this *Antone La Rue* from the equation will not stop whoever it was."

It fell silent for a moment. Somewhere in the distance they could hear the faint clunking sound of old pipes. "Have you given up trying to open the huge safe in the Goering chamber?" asked Maurice.

Jean Pierre looked frustrated. "I've tried to crack the combination on numerous visits," he told Jean Pierre, "all with no results. I thought about hiring a professional, but once he saw the room's contents— much less the safe—there'd be no way to keep him quiet. *A hidden room in the Louvre's sub-basement with hundreds of art treasures worth millions of dollars? A bank safe that may be filled with stolen gold and jewels?*

"We could never pay him enough to buy his silence. Our only option would be to get rid of the man soon after he opened the safe.

That, of course, would create a whole new set of problems. And the death of *one more* person. I think it is time for us to tie up the loose ends, forget the safe and disappear. The sooner we shut down our operation, the better off we'll be."

"I have to say I agree," said Maurice. "Let's forget about the safe, seal the chamber and . . . move on. Perhaps someday, in the future, when they decide to refurbish the Louvre, someone will discover this room, designed by German engineers with a proper heating and cooling system designed to protect its contents indefinitely. It's incredible to me, despite the fact that the chamber is tied into Louvre's main ventilation system, no one has ever deduced that it even exists. The entrance to the hidden chamber is so cleverly designed that unless you know precisely where the access point is, you could never figure it out. We should be thankful for our good fortune.

"I have to give the Germans credit. There are no drawings of its design anywhere to be found. The chamber was built secretly by Goering's engineers, most of whom were killed during the war."

From across the table they calmly looked into each other's eyes. Neither man betrayed his thoughts or dared to look away. "You know," said Maurice, "other than you, Jean Pierre, I am *the last person on earth* connected to Goering's hidden treasures. Even if he passed his secrets onto one of his children or a lone confidant before he died, it's been forty years and no one has said a word. We'd be foolish to completely rule out that someone else may know, but there's never even been a hint. So I have to believe it's just us."

CHAPTER 15

MOTIVES ARE REVEALED

"You know," said Maurice reflecting back on the war, "I will never forget the first time Goering came to the Louvre. It was 1937. I'd been summoned to the director's office for a meeting. At that time, I had been working for the director for almost a year as his personal assistant. Because of my memory and recall, he'd put me in charge of all the functional and logistic details required to run this place. It was a daunting task. I'd no formal training, of course, but over time I was able to do the job quite effectively.

"Now, I don't know if you ever met Director Louis Dequire. He was a mediocre painter, but a very prideful man with a huge ego. With his vast network of political connections, he'd been able to rise to the top position at the museum in very short time. What he did not realize, however, was how much the job depended on a wealth of administrative and organizational skills. Those, he neither possessed nor wanted to cultivate. In me, he saw a person who could take over the museum's logistics, freeing him up to pursue his mission of making the Louvre the biggest and best collection of art, artifacts, and antiques in all of Europe—if not the world.

"I became the go-to guy for all the museum's department heads and assisted them with determining where 90 percent of the pieces were housed or displayed. Just as Director Dequire had envisioned, with me handling all these details, he had more time to research and purchase more art and develop huge exhibitions. Indeed, he can be credited with the tremendous expansion of the museum's Near Eastern and Egyptian pieces and exhibitions. They are quite detailed and extensive and thought to be the best in the world.

"With his efforts focused on continual growth and expansion, he gained the recognition he craved to feed his tremendous ego. Before long, he'd become the most celebrated and famous museum director in all of Europe—possibility the whole world.

"After Dequire met with Herr Goering, it was no surprise to me that Dequire soon wanted to dump all of the details and responsibility on me.

"For years there were countless rumors floating around about Herr Goering. One story asserted that he owned a huge collection of fine art and antiques, most of which had been stolen from German Jews. Of course, this was never publicly acknowledged or even whispered about in our newspapers. We French were naïve and gullible, believing the story he'd told us. He assured the Louvre's top brass he was merely researching the wonderful designs of our exquisite galleries.

"As you know, by then, the Nazis were in the midst of planning what they insisted would be the most majestic and most important art museum in the world. In honor of Hitler, it would be called the Führermuseum and would contain the most spectacular art objects in the history of Western civilization.

"It was a sly approach, effectively disguising what he really was up to. The officials who ran the Louvre were blinded by his flattery. Even at that time, nobody imagined the Nazis would invade France. The idea of occupation was so far-fetched, it was literally unbelievable. Our French leaders desperately wanted to believe what was happening all over Europe could never happen here. They also naively believed that our army was strong enough to keep the Nazi war machine at bay."

The look on Maurice's face was one of intense concentration. There was no joy or happiness in the memories he was revisiting. "My first meeting with Herr Goering was quite formal and businesslike," said Maurice. "He indicated that he merely wanted to look at our buildings. He said he was interested in the architectural plans and how the exhibition rooms were laid out. I must admit, I thought it was somewhat odd that he spent most of his time looking at our top exhibitions, recording what was in them.

"As he strolled through the various rooms, he had his assistant record a great deal of detailed information about each gallery's contents. Foolishly I thought he was admiring how it all flowed. If you understand it all properly, it tells quite a story. I thought he was swept up in our expert curation. Now I can see he was secretly selecting what he was going to take for his own collection and what he would send back to Hitler.

"The docent I'd assigned to lead the tour later told me that Goering had given extraordinary attention to our Northern Renaissance paintings. More specifically, the ones by German artists. At that point I began to suspect his real motives were quite different than what he'd stated to the director and myself during his first visit.

"Herr Goering's second visit revealed more about his actual plans. Again, after meeting with our director, he turned all of his attention to me. I was told at that time agreements were being established for an antique exchange program. He strongly suggested, naturally, I would be in charge of all the logistics and details.

"This, of course was a lie.

"Not long after that, in the spring of 1940, Nazi Germany attacked us. The subsequent *battle*, if you can even call it that, was shockingly short lived. We were literally *run over* by their mobile tank units and pounded by the Luftwaffe, the far superior German air force.

"Guess who was in charge of that? None other than Reichsmarschall Goering.

"The invasion was so swift and successful, Hitler promoted Goering and awarded him with the Knight's Cross of the Iron Cross, the highest award in the Nazi military. After that, Goering became the top-ranking soldier in all of Germany, with seniority over all other officers. He only answered to Hitler. As far as everyone else was concerned, he was beyond reproach. To question even his smallest order would be career suicide, if not a literal death sentence. With this new power and authority, he quickly began to amass his personal fortune with countless soldiers at his disposal.

"During his third visit, Goering's true motives and his master plan became an open book. Of course, he never said any of it explicitly, but I knew what he was doing. I am equally certain Goering knew I had him figured out, but he had all the power. Any form of rebellion or disobedience was pointless.

"On this occasion, *Reichsmarschall* Goering arrived at the Louvre as the conquering hero, to be respected and feared. At our first two meetings, he'd been dressed as a very successful businessman with benign intentions, merely trying to work out the details of artwork exchanges between France and Germany. On his third visit he was dressed in full military regalia with dozens of medals on his chest and a team of assistants in tow. He flaunted his unrivaled power and made it clear he was now in charge.

"At that point, he rolled out his plan, beginning the construction of his hidden, underground cache of stolen art. Of course, he insisted it was a protective bunker for the Louvre's priceless treasures. Even then, there was no reason for anyone to doubt him. He played it off like his love of art and respect for the museum's pieces was the driving factor.

"His plan was simple but clever. All of the government buildings and museums were now under Nazi control. He could confiscate all of the items he'd identified previously for his personal collection. Most would be shipped to Germany. Some, Goering stored in his hidden underground bunker located in a sub-basement somewhere beneath the Louvre.

"Goering knew full well that museums were not going to be the targets of any bombing raids or land invasions, especially not the

Louvre. Paris was denoted as a *free city,* to be saved from destruction because of its importance to Western European history. The most clever part of his plan was to prey on the vanity of our director and other curators. Goering had convinced them he only meant to protect France's most important art and antiques; meanwhile he was collecting them in a hidden bunker below the world's most famous museum. His personal collection was now totally safe and available to him whether the Nazis won or lost the war.

"During this time, his access to all the treasures was unlimited. Before the war had even started, he'd established his special task force, known as the ERR or *Einsatzstab Reichsleiter Rosenberg,* organized to steal the most valuable pieces from the most prominent national museums and galleries in the countries the Nazis conquered. All of it was funneled and inventoried at the Paris office, and the officer in charge answered only to Goering."

Maurice took a deep breath and rubbed his temples. Recounting this painful chapter of the Louvre's history was emotionally draining. He steadied himself and continued. "Of course, I was witness to Goering's frequent visits to his Paris headquarters. Here at the Louvre, he personally reviewed the manifests of all the incoming items. This was his primary method of selecting special pieces for the Führer and his collection. The other German generals who caught wind of Goering's vast operation, the Reichsmarschall either controlled with bribes or threats of physical violence.

"In the beginning, almost all the items he chose were sent back to Germany to his residences there. The rest were shipped to a special underground salt mine, where they would be kept safe until they were sent to Hitler's new museum, to be built in Austria. Endless trainloads of art, antiques, furniture and other treasures were sent to Germany. As the war progressed and the Nazis opened up a second front in Russia, Hitler unveiled a plan he called *Operation Barbarossa.* The first step, of course, was to defeat and occupy Russia. After that, he fully intended to repopulate the country with German nationals, using some of the conquered civilians as slave labor to rebuild the country.

"However, with the vast German military fighting on two major fronts, things began to fluctuate. For the first time, Goering was uncertain the Germans would win the war. He picked up the pace of his operations and started to move more and more looted items into the Louvre's hidden chamber, which was now fully completed and could withstand the largest bombs in the Allies' arsenal.

"Until then," Maurice made clear, "my involvement in all of this had been minimal. I was in charge of small things, like the food service and janitorial staff. After all, we French the inferior people to him, were fit only for this type of work.

"The Nazis never knew about my photographic memory and ability to recall countless details. To throw them off I purposefully made minor mistakes and forgot to fully complete some of their job requests. I worked hard to cultivate their expectations of me, as a typical dumb Frenchman. Being involved with the food and janitorial services, however, required me to work with all the suppliers and vendors. I was essentially given free rein to appropriate the necessary supplies to keep the Louvre operational. I was able to go to the railyards and shipping docks unimpeded to receive whatever I needed. All I needed to say was that the Reichsmarschall had requested these things. In the process I was able to track everything came into or left the Louvre via the railyards. They never suspected a thing.

"As the war intensified after the Allied invasion in at Normandy, the so-called *invincibility* of the Nazi armies began to wane. Hitler's invasion of Russia turned out to be a huge military blunder. The Third Reich started to falter. The outcome of the war started to swing in the Allies' favor. Of course, the fighting went on until mid-1945, but the die was cast.

"As the German army began to evacuate, security at Goering's Paris hub began to decrease. Hardened, disciplined soldiers were replaced by teenage boys who worked for meager food rations. More and more professional soldiers were redeployed to the various fronts. Being a *dumb* Frenchman, I was asked to send our inexperienced workers to the various shipping locations to pack and ship the massive number of art objects arriving in Paris and being reshipped to Germany.

"I remember one occasion when a specially-marked, custom-made crate was designated specifically for Goering's secret room beneath the Louvre. It had arrived from Berlin. Up until that time, only a small team of soldiers handpicked by Goering had been given access to the hidden vault.

"For reasons I still can't fathom, on this occasion I was asked to assist. No one had *ever* been allowed to know the location of the room or its access points. As we moved this special art piece, I was led down a maze of halls and corridors. They assumed I'd get confused and never be able to retrace our steps.

"They were wrong, of course.

"I was the *only* person employed by the Louvre who could navigate or direct someone to a specific location anywhere in the entire complex. I made sure to feed into their preconceived ideas, pretending to be lost and completely turned around. All these years I kept the location secret, waiting to capitalize on the knowledge of its whereabouts and valuable contents. Now, that time has finally arrived and I shall get my reward for all those years of hard work and service to this museum.

"You know, Jean Pierre, I put up with Goering's arrogance, his insults, his supposed mental superiority every time he visited. Not once did he ever acknowledge me as a person or greet me as a human being. Occasionally, he made vague promises that I would be compensated for my efforts when the war was finally over. But when it became clear the Nazis would lose the war, Goering committed suicide. I was the only one left with any knowledge about his secret collection of treasures and its whereabouts.

"I am now an old man. I have given my life to the Louvre, yet I was never really properly compensated for my special abilities. Yes, I made a modest wage, but neither my family nor I have prospered in any way, despite all of my efforts and the value that I bring to this institution. Nothing—and I mean *nothing*—is going to get in my way or prevent me from taking what I deserve for working here for all those years. So, Jean Pierre, let's finish what we started and move on with our lives."

"Yes, my friend," said Jean Pierre, "you have indeed sacrificed and given much of your life to the Louvre with very little reward. I assure you, the time has come for us to collect what we're properly owed. I meet with Hans tomorrow. After that, we will make our final decisions and start closing down this operation."

CHAPTER 16

THE LOUVRE DIRECTORS

Jean Pierre Rolland had been the Louvre's director for over fifteen years. He'd advanced quickly through ranks, much like his predecessor, Louis Dequire. When Dequire ran the museum, his decisions were always politically driven. With his aggressive style, Dequire made it through the management maze with bluffs and promises.

Unlike his predecessor, Jean Pierre was a tall, stately-looking gentleman with minimal political connections. His background was neither in the field of art nor museum management. He'd been educated at the University of Paris and graduated with degrees in finance and business. After finishing school, he started working for a major French airline company. With his financial background, he became a skilled dealmaker, negotiating the purchase of airplanes and consolidating routes all over Europe and the Americas. With his strong business sense and vision for the future, he rose quickly to the top financial position in the company. He became known in the airline industry for his ability to negotiate contracts, make favorable deals, and secure capital for growth and expansion—all of which made money for himself and his company. He was the perfect person to bring the Louvre back to its status as the world's biggest and best museum.

After World War II, many of France's museums were fighting to stay in existence, both from a financial standpoint as well as to maintain their relevance to those who enjoyed viewing antiques and art. The Nazis had plundered so many pieces, the museums were nearly empty. It wasn't until the agents of the Monuments, Fine Arts, and Archives program (MFAA), also known as the Monuments Men, started tracking down and returning these plundered treasures that museums all over Europe began to recover.

The Louvre had been in need of a man who could negotiate and bring back its treasures by whatever means necessary. Louis Dequire was known to have cavorted with the Nazis, specifically with Hermann Goering. He had put his own personal interests ahead of the Louvre's, making his dismissal at the end of the war necessary. This was, of course, positioned as a forced retirement to mask the real reasons for his departure. It allowed Dequire to save face with the public. Not long after he'd retired, however, he was found dead; an apparent suicide, according to the police.

Despite the official story, it was well known within the museum community that Dequire had helped Goering make selections from some of the plundered goods that arrived in Paris. He was even known to have attended some of Herr Goering's special parties. In the eyes of his French associates, Dequire's political ambitions were nothing short of treasonous.

The French people suffered greatly during the Nazi occupation. The atrocities they endured at the hands of the Nazis were well documented. Subsequently, individuals known to have helped the Nazis in any capacity were dealt with quickly and harshly after the war. Thus, Louis Dequire was hardly mourned. He had been branded a traitor who could never be forgiven.

Thus, when Jean Pierre started working for the Louvre, the museum was not only in the throes of a financial crisis, but in the eyes of the French people, it was an organization that had conspired with the Nazis. The war had left a negative legacy on its most famous museum.

Once France's museums were repaired and reopened, many were still missing their most prized and most famous pieces. Tracking down and identifying its stolen treasures was the top priority of the Louvre's leadership team. Jean Pierre's hiring proved to be a wise and fortuitous decision. However, the temptations that came from associating with the rich and famous of the art world would prove to be daunting for him. The world of these elites revolved around investments and collecting precious things. Owning a creation by a world-famous artist was not only a hedge against market downturns, but a status symbol and ticket into the highest social circles of Paris. With his business acumen, Jean Pierre had already achieved his personal financial goals. As he took on the role if director, he turned his attention to building his image and status within the French art community.

CHAPTER 17

THE PAINTING DISCOVERIES

The meeting between Hans and Jean Pierre was not held in Jean Pierre's office, but in a secluded section of the building. There were no phones, only a desk and two chairs. There were refreshments, pastries, and fruit to meet the needs of the two attendees. It was quite obvious to Hans that his host's intentions were to keep the conversation private, causal, and uninterrupted, allowing both parties to express themselves freely in this relaxed atmosphere.

"So, what do you think, Hans? Is the painting a fake? When you stated at the exposition that the painting was in pristine condition, I couldn't agree with you more. And I also believe, like you, it has most likely not seen the light of day for years."

Of course, Hans knew it was not a forgery. The day after he returned from the exhibition at the Louvre, he checked the black book his family used to record their restoration work. There was no question; the numbers he copied off the canvas matched perfectly with what was recorded in the book years ago. Yes, he knew that this was indeed the painting for which he'd been given special instructions from Goering's agents that day in that horrible warehouse near the Berlin railyard. The special, heavy duty packaging made sense to him now. It was required because it was going to France with specific coded information for storage into the Louvre's hidden room. It was all coming together for him now. What a clever scheme! Store and hide some of your most important and valuable treasures at the Louvre. Who would guess in a time of war that an invading captor would do such a thing? With this knowledge, Hans still wanted to examine the painting, being careful not to give away his involvement with it, and also investigate his theory that this museum was housing more missing World War II art. He thought about the impossible task of locating these other missing artifacts in the largest museum in the world. He decided not to give away any of his thoughts about what he had discovered to Jean Pierre. *Not yet*, he thought. *Let's see where the conversation goes first.* The meeting's private location begged the question: what was Jean Pierre's real agenda with him?

Hans responded, "The real value of this artwork cannot be determined without further close examination. We need to determine if this is the original canvas and not a painting over a painting. I believe you have here in your lab the special x-ray equipment that will allow me to look beneath the top painting surface to determine if there is a second painting underneath. It will also be necessary to examine the paints used to determine the painting's age. Once we acquire this data, then I can give you my final assessment as to its authenticity, and I will be 99 percent sure you that have a four- to five-hundred-year-old artwork that is worth a small fortune. If you and the owner allow me to do these evaluations, it will require at least two days. If this painting is from a real art master, then I will be able to provide you with a value and verification of its authenticity. And if it's real, the owners would become quite rich if they decided to auction it off."

Jean Pierre remained silent throughout Hans's analysis. He was quite impressed with what was hearing. He had never really seen the technical side of this man. They had known each other and been friends for years. Not close friends, but they had many common interests. They both loved art and a good French wine. Both of them had lost their wives during the war and had granddaughters similar in age—adored granddaughters to whom they were devoted. But there were major differences in their values. This, he believed, would prevent them from ever working together in a business relationship.

CHAPTER 18

REFLECTION AND RENEWAL

The eighth and final candle on the menorah was lit. It was the final evening of Hanukkah. Chris had participated in each night of the Muller family's celebration. He'd been captivated by the experience— the history and the ancient stories about the Jewish faith that Hans had shared with his granddaughter and her guest.

For Chris, it became a time of reflection and renewal. He couldn't imagine how his body and mind had survived the terrible car accident, and yet, they had indeed survived. Of course, he knew very well his recovery was due to the many dedicated people at the hospital who had put the needs of others, like himself, before their own. How fitting for Chris to celebrate this festival of restoration with the angel who'd seen him through his darkest days.

Refreshed and renewed by the week-long experience, he was more driven than ever to get to the bottom of the mystery of who he was and why he was in a foreign country.

"So, how was your day at the shop today, Chris? You've been working there almost a week. What do you think?"

Chris chuckled and said, "I think you hired the wrong man. I feel clumsy. I don't know the products well and dealing with people on a one-to-one basis makes me uncomfortable."

"You must give it time," Hans assured him. "You know, you have Alana to help you. She's just a phone call away."

"That sounds suspiciously like a TV commercial tagline to me," said Antone. "Hans, are you sure you haven't already retired?" They all shared a good laugh at this.

"The more important question I have for you," responded Hans, "is how's your *personal* investigation coming along? Are you utilizing the computer? Do you have any further information you can share with Alana and me? Any new and exciting details?"

"Well, I'm not sure how exciting any of this might be, but *yes*. I've discovered some very interesting facts that go back to my schooling in Minnesota," he said. Chris began to share the details he'd first seen in his dream and then confirmed online by tracking down a copy of his high school yearbook.

"It's getting late," Alana interjected. She had some thoughts as to how to spend the rest of the evening. "I have a very busy day tomorrow. Can we wait until Saturday and cover all the details with you then? Besides, who knows what else Chris will discover between now and then."

"But of course," said Hans, before adding, "I have some special information I need to cover with the two of you as well."

As Alana and Chris departed from Hans's home, Hans couldn't help but notice his granddaughter slip her hand into Chris's as they disappeared down the sidewalk. Hans had been following Chris's recovery process and his granddaughter's involvement. It was no surprise to witness this bond of togetherness. Hans had also felt the healing power of Hanukkah during the week. Slowly, it had released some of the demons that had been haunting him from his recent encounter with the painting. He smiled inwardly as he thought about his granddaughter's motives. Now his personal goals were in his sight and felt attainable: to fulfill his promise to his beloved Elsa and repatriate stolen art to Holocaust survivors.

Still, he had to admit, he wasn't looking forward to his upcoming discussion with Jean Pierre about his evaluation of the mystery painting. Hans needed to conceal the truth about the masterpiece, no matter how much he had to distort or bury the facts. The history must be righted. He was not sure that Jean Pierre was involved in a scheme profiting from his involvement, but the man seemed suspicious. Exactly how long a conspiracy had been operating and the depth of Jean Pierre's involvement in it—not to mention others at the museum—remained an open question.

Hans was well aware that once the real owners were revealed, shockwaves would be felt throughout the entire art world.

CHAPTER 19

THE NIGHT OF NIGHTS

As they reached the corner of Hans's block on that beautiful evening, Chris and Alana decided to take a cab back to his apartment, despite its short distance away. This last evening of Hanukkah had heightened their feelings for each other. Their passion was palpable.

Alana had also purchased a nice bottle of Bordeaux to celebrate Chris's personal discoveries and she was eager to hear what he had to share.

With the wine decanted and their celebration begun, they relaxed into each other's arms. Their discussion shifted from the past to the present, to the new relationship that was unfolding between them; a relationship that had broadened into a state of pure joy. It was a love that knew no inhibitions, a love which now consummated the intense emotions they felt for each other. Their beautiful, pent-up desires had been held in abeyance these past few weeks, waiting for the right time, the right moment to break free, to be unleased from the bounds of individualism into togetherness. This unveiling of their emotions toward each other was now complete. There would no longer be a separation, but a harmonious conjoining of bodies, minds, and hearts.

How could one imbibe this array of emotions, this intensity of sensations with a lover and still remain coherent?

It could not be done.

One could only relish the feeling and dive deeper into the moment. The two lovers found themselves enwrapped in each other's arms, immersed in a world of emotion and pure love. It was a night of all nights and neither of them wished to ever break the spell.

They talked the entire evening and well into the early morning hours, dozing off from time to time into pleasant dreams about what had transpired, what was said, and what lay before them. The hours were priceless and so rewarding for each of them. They savored every moment.

Eventually, the spell and their embrace was disrupted by the ringing of Chris's phone—a wrong number, naturally.

Anyway, it was time for them to meet the challenges of the day. She, to her beloved job of nursing, and Chris to his seemingly endless quest for his true identity. They agreed to meet for dinner that night at a nearby restaurant to discuss the next steps of their future together.

CHAPTER 20

THE DANGEROUS CALL HOME

"Where on earth have you been?" asked Chris's brother, Scott. "Everyone thinks you're *dead*. Where are you, anyway?"

"Listen, Scott," said Chris, "I have to make this call short. I'm sorry to say, I can only answer *one* of your questions."

"Bull crap, Chris, Mom and Dad are worried sick. Your fiancée is pulling her hair out, on the verge of a nervous breakdown. Your secretary doesn't know what to do with your business and your customers are getting antsy. All of your country club buddies are looking for answers too."

"First, I need to limit my answers," said Chris. "Your phone is probably bugged. Please don't get upset, it's the business I'm in. I need to keep this short for now. Just listen. The less you know about this, the safer I'll be. You too, for that matter. I can't drag you into this.

"I spent the last three months of my life in hospitals and rehabilitation centers. I'm almost 100 percent recovered from a major car accident, but I nearly died. My body is healing, but I have significant memory problems. I'm making some progress gaining it back, but I need to be clear on some of my life's major events to trigger my brain's recall-mode. I got lucky in the crash. A good Samaritan pulled me out of my car before it exploded, but my briefcase with all my identification when up in smoke. The only ID I have left is my passport and a small amount of cash in the hidden passport holder I carried around my neck. And the passport? Well, it says my name is Antone La Rue."

"Who?"

"Never mind. I think I've already said too much."

"Chris!"

"It was a fake identity. I was traveling with a forged passport. The police had no idea who I really was and neither did I for quite a while. It was a hit-and-run. There were very few clues, so the case was dropped. To be honest, I only figured out my real name a few weeks ago, with the help of the trauma nurse who kept me alive during my desperate fight to stay alive. She is truly my angel . . .

"I'm making some progress with my memory, but there are still significant gaps. About three weeks ago, I had a dream about helping Dad on the farm as a boy. It was so vivid, I woke up in the middle of the night in a cold sweat. From that dream, I was able to piece together some of my past, like my high school years in Austin, Minnesota. With the help of the local library's internet system, I searched through Austin's high school yearbooks and the local newspaper. After much digging I was able to find my senior class picture and my real name. I also found you, of course, and all of our brothers. Thank God for all those hockey pictures in the local paper. I think I might have been stuck if we hadn't all played in high school.

"I know I graduated second in my class and had several scholarship offers, but I have no idea which college I went to or who I worked for after that. Thankfully, I've managed to put my early life back together, but after high school, hit a wall. Things are at a standstill. I need your help getting some answers, and I need them quickly. I'm being watched, but I don't know why. I no longer think the car crash was an accident and I'm worried there will be a second attempt on my life.

"Scott, I need to know my history *after I left high school*. My Social Security number, my passport, my internet user IDs and passwords, if you know them. Anything you can get me. I need it all, but here's the thing. Listen, this is serious. Do *not* gather this information over the phone. It *must* be done in person. You can't tell anyone the details of this conversation, not even our parents or my secretary. They will be in too much danger.

"Scott, somehow I think I've put myself in the middle of a huge international art scandal—one that will send shockwaves through the art industry for years. Museums, galleries, private collectors, they all want a piece of me. I need to know who hired me and what they sent me to investigate. I think I was getting close to uncovering something big when the so-called *accident* happened, but I do not know what that something was.

"I need to fill in the blanks of my personal history. Quickly, so I can begin to unravel this complex mystery. I will call you tomorrow. You need to tell me whatever you can." Chris hesitated briefly. His already-serious tone became even more solemn. "Scott, I need you to buy a private phone," he said. "Figure out a way to get me the phone number without revealing it to *whoever* is likely listening to this very conversation. Please help calm Mom and Dad down, but don't share what we have discussed. Not with anyone."

"Chris, seriously. Don't you think you're being a little paranoid?"

Scott heard a very distinct, but muffled, click. Chris had ended the call before Scott had even completed the question. The line was silent. Chris hung up the phone and looked out the window at the clear blue sky. Neither Scott nor Chris heard the final click as all connections ended.

Somewhere in the basement of a nondescript office building in St. Paul's downtown warehouse district, a man asked his recording technician, "Did you get all of that?"

"I did. And you can be damn sure I'll be ready for tomorrow's conversation, too."

"Excellent," said the first man, consulting his clipboard, "let's review what we know. Scott is the oldest son of five boys in the Da Vita family. He is married, has three children of his own, and works for a large multinational company not far from here, in St. Paul. Chris, the brother who just hung up, is the middle son. Wherever the call originated, we know it was from overseas. Chris is the *adventurer*, his family calls him. We know he is whip-smart and has the resume to prove it. He's always doing new things, trying something different, taking risks and pushing himself. He was always 'a handful,' to quote his parents, and has never been known to back down from a challenge. The curious part is, who is he working for now, and for what purpose?"

Why me, thought Scott, after his brother had hung up the phone. *The two of us haven't spoken in nearly a year. Even then, we did little more than exchange cursory greetings and social niceties. Yes, I'm the oldest, but Chris knows I'm swamped by major responsibilities at work, juggling the chaotic schedules of two busy teenage kids and trying to carve out some to be alone with my wife. Or maybe he doesn't remember . . . If only his research had told him to call Steve. He's young, unmarried, and an internet guru who could help Chris easily.*

Then there's this bit about getting a brand-new phone and a number that can't be traced or tied to anyone. And somehow, by tomorrow, I have to get him this information without revealing it to anyone else.

The first two requests were easy, but how could Scott hope to accomplish the third and most difficult request? Scott was upset with Chris. Their conversation had been too short and one-sided. Still, Scott could tell from Chris's voice that the danger was real and immediate.

Scott also began to realize there were some excellent reasons why Chris had chosen *him* to carry out the request. Chris was an ex-CIA operative who'd retired the previous year, after ten years of service. Occasionally, the two of them discussed Chris's career with the CIA in broad, general terms. No case information, of course, but they talked about some of the techniques used by undercover agents to send and receive messages over unsecured phone lines.

There was no limit, it seemed, to the different methods and the cleverness entailed. Most agents used their own system when they were under deep cover, especially if their lives depended on getting secret information back to the home office.

Scott surmised there must have been one or more clues hidden in their conversation. Chris had sent him a message on how to accomplish the task of disclosing the phone number without revealing it to anyone bugging the phone.

Scott thought back to their conversation and replayed it all in his head. *Yes!* It must have been in the comments Chris had made about hockey. Chris had clearly said that *all their brothers* played high school hockey. He remembered Chris's comment clearly: "Thank God for all those hockey pictures in the local paper. I think I might have been stuck if we hadn't all played in high school."

That's not true, Scott thought to himself. One of their brothers quit hockey and joined the ski team. That must be significant for some reason. Certainly, Chris would know only four brothers had been on the hockey team.

But what is it? Scott wondered. One thing they all had in common was their jersey numbers. Each brother had kept the same exact number from his early park-league days all the way up through high school. Each brother's number was different from all of the others. Nobody else would ever know that if they weren't aware of the family's sports history. Those numbers would mean nothing to anyone else, but were very much a part of the brothers' childhood.

Scott went to bed very late that evening, his research completed. Exhausted, he fell asleep, confident no code breaker would ever be able to decipher his message when he called Chris the following day. In the morning, he would buy a disposable phone, request a special phone number, and pass that number to his brother.

Scott didn't hesitate for a second when Chris answered the phone. "It's good to hear your voice again," said Scott, launching into a laundry list of facts. "Harvard business school. Scholarship. Mathematics and business major. Fluent French. Minor in art. Ten years with The Company. Restless and bored, so you quit. Present occupation, unknown.

I'm not even sure you know it yourself. Have fun." Scott took a deep breath and said very slowly and clearly, with metronomic precision. "S . . . C . . . S . . . B, stop. CR, stop. B . . . S . . . P . . . M, stop."

No other word was spoken. That was the whole conversation. Both parties simply hung up.

At the underground office in a secure facility in St. Paul, a frustrated man yelled out, "What the hell was that? He didn't tell us one damn thing we didn't already know. What the hell do those letters mean?"

"Obviously, it's a very clever coded message," the security technician responded. "We need to break it—and fast—or we're going to lose him."

"We can try, but don't hold your breath. I think we should get in touch with the boys in Europe."

It didn't take long for Chris to decipher the phone number.

The letters *SC* were the area code 715. *SB* was 710 and *CR* was 1514. Chris knew Scott was a hockey nut, and being the oldest, he got stuck taking his younger brothers to countless hockey practices. He'd watched so many of their games, without question, he knew all the boys' jersey numbers. The final four letters told Chris the time he should call Scott back: 10:15 p.m.

Chris knew it probably wouldn't take a code breaker long to decipher this new phone number, but he didn't care. One quick private call with his brother an hour later would allow him to get him the rest of what he needed to understand his history. All this new information, along with the use of Hans's computer, should be enough to accelerate the process of regaining his full memory.

At precisely 10:15 p.m., the two brothers exchanged information with complete confidence that no one else was listening. Unlike the previous call, this conversation continued for quite some time, with both parties getting the information they sought. Chris was very careful not to disclose any clues as to why—or what—he was doing in Paris in order to make sure his brother and family weren't put in jeopardy.

Before they finally hung up, they agreed to talk the following week at the same designated time. The new phone would be destroyed; Scott would procure another and pass along the coded number.

This time, there was no secondary phone click following their discussion. Their plan had worked. With quick and clever low-tech methods, they had outwitted the men who'd hoped to tap their conversation.

Armed with voluminous new information and concrete pieces of his history, Chris attacked his memory issues with a vengeance. It was already getting quite late, but he knew he couldn't wait until morning.

He went back to Hans's shop and turned on the computer. As he began to scour the internet for more clues, based on the information Scott had provided, his memory was triggered. His mind became a cascade of incidents and encounters from his college days, his recruitment by the CIA, and the work he'd performed as an undercover agent.

The pieces of his history started to fall into place. It was early Saturday morning when, exhausted from his all-night internet searching, he collapsed on the office couch. As he drifted off into a coma-like dream, he thought how easy it was for him to access all this information about himself. He remembered the hours and hours of training that he'd received while going through his CIA boot camp. Getting his body in physical shape was one thing, but the computer training, learning the various methods of accessing data, was really paying off for him now. He told himself that tomorrow he would break into his own private office computer in St. Paul to complete his identity quest as to why he was in Paris.

CHAPTER 21

THE CONTRACTUAL AGREEMENT

It was late Friday afternoon and Chris was getting ready to close up Hans's shop. It had been a great week for him. The celebration he and Alana shared in his apartment on the last night of Hanukkah was still fresh in his mind and he felt like he was on top of the world. The art shop was also doing well. He'd made some great sales for Hans and he was getting excited about this new and interesting work.

Surprising even himself, he'd quickly picked up on the lingo and skills required to sell expensive works of art to very sophisticated clients. It was almost as if he'd done this before, with prior insider knowledge about the art industry.

Perhaps his background knowledge, from his art minor in college, enabled him to speak with some authority and credibility when dealing with customers. Either way, he could definitely picture himself, with Alana by his side, making a career in art once this mess was finally resolved. At the moment, he was just eager to lock up the shop and meet Alana at the restaurant they'd chosen. Hans's business would be one of the many subjects they needed to discuss.

Unexpectedly, the front door chimed, breaking his train of thought. He instinctively looked to the front of the store as two men entered. The second man stopped at the door, flipped the store's *Open* sign to *Closed* and positioned himself in the doorway with his large, muscular arms folded across his chest.

Chris took a step to meet them, but before he could say a word, the first man barked, "Mr. Da Vita, what are you doing here? You had a job working for us. Did you already spend all the money we paid you?"

Chris was utterly shocked, hearing his real name from a total stranger. He became so choked up that when he spoke, only babble came out.

"We're here to check the progress of your *investigation*," said the man. "By now, of course, you know there have been many stolen pieces of art that vanished during World War II showing up here in Paris and auction houses all over Europe."

"Who *are you*?" asked Chris, feeling a sudden surge of adrenaline. Deep inside his body, a defense mechanism had been triggered. He quickly and silently maneuvered himself into position, ready to overpower the stranger should it be necessary.

"Whoa, whoa, there, buddy," said the man raising his palms as if to signal surrender. "I'm not the enemy here. We've come to check on your progress. We gave you a generous contract, but it's been several months now. Our agreement stated you would keep us up to date, but we haven't heard *anything* from you in quite some time. For a while, we just assumed you'd run off with the money and we'd never hear from you again.

"We staked out your apartment, but it's been quiet for months. We only picked up your trail recently, and here we are. We were going to *stop by for a visit* the other night at your apartment, but we saw you with . . . a woman and decided not to interfere. We assumed she might be tied to your investigation?"

The man waited only briefly for an answer, before pressing on. "So, *Chris*, it's your turn now. You certainly have a lot to explain, but first, have you discovered anything you'd care to share with us?"

Chris's head was a tangle of unspooling thoughts. None of this made any sense. He'd recovered a lot from his past, but nothing like this. He was well aware of his security business back in Minnesota, but he had no recollection of establishing contact—let alone signing a *contract*—with these two mysterious men to perform an investigation in Paris.

Who are they? Who could have sent them?

They looked professional in their attire, but could they be trusted? They knew his real name for some reason.

"Do you—can I see some kind of identification?" he asked.

The two men seemed bemused, as if Chris were joking. After a moment, however, the face of the man nearest Chris fell serious and he showed Chris his badge. They were special investigators with the Paris police. Chris relaxed and mentally lowered his defensive posture. He would have to trust them for now, even as he racked his brain for any knowledge concerning the "update" they'd requested of him.

With no other options to speak of, Chris decided his first order of business would be to tell them the truth about his accident, his incredible survival story, and the memory problems that persisted. He led the men into Hans's shop, well away from prying eyes that may be looking through the front window and began his incredible tale. All told, it took nearly two hours to tell, though Chris was careful not to reveal the nature of his relationship with Hans or Alana. Instead, he told them he'd taken the job so he could pay rent, reminding them that his money and all identification papers had been incinerated in the car fire. He'd had no source of income and discovered only recently his real name and identity.

"That's quite a story, my friend," said the man who'd stood guarding the door. "Of course, we're glad you survived, but now we still need to discuss our contract. Our *client* is anxious to find what information you've uncovered, so please, let's cut to the chase. Have you yet identified who might be behind this illegal scheme of selling stolen art and antiques? As you know, there are master artworks sporadically showing up at different museums throughout France and there's very strong indications they originate from the same source." Chris frantically tried to remember what, if any, evidence he may or may not have discovered.

"Gentlemen, please forgive me," said Chris. "Perhaps if we go back to the start of our relationship, the details of the contract will help trigger my memory. Then, I might be able to recall—and to *share*—the findings that I've made."

"Chris, do I really need to tell your there is big money here for both of us?" asked the first man, skeptically. When Chris still remained silent, he launched into what he knew. "Very well," he said, "we've never met our client. Even now he remains completely anonymous. We receive our instructions through encrypted, untraceable email. We were told to hire someone with your skills and background to investigate where this sudden influx of old-world art, antiques, and master paintings were coming from. The client *demands* to know who's behind this illegal scheme. Someone out there is making an awful lot of money from the sales of all these stolen goods.

"Of course, as you must know, my partner and I aren't doing this in an *official* capacity. This is strictly off the books. A moonlight job, if you will. We only took the assignment to make some additional cash. I'm sure you understand. Living *comfortably* in Paris on a policeman's wages is quite difficult." He smiled briefly, then continued. "The instructions we were given specified that we hire someone who spoke fluent French. Not a Frenchman, mind you, but an *outsider* with excellent knowledge about the field of art and how pieces are bought and sold. Needless to say, this person was also to be an outstanding investigator."

He paused thoughtfully for a moment, the only sound Hans's grandfather clock on the back wall of the shop. "It took us quite a while to find you," the man continued, "but we obtained your name from one of our secret case files. Apparently, you'd worked with the French government before, in our very agency with our top undercover group. You were on loan from the CIA. With your recent retirement from the CIA, your impeccable background, and your own security business, you were—or rather, *you are*—the perfect fit. We knew you'd still have many contacts that you could leverage in your investigation.

"When we first approached you, in the United States, we passed along this information, including a list and pictures of the most prominent items that the Nazis took during the war. Your fee, *if you're successful*, is to be $500,000 US dollars. You were given the first half when you arrived in Paris. The other half will be paid when you *successfully* complete the assignment. Of course, our client is also paying all of your expenses during your investigation.

"When you landed at Charles de Gaulle, you were given a briefcase with the first half of the money, a forged French passport for *Antone La Rue*, with corroborating documentation, as well as a nine-month lease on your apartment and instructions on how to contact us. This was all given to you at a small cafe not far from the airport. That was the last time we saw you. You'd agreed to regular updates, but thus far we've only received minimal information regarding your progress.

"In your only substantive report, you mentioned that you'd located one of the paintings from the list. You also indicated that you were following leads that might identify the source and people who were involved. Since then, we haven't seen or heard from you. Needless to say, we've been . . . *worried*. We stuck our necks out for you and put our credibility on the line. You've been a mystery man to us. As I said, we thought you'd skipped town and left us holding the bag. Now that we've finally found you, it's time to make things right. We can't afford further delays."

Chris pictured the day he and Alana had searched his apartment for clues about his identity.

His special jacket with the hidden pockets containing some money and a special key—not to mention a custom space to conceal a gun—had piqued his interest then. Now, listening to these two men, his mind flooded with specific details as to why he was in Paris. As funny as it sounded to him, that key may be *the* key that would unlock his final memory recall dilemma. All he could think about now was how to get to the airport and get that briefcase. If indeed that's where it was, he vaguely remembered looking for a secluded locker area to put the attaché case with all that money. It didn't get burned up in the car accident, he was sure of that now.

But first, he needed to somehow get these two detectives off his back. "Time!" he shouted out. "I need time to verify that what you have told me is true."

"Of course, monsieur. But we will need to get in touch with our client as well. He controls the purse strings. It's his timetable, not ours. We are merely the middlemen in this whole affair, a buffer to maintain his anonymity."

"I sense you don't believe my story. You're with the French police. You have access to the Paris police records. Check out my story. No doubt they have a case file of the accident I was in, and my condition after the accident."

"That is precisely what we will do, Chris, and we will pass that information onto our client. As far as continuing your involvement in this contract and the status of the money you received, that is out of our control. If you will provide us with your phone number, we will get back to you in a few days and advise you if our client wishes you to continue."

Chris's head spun with all the information he'd just learned, but he managed to blurt out a statement he hoped would give him the chance to complete the contract he'd committed to: "I will complete this investigation with or without your client's approval. This entire affair has changed my life. My memory and recall abilities are tied directly to solving this case. I believe only when I have completed this assignment will I regain my total memory. Furthermore, I believe my accident was planned, therefore my life is still in danger—I was getting close to identifying the leader and sources behind this scheme. When you guys hired me, you never told me my life could be in danger; that was not in any contract. To me, it was a simple investigating job. I was selling my skill, not my life. You people should have been more upfront about the dangers I would face. I should be getting additional hazard pay for what I'm doing. You tell your client I will finish this job. The game is changed, gentleman. I fought hard these past few weeks to regain my memory, made some great steps and progress in this endeavor. I have gone from zero knowledge about myself to almost full recovery. In the process, I've lost months of my life. I almost *lost* my life. With what you have told me tonight, once I track and verify this information and recover that attaché case, that should complete the linkage for me. I am sure of it. In fact, I guarantee it. I also know how much progress I have made here in Paris."

"Well, Chris, you will get no argument from us. In fact, if we can assist you in any way, let us know. We have access to all the police files in France. We can provide you with information even your CIA people can't. We, too, have an investment of time, labor, and favors that we owe people. There is no paycheck for us unless you are successful."

Yes, Chris thought, *I might just need their assistance in the future.*

The meeting finally broke. It was well past midnight when Chris switched off the lights in Hans's shop and locked the door. *I need to call Alana,* he said to himself as he walked down the street.

CHAPTER 22

AN UNDERCOVER MISSION

"Alana, I know it's late. I'm sorry I didn't call—"

"Oh, Chris, thank God it's you," said Alana, cutting him off. "I was worried sick about you."

"I'm fine, everything's fine," said Chris, urgently.

Alana sounded like she might cry. Chris could hear her breathe deeply, trying to calm herself down. "After I didn't hear from you, I came to your apartment. I couldn't bear the thought of not knowing where you were. I'm still—please come home as quick as you can."

"I'm only ten minutes away," he said. "Please, try to relax. I've got so much to tell you. Things you'll hardly believe. Pour us each a glass of wine. I'll be right there."

They met at the door of Chris's apartment and shared a long, tender embrace. Chris could feel Alana's heart beating against his own chest. As they held each other, its pace began to slow. The feelings that bonded their bodies together as lovers overpowered the fear and trepidation about the unknown. Safe in each other's arms, they knew they could face it together.

"We have so much to discuss, I fear there may not be any sleep for us tonight," said Chris. He knew in his heart that he needed to tell Alana *everything*. There would be no secrets between them.

As he predicted, it was nearly dawn when Chris finished telling Alana everything he'd learned about his real identity, his suspicions about the car accident, and his unexpected conversation with the two police officers. He wanted Alana to know that there might be danger ahead for both her and her grandfather simply because they knew Chris.

"We must get to the airport now and find that briefcase!" said Alana. "Hopefully it will contain information that supports what you've learned. Perhaps it will also validate this supposed contract of yours. It could be the final piece of the puzzle that brings everything into focus and unlocks your full memory. The case simply *must be* in one of the private storage areas at the airport. Come, let's leave now," she said, holding his hand as she stood. "We can beat the rush hour traffic and be back in a couple of hours."

"I like your thinking, Alana, but no, I think we should wait," said Chris, coaxing her to sit back down. "The bigger the crowd at Charles de Gaulle, the safer we'll be. We must assume that I'm being followed. Plus, there are security cameras everywhere. We don't yet know who our adversaries are or how deep this goes. We'll take the train to the airport at the peak of rush hour. I'll also wear a disguise. We'll go separately. You will meet me in the luggage area with a large, empty backpack."

Chris had surprised even himself saying this. Instinctively, his thought processes had switched to those of a seasoned CIA agent who worked deep undercover. With unknown dangers threatening both his own safety *and* the safety of the woman he loved so deeply, it all came rushing back. His analytical thinking, the years of training he'd endured, the painful lessons he'd learned from past experiences in similar circumstances—all of it came naturally now. His subconscious brain had risen to the challenge with lightning speed.

The couple locked in a final embrace, exhausted, and fell into a deep, dreamless sleep.

The Charles de Gaulle Airport stood as one of Europe's major hubs for international travelers, named in honor of France's most famous World War II general and the statesmen who led the French resistance against the Nazis.

Chris had been to this airport countless times in the past. It was a central point of contact for receiving assignments and giving status reports to his boss at the CIA. Even now, if necessary, he knew he could tap into some of the assets there if he needed them. He'd left the agency with high marks, on the best of terms, his boss begging him not to go. There was a promotion coming soon, his superior told him, but that was not the issue, Chris had assured him. Chris's job was interesting and challenging, though obviously quite dangerous. He loved the excitement, but his roots were deep in small-town America. He wanted to start a family, settle down in a solid Midwestern community amongst his family and friends. He wanted his children to spend time with their grandparents. He and his brothers grew up in a wonderful, loving environment in a small Minnesota community. That could never happen if Chris remained an active field agent working in secret for the CIA.

Coincidentally, over the airport loudspeaker, Chris heard the announcement of a Delta flight arriving from Minneapolis-St. Paul. It was probably the same flight, he reasoned, that had brought him to Paris several months ago. Same arrival time, same gate, and most likely, using the same luggage carousel.

The announcement that had interrupted his thoughts brought his mind back to why he was at the airport in the first place. *I need to retrace my steps*, he thought, *and follow the passengers to the baggage area.* His thinking and actions were now natural, not forced. He felt totally at ease and under control. He could feel his confidence rising. He knew what he had to do.

As he made his way through the huge complex of buildings and numerous corridors, he remembered receiving a briefcase from the two Paris policemen. With each step, it became more clear and vivid in his head. He remembered the location of the storage locker he'd rented. He'd used these very same lockers to store electronic equipment, weapons, money, secret documents—you name it. In the short term, they were convenient and as good as a bank's storage vault. There were thousands of such lockers all over the airport. As long as he took the precaution of not letting anyone see him using the locker or giving the security camera a good look at his facial features, he and his *deposit* were safe. Chris knew this because he'd investigated this particular section of the airport in the past. After a painstakingly thorough examination, he'd determined this was the safest place to store his most important items. The apartment where he lived could be broken into easily. He was also gone much of the time, for many days in a row, giving robbers ample opportunities to survey the place and break in.

He located the large bank of storage lockers tucked away in an area not too far from the restrooms. He decided to first pass by them, casually noting their numbers, making sure he had a key that matched one of them. Satisfied, he continued to the restroom and paused briefly, taking note of the security cameras before continuing on to the water closet.

There, he checked his disguise in the mirror. He was still not sure he could trust the police officers. The rule of thumb undercover is *don't trust anyone.* Perhaps the two men only wanted to get their hands on the sizable down payment Chris had already received and eliminate him from the picture. It was certainly enough money to disappear for a while. *Don't take any chances,* he reminded himself. *Those police officers may have been trying to confuse you so they could steal the money themselves. It would be easy to convince their client that I ran off, back to America.*

With their police connections, there was a decent chance they were watching Chris right now, carefully tracking his movements with the help of the security cameras. His original plan was for Alana to bring the backpack to the baggage area, where they could put the briefcase in it before they left the terminal. Instead, after consideration, Chris had told her to meet him at the railroad station, a short walk from the airport, so she wouldn't appear on any of the airport's security cameras.

Just as Chris had planned, foot traffic in the baggage claim area was at its peak. Chris slipped out of the restroom into the sea of people with the locker key in one hand and the empty backpack in the other.

In less than a minute, he'd located and opened the locker, quickly stuffing its contents into the backpack. Naturally, he made sure the entire process was completed with his back to the security cameras. He also positioned himself to cover the locker with his body, so whatever he removed couldn't be seen.

In a matter of minutes, Chris was out of the airport, walking toward the train station and his rendezvous with Alana. *If you want to lose someone,* he thought to himself with a grin, *go to any large train station in a large city anywhere in the world during rush hour and you're home free.* Chris had used this strategy many times when he'd worked as an undercover agent. Now, the time was right to employ it yet again.

With the backpack strapped securely to his chest, Chris performed his usual sequence of evasive maneuvers to prevent anyone from following him to Alana. He also quickly altered his looks, removing his jacket and changing his hat while disposing of his fake mustache. Before long, he and Alana met up on the prearranged train platform. No words were spoken. Alana had already purchased their tickets and they disappeared into the highly congested train.

CHAPTER 23

SPLITTING THE WEALTH

Jean Pierre and Maurice were meeting in their secret room at the Louvre. It was here that they'd developed their methods to sell the treasures hidden in the underground chambers. They'd discussed each item to be removed and exhibited at museums across the continent before they would be sold.

At first, they chose less conspicuous, lower-value pieces. There was very low probability that these items would be recognized as stolen during the war. After all, the pieces had come from many different countries and their original owners would now be dead.

The money they received from these sales wasn't great but, over time, accrued to a significant sum. These funds were then deposited into two separate bank accounts, one for Maurice and one for Jean Pierre. Each account had been opened with a forged passport under a new identity. The men shared the spoils equally, as they'd agreed to at the beginning. A separate fund was established to pay middlemen and other expenses. After the success of their initial venture, the pair fine-tuned their process and decided to start selling the more valuable pieces from Goering's secret collection.

Jean Pierre, with his international experience and extensive travel schedule, was able to discreetly sell several high-quality pieces. His travels often took him to Switzerland for meetings with financiers, collectors, and art auctioneers. The international banks located there, of course, were the perfect place to hide money safely away.

As with most illegal schemes, greed began to influence the pair's operations. After being incredibly careful at the beginning, their unqualified successes made Jean Pierre and Maurice eager to unload some of the more lucrative pieces to private collectors and smaller museums. Their profits were steady and getting bigger all the time, but still, they wanted more, faster. They wanted to squeeze as much money out of the art community as possible and vanish with massive fortunes, assuming new identities and living new lives.

As they released more well-known pieces from Goering's hidden chamber, however, the risk of being discovered grew exponentially. The value of these objects far outweighed the lesser-known pieces. They told themselves if they achieved their financial goals quicker, they could cease their illegal operation sooner. But with huge sums of money flowing into their bank accounts, they were more inclined to keep pushing their luck than winding things down.

Inevitably, some of the pieces were identified by a very rich, well-known, French art dealer who was notorious for buying, selling, and trading gray-market art and antiques worldwide. These illegal transactions had made him a fortune, but somehow, he'd evaded law enforcement. Because of his success in these questionable markets, he was quietly sought out by private collectors and unscrupulous museums to sell certain infamous items—no questions asked. Enormous sums of money changed hands in these transactions, based on dubious chains of provenance. This particular dealer was willing to take such risks, constantly skirting the edges of international law.

When World War II ended, the market for masterpieces exploded. Meanwhile, the countries that had been plundered by the Nazis were clamoring to locate and repatriate the art stolen from them. Enormous fees were paid to reacquire many of the items, rather than fight court battles that could drag on for years. Museums quickly realized, if they didn't pay to get their national treasures back, they may never see them again. The pieces would simply vanish into private collections. This art market was huge, lucrative, and full of untold opportunities for ruthless art dealers willing to walk this fine line of illegality.

Of course, this particular mystery art dealer was not interested in blowing the whistle and shutting down this market. Rather, he believed it was an opportunity to increase his wealth and sell even more art to customers who didn't care who had owned it in the past. His intentions were crystal-clear: he would hire someone to find the source, identify the individuals behind the scheme, and offer them a better, safer way to sell these illegal goods, with the implied threat that he could have them arrested any time he chose. Naturally, he would demand a generous portion of the profits for his expertise and *silence*.

With this objective in mind, the secretive dealer discreetly hired two special investigators from the Paris police department who had resources to get the job done through back channels and with absolutely no traceability to him. He'd been told the investigators were getting closer to cracking the case, but he was very eager to work out his *arrangement* with the people running the scheme.

The small table in Maurice and Jean Pierre's secret underground room was covered with pictures and documents. In the center of the table, on top of everything else, was a plain, unassuming ledger book with an astounding number of entries, all carefully written in the same neat handwriting.

"Well, Jean Pierre, I think it is finally time to shut down our secret operation," said Maurice, leaning back in his chair. "As you can see in the ledger, we've been more successful than we ever imagined. Yes, we could keep going. There are thousands of items here we could sell. Not to mention, the safe we've been unable to crack. I suspect it contains some incredibly valuable art objects, but recent events have got me on edge. I'm afraid we may be found out. That hit-and-run survivor is still out there somewhere. Your son reported that a man seen on one of our security cameras looks very much like the person we tried to . . . *eliminate*. And of course, there's also our friend Hans

Muller, our quiet art restorer, performing his evaluation of our four-hundred-year-old master painting. It seems to me that painting has some sort of special significance for him. I have yet to find out what it is, but it makes me uneasy. Too many people are getting too curious."

"Reluctant as I am to admit," said Jean Pierre, "I have to agree. Hans and I are scheduled to meet on Friday to discuss his final findings. As you know, that master painting will be our last and most lucrative item. God knows, it could be worth as much as nearly everything else combined. Believe me, once that is sold, we will close down this operation."

"You will get no argument from me," said Maurice, "however, we do need to finalize our equity agreement. I was surprised to see your records on what has been sold to our clients *do not agree with mine.*"

"What—?" Jean Pierre sputtered, shifting uneasily in his seat. "What do you mean to imply, Maurice? Of course, my records match yours. I'm not going to sit here—"

"Don't take me for a fool, Jean Pierre," said Maurice, quickly cutting him off. "I know the location of every painting, every sculpture, every artifact, every piece of *parchment* that is in Goering's treasure vault. Hell, I even can tell you where each item is located, what it's next to, if it's ever been moved, and the exact condition it's in. Or have you somehow forgotten about my special talents and recall abilities?"

"But—but you informed me, not so long ago, that these skills of yours seemed to be fading," Jean Pierre protested.

"Ah, yes, I did, *but that was just a ruse,*" said Maurice, an air of menace in his voice. "For a while I suspected you were removing objects when I wasn't around, trying to hide that fact from me. Perhaps you meant to tell me, but somehow forgot?" Maurice slammed the ledger shut, picked it up, and shook it in Jean Pierre's face. "This ledger proves you've been going behind my back." Maurice slammed the ledger down. "I played *you* like I played *the Nazis.* Hell, you're no different from Goering or Louis Dequire. Liars, cheaters, thieves—all of you treating me like I'm a nobody, harnessing my abilities and knowledge for your selfish goals. I've lost all respect for you. I can't trust you at all."

"Listen to me, Maurice," begged Jean Pierre. "Please, just listen to me: I was the one who came up with the system to get rid of these valuable pieces without being caught. I took all the risk, setting up phony bank accounts and phony documents to sell these items. I stuck my neck out for you. Hell, you could never make even *one* of these deals. Without me, you'd be nothing. You and your family have got money to last two lifetimes. Perhaps I got carried away, but I took all of the risk. Every sale that was made, *my life* was on the line."

Maurice breathed deeply, staring at Jean Pierre with unforgiving eyes. "Our original agreement," he said, "was that the money from Goering's stolen treasures was to be split fifty-fifty. An agreement is an agreement. It's your word and *your honor*. If you don't have that, then what do you have?" Jean Pierre glanced at the table, unable to look at Maurice. "When you came to this museum, you had *no idea* about this room and its treasures. If I hadn't showed you, you'd never even know it existed. Not one thing would have been sold if it wasn't for *me*. I shared my secret with you. I'd kept quiet for over four decades, biding my time. At any time, I could have gone to the police and retired with the reward I'd be given. I trusted you to be my partner and *this* is how you repaid me."

Maurice picked up the ledger again, slowly this time. He deliberately flipped through the pages until he found the one that he wanted. He spun the open book toward Jean Pierre and set it down in front of him.

"By my calculations, there are forty-five objects missing from the chamber that are not accounted for in this ledger. I'm going to give you *one chance* to tell me the truth. Were they sold? If so, where is the money? Did you open yet another secret Swiss bank account? You see, Jean Pierre, I've been taken advantage of before, and I have been watching you, tracking the items removed from the chamber to see if they show up on your list of items sold. Guess what? There are no entries for the forty-five missing items. That's a lot of money, you know. How do you explain it?"

Jean Pierre listened intently. He recognized the disdain, even hatred, in Maurice's voice. He couldn't quite believe this man possessed the ability to track all the items stored in the hidden room. Indeed, Maurice knew *precisely* that forty-five pieces were missing. Jean Pierre was amazed by this seemingly unremarkable man's incredible abilities.

Jean Pierre had taken only smaller objects: porcelain; jewelry; and minor, portable paintings. The vault was filled with hundreds of bigger, more expensive pieces—everything from paintings to tapestries, sculptures, rare books, and more. Without question, Jean Pierre had grossly underestimated Maurice. His only recourse now, he reasoned, was to come clean and try to work out a favorable agreement, one he hoped would undo the contempt Maurice now held for him. Jean Pierre was rattled. He wanted nothing more than to finish their business and part ways.

"Yes, Maurice, I confess I removed some small pieces from the room. Nothing more than trinkets, really. But I am not selling them. These *trifles* are of low value, little more than an afterthought, pieces that we most likely would have never sold through our operation."

Their tense conversation continued for some time, with Jean Pierre desperately trying to talk his way out of it while Maurice seethed with anger and mistrust. Finally, Maurice had sufficiently vented and financial arrangements were made. Jean Pierre agreed—once their operation finally closed down—that Maurice would be fully compensated for half the value of the items Jean Pierre had smuggled from Goering's chamber.

Maurice was still more than a little suspicious as the men finally parted ways. He doubted their verbal agreement would ever be carried out. As his anger and frustration climbed even higher than before, he began to work out a plan for his greedy, selfish companion. Thankfully, he had full control of his secret Swiss bank, one that already contained more money than he could spend.

But it's not just about the money, Maurice thought to himself. *Jean Pierre let greed cloud his thinking. I've seen it in his eyes, just as I saw it in*

Goering's all those years ago—the insatiable desire to own and acquire more, the desire to have it all. He felt the heat of anger coursing through his veins. He unconsciously clenched his teeth and balled his hands into fists. *All my life I've been cheated,* he thought. *I was cheated by the Nazi general, cheated by the Louvre's former director, and cheated by Jean Pierre, a man I thought I could trust. This is the last straw. I've been cheated for the last time. I'm sick of getting screwed over by people without my talents. Trust is earned, not given. Jean Pierre failed the test.*

Thankfully, even now, there were only two people who knew about the hidden chamber in the Louvre's sub-basement. But how could Maurice trust Jean Pierre to abide by his word and *never* go back to the room containing countless treasures? And then there was his family to worry about, his wife and children. Their lives could be in danger, too.

Jean Pierre will always be tempted to keep going back for more, thought Maurice. *He will never have enough money, enough treasures, enough of anything. He will end up in jail or dead. No, I cannot—will not—leave this decision to chance. Jean Pierre must be dealt with, but the timing must be right.*

It slowly dawned on Maurice that he was also in danger. *If Jean Pierre takes steps to get me out of the way,* he thought, *the director will have total control of all the remaining treasure. Nobody would stand between Jean Pierre and the hidden room. Does my greedy partner already have plans to get rid of me?*

CHAPTER 24

BRIEFCASE RECOVERED, CONTENTS CONFIRMED

Chris and Alana agreed: once the briefcase was in their possession, they would find someplace secluded, away from the train station, to examine its contents. There was no way they would take the briefcase back to Chris's apartment or Hans's shop.

Instead, they'd picked a location in the art district, close to the art school, where large backpacks were common attire for people walking the streets. Alana had suggested a small cafe that she'd frequented while attending night school. She knew her grandfather desperately wanted her to take over his art business, but her true love had always been nursing. She thought taking art classes at night might help to appease him.

It was now mid-afternoon. The cafe wasn't crowded and they were able to get a table in the back, away from most of the other customers. They ordered a light lunch with wine and then requested not to be disturbed.

Finally, the moment of truth had arrived. The stress from getting the case had subsided somewhat, but Chris was anxious to see its contents. His mind started racing again, wondering if he might find concrete information to validate what he'd been learning. Every day now, he had short but detailed flashbacks connected to the briefcase and the two men who'd given it to him. Before opening it, he said to Alana, "I think I know exactly what's in this case . . ." Unlocking the latch, he said, "Don't be surprised by what you see. I will explain everything."

Their eyes were drawn to a gun with a silencer. It was loaded and ready to shoot. Alana was visibly startled. She began to speak, but Chris placed his finger gently on her lips. "Not here," he said in a whisper. "I will explain everything. I promise."

Alana watched Chris as he mentally inventoried the piles of cash and documents. At last, he found the main thing he'd been looking for: his American passport. He flipped to the picture inside the cover. There was his legal name, Christopher Leonard Da Vita, from Austin, Minnesota.

A sigh of relief escaped his mouth became a huge smile of satisfaction. Finally, he was fully aware of his true identity and why he'd come to Paris; the two major questions that been haunting him. His quest to restore his memory was a major success.

He shut the briefcase momentarily to think. "We need to find someplace even more private where I can bring you fully up to date. I know you have questions about me and the contents contained in this case. Alana, we need to find somewhere safe to store all this money."

Alana could hear a distinct tinge of desperation in his voice. The happiness she felt at seeing his beautiful smile of success faded, quickly overtaken by apprehension.

Chris was concerned for Alana's safety, a fear magnified greatly by his possession of so much money—and the gun. If there were reasons to feel paranoid and cautious before, they had doubled now.

In hindsight, Chris wished he had pressed harder to have his payment deposited electronically into his business account to avoid this exact situation. He was told at the time his anonymous client *demanded* a cash payment. The only paper trail to this entire affair was a single-page document he'd signed, accepting the $250,000 for his special art investigation. At that time, he'd backed down on his request for an electronic payment. Starting a new business required money and here was a chance to earn some easy cash, performing a sound, straightforward investigation. *How did this simple job put me in harm's way?* he wondered. The only answer now was to solve the problem and fully neutralize the danger. He remembered the words of his father when he was young. Looking out at a lush green cornfield after a grueling spring and summer, his dad said: "Nothing is ever quite as easy as it seems." *Lesson learned*, thought Chris. *Thanks, Dad, wherever you are.*

CHAPTER 25

THE TWO BROTHERS

"There is so much I need to tell you, Scott, I don't know where to begin," said Chris, anxiously holding onto his phone.

"Then maybe I should begin," Scott responded. "I don't know what's going on there, but you've got a whole other set of problems here in Minnesota. Everyone is clamoring to get a piece of you: your secretary, Mom and Dad, your fiancée." Scott's voice became even more accusatory. "Do you even remember you *have* a fiancée? Darlene, in case you forgot, and she is driving me nuts. She doesn't think you love her anymore and I don't blame her. You haven't even *tried* to get ahold of her. We had her over for dinner last week, to try to cool her down, but all she could talk about is how you've been avoiding her. She's been so upset with you, she removed your engagement ring. Now she's telling me she's going to track you down in Paris."

"How does she—what did you say? *You* told her I'm in Paris!"

"I had to get her off my back somehow. She's been driving me crazy, calling me three times a day. I have a job, you know. I've tried to explain to her you're in the middle of a very difficult case, that you're working undercover, but she won't listen to me."

"You have to stop her, Scott. I'm embroiled in something *huge* in the art industry and it's truly dangerous. I fear for the safety of anyone who even knows me. I've recovered most of my memory, with your help, and I finally found my briefcase with all of my notes. I can't get into the details right now, but I'll give you the main idea, pieced together from my research.

"About seven months ago, I signed a very lucrative contract to investigate how stolen World War II art and antiques were suddenly showing up in European museums. I was getting close to revealing who was behind it and what their methods were, when that truck hit and nearly killed me.

"I am positive now it wasn't an accident. Some group tried to silence me, and they almost succeeded. Whoever these people are, they knew I was getting close and they tried to take me out. They're ruthless. You must stop Darlene from buying that ticket and coming here. I'm still in grave danger, probably more than ever. Tell her I'll call her this weekend. I'm worried her phone might be bugged, but I'm willing to take the chance, if it will appease her.

"This scheme is big and ugly. If the details ever get out, the art industry could be paralyzed for decades with lawsuits and insurance claims. The high-end art world would never be the same. I need more time to complete this assignment. See if you can hold her off for at least two more weeks."

Scott had finally calmed down. "Chris, I'll try. You know that. But she's a very strong-willed person. I've seen a side of her that doesn't bode well for you. Especially with the business you're in. I don't exactly see her coping well with all of your travel and secrecy. I hate to say it, but if I were you, I would definitely give some additional thought to the idea of marrying her when your contract is over."

Deflated, Chris said, "Well, big brother, as you know, there was a time not long ago when I truly believed she was the one for me. We'd been dating for years when she pressured me to make a decision. She was overjoyed about the wedding. I understand her disappointment."

Chris paused for a moment, trying to find the right words. "The things that have happened to me these past six months have changed the entire direction of my life. Not knowing who I was, where I'd come from . . . My beliefs, my values, my goals—what I want to do for the rest of my life and who I want to spend it with—well, they've been dramatically altered, to say the least.

"I've totally depended on others these past months. And believe me, I mean *totally*. EMTs, doctors at the clinic, my trauma nurse, Alana—they all sacrificed huge amounts of time and energy to save me. I'm only alive today because of their skills and their dedication. If I survive this case and fulfill my contract, I stand to make a lot of money, and maybe I can repay them. Chris, when this is all over, you will definitely see a different person."

"I'll be the judge of that. You've definitely changed from our time back on the farm. I look forward to the day when that old, fun-loving Chris is back again. You've always been so confident in your abilities. With the successes you had in school and with your work, you've proven you can overcome any challenge and get the job done. I have to tell you, though, sometimes the family thinks you need to come down off your high horse and think about others. Your 'me, me, me' attitude needs to change."

"Yeah, yeah, Chris, I hear you. And you're probably right, to some extent." Chris let out a little chuckle. "Sorry to say, we'll have to discuss my character flaws at a later date. We've got more important things to discuss."

"Okay, Chris, you're right. Your *second* major issue back here is your security business. You need to contact your secretary soon. She's been telling me that things are hanging by a thread. Your customers are threatening to leave. Apparently, your employees are not performing to their satisfaction, and your bank account is dangerously close to zero.

"I can help you out financially, if you need it, but only for a short time. Sophie and I have to save for the kids' college. They're both growing fast and it's getting hard to keep up with their demands. It's all about their needs now. It's a daily issue." Scott sighed and sounded wistful. "Sometimes I think Sophie and I should have brought them up on a farm, where they would have a better appreciation of family and how to earn an honest buck."

"I'm sorry I got you involved in this mess," said Chris. "I'll make it up to you, somehow. You were one of the major keys to unlocking my memory. The dream I had about our childhood, the farm, and playing hockey shook up my brain and put me on the path of remembering. If it wasn't for your help—and Alana's—I would have remained a fictitious person in search of my true identity for the rest of my life.

"Scott, please don't quit on me now. There are only a few more things left to do to complete my investigation. But I need you to do some things for me quickly, aside from calming down Darlene.

"First, you need to get rid of this phone as soon as you can. Don't ever use it again. Get another new phone, with a new phone number. I know it sounds paranoid, but my paranoia is what's kept me alive. I'll give you the alias email address I established in Paris. Send the new phone number there. I'll replace mine as well. Also, open a new account with a different bank, one that will allow you to easily receive offshore money transfers. I will need to get your new phone number—and the new bank account number—as quickly as possible.

"As soon as I have all the information, I'll wire $9,500 to your account. Use it for the expenses you've already incurred. Meet with my secretary personally—no phones, no computers. Tell her that I'll transfer $100,000 into my business account. The money will be coming from an art dealer's bank account here in Paris. The name on the account is Hans Muller. He hired me to tend to his art store and has allowed me access to his computers. Without him and Alana, who's his granddaughter, I would probably be lost on the streets of Paris.

"Tell my secretary she can use the money to make payroll and pay the bills. She's also going to need to purchase a burner phone. I need to give her some special instructions on how to handle the additional money she'll receive later. And I will need her to get ahold of some of my CIA buddies."

"Chris . . . is this art dealer a legitimate businessman?"

"Yes, I took a job with him to pay my bills. Mr. Muller deals with very expensive antiques and masterpieces from all over the world. His family has been in art restoration and repair for three generations. I'm in the process of doing a complete investigation on him and his background.

"Somehow, and this is an unbelievable coincidence, I think he may be tied to the mysterious master artworks that are showing up all over Europe. The art underworld is huge. Museums and private collectors are willing to pay millions of dollars to purchase great works. All of the items *should be* returned to their original owners or the museums they were stolen from. I'm afraid some were already purchased by anonymous private collectors and they'll never be seen again in public.

"It appears that these items were taken by the Nazis during the war. Naturally, the provenance of each piece will have to be traced, and the owners identified. If I can find out where these items are coming from and where they're hidden, not only will I complete my contract, I'll also uncover a massive cache of lost art that some people lost their lives to protect.

"Get on the internet and look up lost art from World War II. You won't believe the quantity of treasures that were shipped from Nazi-occupied countries to Berlin. It's staggering. Many of these treasures were since returned, through efforts of special organizations established during and after the war. But there are still millions of dollars' worth of antiques still unaccounted for.

"You know that I've always been a World War II buff and that I took classes about old world art in college for my art minor. Historical art is one of my passions. It's the other reason I took this job. Little did I know what I was getting myself into.

"Anyway, getting back to Hans . . . He receives and completes wire transfers for his clients weekly. I've been doing them for several weeks. It's only recently that the two men who hired me turned up at the shop to get a progress report for their *anonymous* client. Of course, I had no information to give them, as I had no memory from that lost period of time—or even a sense of what I was hired to do.

"After a long conversation about the details of the contract—and down payment they'd already paid me—an avalanche of puzzle pieces started to fall into place. Suddenly, I remembered key events and places, including the location where I'd stored my briefcase—the very same one containing the down payment I was given the day I arrived in Paris. That was a key moment for me. When I actually retrieved the briefcase and inspected its contents, I also found my American passport and other supporting documents that confirmed my real identity."

"Just how much, exactly, are you getting for putting your life in danger?"

"In total, it will be $500,000 in US currency. Half was paid up front, the other half will be paid when the work is completed. It's legitimate income for my business and obviously it will be taxed. I know how it must sound, but everything's by the book. I don't need Uncle Sam and the IRS breathing down my neck. That's the other reason I need to contact my secretary, to make sure all this income is recorded properly."

"Well, as we say in America: *no risk, no reward*. Little brother, that's quite a reward if you can pull it off and walk away with your life."

"I have to say, it doesn't even *come close* to covering what I've been through these past seven months. Had I known about the risks up front, I can't imagine I would have ever taken the case. I spent the past ten years of my life in a job with high risk, intrigue, and of course, plenty of danger. I just wanted to settle down and lead a normal life, with a wife and kids. The plan was merely to build a nice security business and be *just like you*, big brother.

"I know it's going to take you a day or two to do all the things I've asked for. I know you have a life of your own, but there's real urgency here. Do the best you can. That's all I can ask. Call me as soon as you get your new phone. Please tell Mom and Dad I'm not in any danger. I trust you haven't told anyone else about this?"

"Steve's asking lots of questions, but he's so busy implementing a new computer system, you've drifted off his radar. He's up to his eyeballs in work."

"I do need to get ahold of Brad in New York," Chris interjected. "With his art knowledge and his contacts with the museums there, he could do some research for me, if he's willing. What I'm doing here is right in line with his field of study. He could be very helpful, if he has the time. Please give him a call. Tell him he'll be receiving a rather *unusual* email from me about a fictitious art dealer in Paris. He needs to open the email. He won't recognize the address but tell him it won't be spam. I'll need a quick response, but it should be no trouble for him. Is Rich around?"

"Only when he wants to be," said Scott. "He has a new job. Same company, but now, he has bunch of representatives working for him. Travels every week and hobnobs with millionaire business owners and the like. Most of them like to hunt and fish, and you know that's right up his alley." Scott gave an appreciative chuckle. "He's got the job we'd all like to have—wining and dining customers on the company's dime while pursuing your favorite hobbies."

"Well, Scott, I guess you're stuck with me. That's what you get for being the big brother."

"Well, all I can say to you, Chris, is get this job done *and come home safely*. Of course, you owe me big time, and I'll want to collect my pound of flesh from you."

The phone lines disconnected with no secondary disconnections. Good. Chris's security methods were working.

CHAPTER 26

AN AGENT'S MIND

As he turned off his cell phone, Chris began to focus on how to complete his contract. He was keenly aware that he was exposed to impending danger. By extension, so were the people he loved. It was a potentially deadly situation, a scheme that could get him—and others—killed. It was definitely *not* what he'd imagined when he took the job. With a wealth of background knowledge and his skills from his stint with the CIA, by all rights, this should have been easy. A quick, foolproof way to earn quick money for his business.

His undercover assignments for the CIA had given him total freedom and control of his decisions, without involving any others, especially those closest to him. Now, a wrong decision could compromise his mission *and* jeopardize Alana and Hans. Innocent people had been unwittingly pulled into this web of deceit and corruption. Chris's plan to get out of this would have to be flawless, and he was running out of time. He needed to be done with it—*now*. There were simply too many risks.

In his ten-year career with the CIA, Chris had completed many complicated assignments, most of which were more complex than this job. His skills were still deeply ingrained, part of his subconscious being, but now he was without the agency's support and the stakes were higher than ever. Thankfully, he'd retired less than a year ago and could call upon many of his former contacts.

As unbelievable as it sounded, Chris sensed there was a strong connection between what he'd been hired to do and Alana's grandfather. Chris knew Hans had reacted intensely to one of the Louvre's newly exhibited paintings—a response that went far beyond mere admiration. It had been deep and visceral. It wasn't much of leap to think Hans may have seen it before. *That painting must have been missing,* Chris thought. *Where could it have come from? Does the painting's anonymous owner have more than one piece in his possession? Why has it appeared now? Could it be part of a recently discovered collection?*

Chris had heard several stories about high-value art pieces suddenly showing up out of the blue. Someone's quiet old granny dies, the kids go through her belongings, and they find a famous painting in the attic or cleverly hidden in the wall of her bedroom. All this time it had been in her possession, but she'd never breathed a word of it to anyone, not even her family.

Reluctant as he was to do so, Chris began to evaluate Hans's personality traits and patterns. Until recently, Hans had traveled extensively all over Europe for decades, establishing and cultivating personal friendships with the directors of virtually every notable museum on the continent. Hans had access to their work rooms and storage areas while he performed repairs and restorations. From a purely logistical standpoint, he was the perfect person to implement a plan for covertly selling stolen treasures from the war.

No, Chris thought. *It's not possible that Hans is intentionally part of the scheme. He's not only gentle and kind, he's a man of principle, a man with strong faith and values, steeped in honesty and integrity. If Hans is involved at all, he must be an unwitting accomplice—little more than a pawn in someone else's game.*

What, then, was the connection if there even was one? Had Chris gotten carried away? Chris knew Hans had been making frequent visits to the Louvre to determine if the painting he'd been asked to evaluate was authentic. Serendipitously, it had been one of the paintings Chris studied before he'd even taken the job, though like all his other notes, leads, and transcriptions, the photos of it he'd been given by the two Paris agents were destroyed in the accident.

Chris suddenly felt compelled to see this masterpiece for himself. *I mustn't make any conclusions until I've seen the piece in person*, he thought. *If Hans actually is somehow connected to it—in any way—I'll need to have proof. Without hard evidence, this is all speculation. No one else would believe it.* He laughed silently. *I'm not sure I believe this crazy story myself.*

It pained Chris to know that his precious Alana, an innocent bystander in this whole affair, may have unknowingly been pulled into this nightmare from two different directions: her grandfather and his close connections to the art industry, and Chris himself. The patient who she'd selflessly nursed back to health, with no other goal than to see him recover.

Should I share all of this with Alana, he wondered, *or will that put her in more danger? Should I tell Hans?*

Since he planned to wire-transfer a portion of his down payment to one of his accounts through Hans's business account, he had to have some explanation as to where the money had come from.

After some thought, he decided to tell them both at the same time. That way, he could study their reactions for any clues as to whether either of them were involved.

Chris also worried about the phone call he needed to make to the two Paris police officers. He needed reassurance that he would be paid in full when the job was complete. He was definitely not going to give them any information about Hans Muller until their deal was rock solid.

As all of these facts churned in his mind and he tried to put together an action plan, his cell phone rang. It was Alana and he could tell by her voice she was frightened.

"My grandfather called me," she said. "He wants to meet with us tonight at his shop. He sounded pretty worried. I . . . I fear for his life. Lately he's spent more time inside the walls of the Louvre than his own shop. He's also made numerous calls to his closest colleagues at the other museums, all across Europe. I can't get him to share any-thing with me, and that's not like him. Ever since I was little, he's told me everything. Chris, I'm terribly worried. What should I do?"

As a trained CIA agent, Chris knew how to keep his tone firm but relaxed, betraying no emotion. "Do *not* say anything more," he said. "I'm on my way to the shop now. I'll use the back entrance. Keep an eye on it. I don't want to be seen at this late-evening family gathering." He paused for a moment and spoke in a clear, authoritative voice. "Listen to me, Alana," he said. "You have to stay in control. Act as nonchalant as you can. I'm sure the shop is under surveillance, either by the Paris police who hired me or whoever's running this illegal art operation. Probably both. I can't give them the impression I still work for your grandfather or that I have all of that cash. Just act normal, stay calm, like any other time you've gone to work there."

Chris slowed his heartbeat the way that he'd been taught. "There's so much I need to tell you and your grandfather," he said. "I desper-ately need his help. Alana, you have to trust me. I need to use your grandfather's bank account. I don't need money, I promise, just a via-ble account to wire the money to my bank. I will see you soon. Please be careful, my love."

CHAPTER 27

THE MEETING OF DISCOVERY

It was past closing time at Hans's shop. From the street, the building appeared empty. A small security light blinked in the darkness, but there wasn't enough light to see the outline of the door that led to the small back room where repairs were performed and shipping containers were stored.

Hans was there, alone, feverishly skimming through various documents and old pictures strewn haphazardly around the worktable. In the midst of this jumble of paper sat the small, well-worn, black ledger with neatly written columns of dates, names, and other details. Hans was busily double-checking the ledger against this small mountain of work orders, receipts, and shipping manifests. He didn't hear Alana and Chris come into the room.

"What are you doing, Grandfather?" Alana asked, feeling a shiver run through her body. "What are all these documents? Where did you get all these papers and pictures? What does all of this mean?"

As the tired man looked up, she couldn't help but notice how frail he suddenly seemed. The excitement from the blessings they'd shared during their Hanukkah celebration had drained away, replaced by a feeling of despair and hopelessness. Hans took off his glasses, folded them slowly, and looked up from his work.

"I believe I may be in grave danger," he said, "a danger which your grandmother and I lived under when we were held captive by the Nazis during the war." He sighed deeply and looked at Alana, his eyes slowly welling with tears. "I no longer fear for my life, only for yours. You must leave Paris, and soon. What I'm about to tell you will turn the art world upside down. That is . . . if I ever get the chance to reveal the true facts of the story.

"Chris, I dragged you into this, especially after what you've gone through these last few months. You see, my most valuable possession is my granddaughter. I've been closely watching your relationship with her, watching your love and affection blossom. I can see that the union you're forming is one of joy and love.

"You have my blessing.

"I, too, had this kind of love with my dear Elsa. We were insep-arable until the war destroyed us. Chris, you must take Alana back to America. It might be the only place she's safe. I don't know if you have a job or money or any way to support the two of you, but I can provide whatever it takes. You can open up a small art shop, maybe in New York, or wherever you'd like. I have many contacts there and I know they'll help you, for my sake."

As Chris listened to Hans, his mind searched for the link between Hans and this bizarre scheme. He decided to listen to the rest of Hans's story before revealing his true background and own ties to the affair.

"I will honor your request," said Chris. "You've been there almost from the beginning, watching our relationship grow into one of love and devotion. Like your dear wife Elsa, Alana is the most precious person in my life. I will do whatever is necessary to protect her."

Chris knew he must press forward to learn the truth. He decided to seize the moment. "I know I can help you," he said, "but you have to share the entire story. My memory is almost fully recovered now and I have contacts and resources at my disposal that can solve your prob-lem. Please, you need to tell me the truth about what's happening."

Hans knew Chris was right. He was tired of shouldering the burden, the weight of his secrets, all by himself. "Some of the papers you see on this table," he began, with a sweeping gesture, "go back two or even three generations in the Muller family archives."

Hans felt his body tighten, as though it were physically trying to prevent the truth from escaping, but the time had come to finally reveal what he'd been holding back for decades: his reluctant involvement in Goering's plunder of treasure from all over Europe. Yes, at last it was time to divulge the cruel atrocities that he and his wife had seen from the railyard prison that housed them; the seemingly endless procession of days they'd spent peering out the dirty workshop window, searching desperately for any glimmer of hope. Instead, Hans and Elsa had watched, numbed by the horror, as train after train after train left the railyard, packed with Jews being sent to their doom at the Nazi's numerous concentration camps.

All the while, Hans had been forced to do Reichsmarschall Goering's bidding in exchange for the safety—*the very lives*—of his mother and children. Hans's unique talents had saved his life, but it came at the cost of protecting treasure that had been stolen from the very people packed on the trains, on the way to their deaths. He wished he could have walked away from that agreement so many years ago— but that was impossible. He'd been virtually powerless at the time. He made the only bargain he could.

For years all of these feelings had been hidden in the deepest recesses of his mind, and Hans intended for them never to emerge. With recent events, however, he felt he no longer had a choice. He must speak out and reveal everything he knew, no matter how painful it was. Past wrongs must be righted. He must pull the curtain back and expose the bitter truth his role in it to the police. Justice must prevail.

"Alana, you know some of our family history, but what I'm going to tell you tonight won't be pleasant. Honestly, it's very difficult for me to even discuss it, but this is no longer about me and my feelings. You need to know the truth, from the very beginning.

"My grandfather Manfred—your great-great-grandfather—was a highly skilled artist. He made a living selling his own art at the turn of the century and supported his son—my father and your great-grandfather, Otto—and his family this way. But then the Great War came, and no one buys art when they don't know where their next meal is coming from. When the fighting finally ended and Germany surrendered, millions of lives were lost and whole cities were destroyed. That war crippled our nation, our economy, and our people. We lost large swaths of territory and were forced to pay reparations. The world soon fell into a deep recession. Jobs were incredibly scarce. People were scrambling to feed their families.

"Thankfully, the elders at his synagogue banded together, scraped up whatever money they could and hired Manfred to restore the stained-glass windows, murals, and other precious artifacts that had been damaged.

"With his special artistic talents, Manfred soon became known as the top artist for essential repairs and restorations in Berlin after the war. As is still the case today, there were only a handful of art conservators who could be trusted on Old World art. It is meticulous, delicate, time-consuming work; an art form in itself, you could say.

"Manfred's work was so good, he was hired by museums and private collectors. He realized he could make a fortune working with high-profile clients. He started a business and followed his passion for art. His shop was very successful and our family prospered. Otto followed in his footsteps. Like his father before him, Otto became highly skilled at art restoration. By the time he was in his early thirties he was his father's equal, if not the greater of the two. Between the two of them, the services and volume the shop could offer literally doubled.

"As for me, as a boy I attended school during the day, becoming my father's apprentice when I was old enough. Watching and listening to my father and grandfather in the evenings, I learned the trade as well. Together, through the years that followed, my father and I created an even more prosperous business, well known in Berlin and throughout Europe.

"We had a beautiful shop right on the Kantstrasse in Charlottenburg, a largely Jewish suburb of Berlin and a hub of Jewish culture. I was in my early twenties when I officially started working there, though I'd spent a great deal of my early life there by then.

"It was a joyous, exciting time for me, working with my father and grandfather, learning the secrets of mixing and blending paints, how to duplicate brush strokes that were used by various famous artists, and all of the crucial skills a restorer needs.

"I was driven to become as good as they were in the restoration process. How rewarding it was, not only to see these magnificent works of art but also to touch and bring them back to their original glory.

"During my time working there, I saw hundreds of world-class art pieces pass through for restoration and for sale. Of course, I got hooked on the Old Masters and their masterpieces. That's when I decided I would follow in the footsteps of my father and grandfather, growing and building the business.

"At the time I was also attending art college and met Elsa, the grandmother you never had a chance to meet. She was the love of my life and I was smitten by her charm and personality from day one. She was fun-loving and soon we did everything together. With her light blue-green eyes, she could charm you into doing anything she wanted you to. Our common interest in art drew us together like magnets. We became close friends and, eventually, lovers.

"Her family was from Switzerland, near Lucerne. She'd planned on getting a degree in fine art and then doing advanced studies in European art. Our lives were filled with joy, love, and family, until January 30, 1933, a date I will never forget. That was the day Hitler and his Nazi party seized control of the government. He called it a revolution and named his movement the Third Reich—the third and final German empire. From that point forward, Jews, communists, immigrants, and political opponents were relentlessly persecuted. Little by little, the Nazi noose of aggression strangled off the rights of our people, destroying our freedoms.

"Hitler didn't waste any time implementing his terrible plans. Soon after he'd taken control of the government, he began to enact harsh regulations and severe restrictions which ultimately led to the Holocaust.

"One day, a large, well-built man dressed in a perfectly tailored suit walked into our shop. I'd never seen him before, but he addressed me by my first name and asked to see my father immediately. I was shocked and intimidated by his strong, authoritarian voice. I'd been working in the shop for some time, handling orders and doing minor preservation work for our customers. No one had ever offended me before, but this man did. It was the tone of his voice, his mannerisms. He spoke to me like I was the scum of the earth, a sub-human animal who didn't even deserve common curtesy. He was a man you would truly hate after your first encounter, and I most certainly did.

"After he'd given my father instructions, he left as quickly as he came. Outside, I saw him get into a chauffeured car, along with a co-terie of bodyguards and soldiers. I remember thinking, *There goes a person I hope to never see again.* Shortly after this visit, that man came to control all aspects of my life and Elsa's for the next three years.

"After he drove away, back to Berlin, my father immediately closed up the shop and ushered me back to his work room. There, he sat me down and said, 'Son, I've prepared for this day. I've been expecting it for some time. Under Hitler's new regime, every Jewish business in Berlin—and all over the country—will be destroyed and the owners arrested. It's only a matter of time. This Hitler, der Führer, who rules the government with an iron fist, has vowed to get rid of the so-called vermin he says has destroyed our country. Hitler has openly stated, even preached, that Germany lost the First World War because it was corrupted by communists and Jews.'

"I'd never seen my father so serious. 'Your family must prepare to leave Berlin, and soon,' he said. Then he got up, walked over to his work bench, and pulled out the old wooden cabinet which held all the special tools he and my grandfather used to perform their restorations.

"In a matter of seconds, he'd released the back panel of the cabinet, exposing a number of secret compartments. The first item he removed was a small black ledger, the very book now on the table in front of you. It was my grandfather's, then my father's . . . and now it's mine."

Hans reached across the table and picked it up. "This plain black book lists all the important paintings our family has restored over the past three generations. It identifies each piece's owner, the date the work was completed, the type of restoration performed, and—this is crucial—its appraised value at that time.

"Every job, once completed, was marked with a coded signature, an inconspicuous series of numbers that identified who did the work, when they performed it, and where. Those numbers can all be traced back to this black ledger." Hans slowly fanned the pages. Virtually every page was covered with writing from top to bottom. "There are hundreds of entries inside. You're looking at, perhaps, one of the most important books of provenance in the world. Our meticulous notations and records are concrete proof of ownership before the war. We used a system of coded numbers precisely because it couldn't be forged. No one else knew our system, but the documentation is flawless and can be used in any court in any country throughout Europe to identify the original owner of these masterpieces.

"Unfortunately, my recent involvement with the Louvre has put me squarely in the middle of an illegal scheme to sell some of the looted plunder accumulated by Hermann Goering and his minions. The painting I was asked to appraise, I personally restored in 1938 for Goering himself. I identified my hidden marks on the back of the painting. The museum also has the original custom shipping container that I built when it was sent to an unknown German location. I was told it was one of Goering's most prized pieces. Many times, during my repair work, I was tempted to damage or destroy this beautiful work of art, just like he'd destroyed the lives of so many of our people, but that would have sealed my fate. I got to the point where I was willing to pay the price, but I could never abandon Elsa and my family.

"This book, this inconspicuous black ledger that has been hidden for years, will corroborate its authenticity and prove its original ownership. Legally, of course, it wasn't Goering's painting. His men had *confiscated* the piece from a major Jewish collector and brought it directly to Goering. There was nothing discreet about it. In fact, that was the point. The confiscation and destruction of private property was just one of the many ruthless tactics the Nazis used to crush and demonize their victims. I can also say with 100-percent certainty this painting hasn't seen the light of day since I personally packed it for shipment.

"All the pictures and documents here on the table identify the paintings, sculptures, tapestries, and other stolen objects that have been shown in exhibitions throughout Europe curtesy of so-called *anonymous owners*. Many of these pieces subsequently sold for huge amounts of money. There are some thirty-seven entries sent to me that I've matched with pictures of various pieces shown as part of museum exhibitions.

"Over the past two weeks, I've personally spoken to all these museum directors and curators. Each of them has confirmed the procedures used by these underworld criminals were the same. They received the artwork from an anonymous source, along with instructions for the specified length of time the artwork was to be displayed. After generating interest, the piece would then be auctioned off to the highest bidder. It's an unusual practice, but it's been done before. Many private owners and major collectors wish to remain anonymous for legitimate reasons, sometimes to avoid drawing unwanted attention to their expansive collections, in many cases to avoid a certain country's tax laws.

"In some cases, their methods were quite clever. Of all the items represented here, only five museums were used more than once to exhibit a stolen art piece. One can only guess the number of stolen treasures that were shipped to distant countries and the United States. We will probably never know the actual total, but none of these masterpieces will ever be repatriated if the scheme isn't exposed. You can well imagine the magnitude of the legal issues that will follow once this criminal enterprise becomes public knowledge, but the truth must be told. After all these years, I finally have the opportunity to free my conscience of my past deeds."

Hans held the small black ledger delicately, as though holding it too tightly would make its contents disappear.

"This book can never fall into the wrong hands," he said. Alana and Chris could see the pressure inside Hans was coming to a boiling point.

"It pains me to say, someone at the Louvre must be tied to this scheme. It's not a one-man operation, either. This kind of plot requires a financial person who understands how money can be manipulated, laundered, and transferred internationally without arousing suspicion. A person who can manage the complex logistics without leaving an obvious paper trail. A person who travels regularly, without restrictions, as part of their job.

"Beyond that, you also need someone with total control over the shipping and receiving departments. They not only need to understand the numerous steps of moving high value pieces in and out of the top museums; they also need to know how to doctor the paperwork, omitting or deleting key pieces of information from the museum's records.

"At this point, I'm quite sure both of these people must be employed by the Louvre. It makes perfect sense everything is coming from there. And yet, there have been no reports of missing or stolen items, indicating these pieces aren't coming from the Louvre's official inventory. Therefore, I strongly suspect, somewhere in the Louvre there's a cache of hidden treasures that have remained *outside* the Louvre's inventory system; pieces that have been sequestered out of sight since the war. It's the only way this makes sense. The trail of paperwork—the little that we have—seems to indicate the point of origin begins at the Louvre.

"As far as I know, there's only one man who understands the complexity of the Louvre with its maze of hallways, back corridors, sub-basements, and storage rooms. That man, Maurice Devenue, works for the director. While I was conducting my assessment and appraisal of the master painting, I spoke to him at length and learned his background.

"He's worked in almost every capacity there for forty-five years. Presently, he's in charge of shipping and receiving, the same position he's held for the last ten years. Nothing goes in or out of the Louvre without his knowledge and approval. Not only that, this man has a photographic memory. I've researched people with this type of mind. It's called *eidetic memory*, or total recall memory. As you can imagine, there are but a few people in the entire world with this ability.

"With his incredible abilities, he's a perfect fit for the Louvre's labyrinths of corridors and storage rooms that have been added haphazardly over the years. Maurice also mentioned he personally met Hermann Goering. Unsurprisingly, their many interactions happened when the Nazis were using the Louvre as their central collection point for confiscated art, their base for sorting and shipping looted and stolen goods back to Germany for the so-called Führermuseum. Not coincidentally, I believe, the paperwork Maurice provided me was clearly forged, naming Reichsmarschall Goering as the piece's last-known rightful owner."

Alana's mind flashed back to the day she and her grandfather had attended the special preview at the Louvre. She remembered vividly the expression on his face as they left. "Is Jean Pierre involved?" she blurted.

"I don't know for sure. I don't have any proof, but he canceled our meeting. When he called, he sounded quite upset about something—I don't know—something he clearly didn't want to discuss. We rescheduled for Friday. I got the sense he was just buying time. So far I've been very cautious. I have not disclosed any of what you just heard to anyone else. Not to Jean Pierre or the other museum directors I've spoken to. He sees me merely as a very knowledgeable art restorer. He doesn't know a thing about my past, my involvement with Goering's art collection, the work I did for him or my black ledger. I'm sure it will be a very interesting meeting on Friday. I'm not sure how much information to reveal or what kind of information I should give him."

"What if he's the *instigator*?" asked Alana. "What if he's the mastermind, the brains behind this horrible scheme? If he learns about your involvement in *this painting* and the hundreds of others like it that you worked on, what will he do? What if he discovers your secret black ledger?"

"Well, then he will have two choices: bring me into the partnership or get rid of me entirely. At that point I fear, my dear granddaughter, he will seek to silence you too. And if he takes care of us, it will be the end of the Muller family. There will be no heirs, no one searching for us or demanding to know where we are. Jean Pierre must know that. We will conveniently disappear without so much as a trace."

Alana felt a cold shiver run down her spine. Chris put his hand on hers and tried to calm her. Chris's hand felt warm and reassuring. Alana relaxed, but only slightly. She was still gripped by fear.

"I've known him for a long time," continued Hans, "but we've never been very close. There's a tremendous fortune at stake, enough to live in luxury for many lifetimes. I fear the equation for him is quite simple. It's a matter of survival. He's close to achieving his goal and he will eliminate anything or *anyone* that stands in his way."

CHAPTER 28

TIME FOR DRASTIC ACTION

As Hans disclosed his connection to the stolen masterpiece currently on display at the Louvre, Chris quietly gathered a handful of pictures from the table and looked at them. Within minutes he'd identified several of the pieces he'd been hired to track down. In fact, he was staring at one now. It was one he'd seen at the Musée d'Orsay before his accident. It was a lesser-known masterpiece by Rembrandt, stolen not long after the Nazi invasion of Poland in 1939. The piece was considered a Polish national treasure.

Chris's first impulse was to interject and share this knowledge with Hans, but he stifled the urge. Everything was unfolding perfectly. Chris now realized Hans was not a party to these callous crimes, but a victim of them. Chris's thoughts turned to Hans and the nightmarish events he'd silently carried in his heart all these years.

Chris could no longer be silent.

"Before we go any further with this bleak, but I believe accurate, analysis of our present situation," Chris said, "I need to share with both of you recent discoveries about myself. I think my background in art and experience as an investigator can help get us out of this mess. Together, we will devise a plan to solve the potentially life-threatening problem we're in."

"But, Grandfather, we have another option," Alana interjected, before Chris had a chance to share all his recent findings. "Chris can give the money back to the people who hired him. We can all leave France and live in the US. I will retire from nursing and do what you've always wanted: learn the fine art of restoration. You can teach me how, as your father and grandfather taught you. We can leave this horrible mess behind and build a new life, with a new business in New York."

"Oh, how I wish we could make that happen," said Hans, "but I cannot escape my true destiny. I owe too much to the people whose treasures were taken by the evil Nazi regime. Thousands were victimized by that monster Goering. I've stayed silent too long. This black ledger can—and must—reveal the truth. I will not allow others to desecrate the victims by profiting from these horrible acts.

"It's been eating at me for years, polluting my subconscious. When I was forced to work for Goering, I made promises to myself that someday, somehow, I would make things right for the people who'd been stripped of their most prized possessions and sent to the camps. Other than my deep love for Elsa, that promise was the only thing that kept me going during those miserable, desperate years of war. It was the hope we'd both survive to one day right these wrongs that kept me from giving up and getting on one of those trains, bound for who knows where.

"I won't let fear silence me. I didn't surrender to it then and I won't surrender now. I will never forget *day after day* watching as trainloads of women and children left the train yard, sent away to what we learned were horrific death camps. We didn't know it at the beginning, but we were watching the Holocaust unfold right before our very eyes, as we were imprisoned by the devil himself, forced to do his bidding. I will not run from my obligation to seek justice, even if it costs my life."

With that, Alana broke down and started to sob. She had been pushed past the breaking point. She couldn't bear to think about losing her grandfather. She'd never known her mother, who died giving birth to Alana. Her uncle, Hans's son, had died of an unknown illness in his teens. The woman who'd raised her from birth, her mother's sister, had recently passed away. Grandfather Hans and Alana were all that was left of the Muller family.

Chris rushed to her side, pulling her gently to his chest in a strong, loving embrace. "Nothing is going to happen to you or your grandfather," he told her. "I promise."

"How?" asked Alana, pulling her head away to look him in the eye. "How can you me promise that? Your life is in danger too! How can you promise *me* any of this will work out when you don't even know what will happen to *you*?"

"Breathe deeply, my love. I know it's hard but try to relax. I will explain everything."

As the trio's intense emotions started to ebb, Chris brought Hans up to date. He told him about his numerous online searches and how he'd found his yearbook, the key that began to unlock the mystery of his life. He told them how seeing the briefcase full of money had triggered another flood of memories. He told them about his ten-year career as a CIA operative and his current job as the founder and owner of a small security company. Then, he told them about his most recent conversation with his brother Scott, who still lived in their hometown of Austin, Minnesota.

All this information was totally new to Hans. "The incredible irony of the whole situation is unbelievable," Hans blurted. "How do we proceed? I believe the people behind this scheme are now running scared. The walls are closing in and they want out. They're going to shut things down, cover their tracks, and clean up any loose ends that might jeopardize their plan to escape. Chris, I believe you and I are two of those loose ends."

"I think your analysis is spot-on," said Chris, "and time is of the essence, but before we put together a plan, I need to contact my old boss at the CIA. He owes me a favor and we could definitely use some additional help."

Chris once again transformed into the CIA agent he used to be, taking charge of the situation. If he didn't, he knew, three lives could be lost. "The first item on my list is protecting you and Alana," said Chris, forcefully. "It's a precaution I have to take, so don't object. Now listen carefully—both of you need to maintain your normal daily routines. They likely already have someone watching you. We can't afford to let them know we suspect anything. All of us need to stay calm."

Chris turned to Hans, speaking with assurance. "Hans, you need to call Jean Pierre and postpone your Friday meeting. Tell him you need to do it Monday; you're completing an art restoration project for a private collector. But you're not going into the Louvre again without some special equipment that I'll put on you. And under *no circumstances* will you take Alana with you. In fact, it's best that the two of you remain apart, other than in your shop or at home. Now, I need to go make two very important phone calls. We'll meet back here tomorrow after the shop is closed for the day. Alana, you and I need to arrive separately. Both of you, stay safe and stay in control. We'll all see each other tomorrow."

CHAPTER 29

THE AGENCY AND
THE CONTRACT

"Hello, Chris, I've been waiting for your call," said Jay, his former boss.

"Why am I not surprised?" Chris responded. "Are you going to tell me you're involved in this operation?"

"Not by choice, I assure you. Interpol *strongly suggested* that the CIA might want to participate in an investigation about rare pieces of art and artifacts suddenly leaving Europe, exported to other countries, *especially* the United States. All told, they say the scheme's worth hundreds of millions of dollars. As you know, of course, there's always been steady business in the underground world of forged and stolen art. The huge sums of money currently flowing into and out of other countries—most of which bypass local duties and tax laws of the governments involved—well, it's highly illegal and the countries in question want to shut it all down.

"Apparently, the one thing that really has the art world in a frenzy is that the vast majority of these pieces have been missing since World War II. They were presumed lost because not one of these pieces has seen the light of day since the war. You and the Muller family, my friend, have been unknowingly caught up in some highly illegal and potentially dangerous affairs. These people don't play around. That's all I'm going to tell you over the phone, Chris, or should I say, *Antone La Rue*? And you thought you could quit and make some easy money! My friend, this is what they call a *rude awakening*.

"I'm in Berlin at the moment. We need to meet as soon as we can, but not in Paris. I'll make all the arrangements for the two of us to rendezvous in a little town called Bayeux. Perhaps you've heard of it? It's quite close to the Normandy beaches and a top visitor attraction. We will pose as tourists, there to visit the beaches where our grandfathers landed during the D-Day invasion.

"You know the drill. I need you to look like a typical American tourist, shopping and spending some of that *hard-earned cash* you've made. This quaint vacation town will be the perfect place for us to avoid attention while we bring each other up to speed and plan a strategy to get you out of this mess. Perhaps we can even imbibe a few of the outstanding local wines. But, Chris, here's the deal, I don't want any other foreign agencies to know we're working together. You have to get out of Paris; that place is crawling with agents from all over the world. It's a very dangerous environment.

"There is a Rail Europe train leaving the Gare Saint-Lazare at 18:09. It should arrive in Bayeux at 20:17. I'll meet you at the station, but I will arrive well before you. I'm traveling via an agency plane.

"Chris, I'm sure you're aware you're likely being followed. Unfortunately, since you're no longer an agent, there's only so much I can do for now. Use the evasive techniques you were taught. You're going to be on your own until we meet in Bayeux."

CHAPTER 30

EVASIVE ANSWERS

Chris needed to contact the two Paris police officers who had recruited him. He'd already decided how much information he'd pass along; hopefully it would be enough to satisfy them *and their client* for the time being.

As he prepared to dial the secure phone number they'd told him to call, Chris thought, *It would be great to collect the remainder of my fee. Heaven knows I've earned it.*

The police officer who answered the phone told Chris they would meet at the restaurant close to the airport where the three of them had conducted their first meeting in France. It seemed like a strange choice to Chris, since standard operating procedure was never to use the same point of contact more than once. *If you want to stay alive in this business, you have to be smart*, he thought. No doubt, they were up to something. Reluctantly, he went along with the plan so as not to arouse suspicion.

Unlike the first time Chris came to this restaurant, this time he walked through the door with all his senses on high alert. The first meeting between the parties had been purely transactional, to finalize their contract and secure the 50-percent down payment. The situation had become considerably more complicated. Now, people's lives were in danger. People important to Chris. People he loved.

The first thing he noticed as he scanned the main dining area was the crowd, how they were dressed and grouped. Situational awareness was crucial. At any moment, a seemingly insignificant detail could prove to be the difference between life and death. This fact had been hammered into his head all throughout his tenure at the CIA.

As his eyes carefully swept the restaurant, Chris noted the location of several strategically placed, partially hidden security cameras. It struck him immediately that these slime balls must have already secretly recorded his voice, if not his image too. *Boy, was I naive when I took this assignment, thinking it would be a simple, straightforward investigation for easy money.*

He noticed the two undercover Paris police officers sitting in a booth in the back corner, away from the bar. Their eyes met momentarily, acknowledging each other. Chris slowly made his way over to their table and joined them.

"This will be a short meeting," he said, flatly. "I'm not too happy with your choice of venue, so I won't be discussing my confidential findings here. And if you two think you're going to get my report on tape and then get rid of me, guess again. I had some doubts about your supposedly benign motives for my investigation originally, but I trusted you. Whatever you've dragged me into is *not* what you requested of me. I've discovered a number of facts about who's involved in this illegal art scheme, but you're not going to get any of this information today, least of all in this restaurant."

Chris leaned in toward the men and said unemotionally, "Before I reveal anything, I need two things from you. First, an acknowledgement that your client will fulfill his part of our contractual agreement. Second, as we discussed at our last meeting in Hans Muller's art shop, I need copies of the documents that were lost in my car accident. Everything. As you know, all of my previous notes and findings—the information I already gave you—went up in smoke. I need all of it or I won't go any further.

Silence is golden, they say. The two officers looked at each other. Neither wanted to speak. Chris's aggressive stance had put them on the defensive, knocking them back on their heels. Finally, the officer who'd originally presented the plan spoke.

"We made contact with our client and passed on your statements," he said. "He agrees to the conditions that you require to fulfill this contract. He, in turn, asked us to pass along his regrets with regard to the physical and mental injuries you sustained in your accident. We, my partner and I, received the green light to assess your current mental state and release you from this contract if that's what you want. The money you've already received is yours; you earned it. In turn, you must give us every scrap of information you already gathered. Even the most insignificant detail. Our client paid for all of it and that's what he demands to be given.

"However, if you decide to continue with this assignment—and we believe you are willing and mentally able to do so—our client is offering you an additional $100,000 with the proviso that you *accelerate your efforts* and complete your investigation as quickly as possible. He's quite reluctant to . . . *let you go*, since that would set things back, but I believe he is willing to, should there be any . . . *problems*."

Chris's head swam with competing thoughts. Whoever this client was, he desperately wanted to get any information he could as fast as possible. Chris thought about his recent conversation with his ex-boss at the CIA. There were huge amounts of money changing hands in this underground world for forged and stolen art, Jay had said. *It's a very dangerous environment.*

The fact is, Chris thought again, *once I pass my information to the client, I'm disposable.* He could picture the headline in the newspaper back home: "Small-town Security Man Disappears." In France, his disappearance wouldn't even make the evening news. Jay's keen remarks were perceptive. Chris knew he must heed them well.

Even so, he had the palpable sense that these two—and their client—were not the perpetrators of his hit-and-run accident. He still didn't trust them, but there was someone else out there who wanted him to vanish. His chances for survival, if he continued, didn't look very good. His needed to buy some time. He decided to agree to their deal *for now* and leverage Jay's resources to escape this nasty predicament.

"As I stated at our last meeting," said Chris, "I will see this through to the end." *With or without you or your client's permission,* he thought to himself. "You recording this conversation?" he asked.

"Yes, as we did at that first meeting," said one of the cops. "Our client demanded proof that we'd hired an American and that the down payment was delivered in person. Our client doesn't fully trust anyone and wanted to be sure his instructions were followed to the letter. You see, even in the world of underground transactions, trust is not a given. It must be earned. And money, lots of money, can alter the outcome of contractual relationships."

The man lifted a briefcase and placed it on the table. "We anticipated your request," he said. "We knew you'd be thorough and prudent, as you've been from the start." He put his thumbs on the latches and paused, as though for dramatic effect. "In here we have a complete set of all the documents and photos you were given at our first meeting, as well as half the bonus money. To assure you keep working for us," he said, popping open the case to confirm its contents, "here is an additional $50,000." He closed the case quickly and locked it, sliding the keys across the table.

As Chris reached for the keys, he said, "When I was young, my mom always said, 'In for a penny, in for a pound.'" He put the keys in his pocket, slid the case off the table, and set it on the floor by his foot. Momentarily satisfied, he told the two men that the stolen paintings were very likely originating from the Louvre. Sensing their surprise, he noted, "I'm closing in on the men running this operation. The photographs you brought will help me triangulate the source."

Chris stood up from the table, his mind flashing back to all the pictures and documents Hans had spread out in the back room of his shop the night before. Hans and Chris were confident Jean Pierre and Maurice were the masterminds behind the scheme. If he wanted to stay alive, however, timing the release of his theory and its supporting details was critical. His plan was to feel things out with Jay. Jay's contacts at Interpol and inside the French police could deal with the perpetrators discreetly, in a way that didn't tie things back to Chris or Hans. It was a game within a game and Chris needed to play it perfectly or suffer the consequences.

"We'll meet again soon," he said. "By then, I'll have the information your client requested."

Chris knew their conversation had been monitored, which is why he'd kept things vague and only shared a dubious clue about the Louvre. It wasn't much for them to go on and was very likely something they already knew. It was the details that were elusive. There, Chris had an edge.

He left the restaurant with a clear plan already formulating in his head. His former boss at the CIA, a man he'd trusted with his life during his time at the agency, would be invaluable. The timing of their rendezvous was perfect. Chris envisioned the eminent dangers that lay ahead for both himself and Hans, but they weren't anything he hadn't dealt with before. Vigilance was key. It was more important than ever to notice every detail and always have an escape route. It could save his life.

CHAPTER 31

A CALL TO ACTION

Chris headed back to Charles de Gaulle, initiating some of his best evasive maneuvers to rid himself of any potential followers. Once he was finally certain he was no longer being watched, he left the crowded airport and walked to Gare Saint-Lazare, arriving in plenty of time to buy a ticket to Bayeux in the first-class coach. Ticket in hand, he called Alana and brought her up to date. They'd been living together for several weeks now and kept each other apprised of their daily schedules, both as a matter of safety and because they enjoyed checking in during the workday.

Chris informed her that he would be out of town, doing some research. It was premature to let her know that he'd already enlisted help from his former CIA colleagues. She was better off not knowing and he didn't want her to be consumed by potentially false hope. He assured her that he'd be back in time to make their meeting at her grandfather's shop the next day.

The train ride to Bayeux was only two hours, but it gave Chris plenty of time to review the contents of the briefcase and carefully repack them in his backpack. Tourists don't carry briefcases, of course, so he wiped it clean of all fingerprints and left it in a storage compartment near the back of the train.

He arrived at the station late, as was so typical of the French rail system. It was an ordinary small-town depot—one agent selling tickets, no porters to assist travelers, and no congestion from arrivals and departures. For a moment, it reminded Chris of the many trips he'd taken on Amtrak, passing through small rural towns in Minnesota and Wisconsin as he traveled to and from college.

The two-room depot was almost empty and his former boss was nowhere to be seen, so he continued toward the taxi stand, where only two cabs waited. As he approached he noticed a man staring at him through a cab window with a slight smile on his face. It was indeed his former boss and friend, Jasper Ludicina, the man everyone called Jay.

This was the man he'd worked for as an undercover agent for almost ten years at the CIA, a man he grew to respect and trust like no one else. A man with a strong moral compass and deeply held values that everyone respected. A man dedicated to his profession and loyal to his country.

Jay had joined the agency fresh out of the University of Notre Dame and worked himself up through the ranks to his current position: assistant director of the CIA. He was intelligent, highly skilled, and very analytical. Agents that worked for him were amazed, and thankful, for his meticulous attention to detail before he assigned them to a field operation. When given an assignment by Jay, an agent knew that it was well planned to minimize the risk to all operatives involved.

As Chris opened the door and climbed into the taxi, the friendly smile on Jay's face released some of the anxiety that had been steadily building in his body these past few weeks. Here was the man Chris knew he could count on when the chips were down, especially if he was in trouble.

"Well, Chris, I have to admit, you sure look like a tourist to me," he said. "I like your outfit, it's right out of Farm Country, USA. And that tourist book in your hand, with the *Visiting Normandy* title? Nice touch. Should we check the soles of your shoes for Minnesota manure? I'd swear you came straight from the barn."

"Very funny, Jay. Very funny. It's good to see you, too."

"Well, it's been a long day for both of us, so we'll have quick dinner in town. I made reservations for both of us at the Logis de Saint Jean in Bayeux, a quaint and quiet bed-and-breakfast where we can do some friendly catchup on current events. Tomorrow, I scheduled a four-hour tour of the American invasion beaches, Omaha and Utah. As I'm sure you know, the code name for that massive invasion on the Normandy coast was Operation Overlord, the largest armada of navy ships ever assembled in one time and place. It involved millions of army and naval personnel, not to mention pilots and commanders on the ground. I know you're a World War II buff, an interesting connection to your current situation, wouldn't you say?"

"Typical Jay," Chris responded, with a broad, friendly smile. "I knew you'd put together a plan that covered all of the details, but even I'm impressed. You amaze me. To think we haven't seen each other in over a year. It's like I still work for you."

Because of its close proximity to all of five of the invasion's landing zones, Bayeux was now a major tourist destination. Somehow it had escaped the ravages of the war and maintained its Old World charm. There were dozens of small inns, restaurants, shops, and tour services available. "This is a booming town in the summer," said Jay. "Fortunately for us, in early January there's very little action. Our choices for cuisine are wide open."

They chose a small, quiet bistro with local food specialties. As Jay had predicted, the place was almost empty—the perfect setting for the important conversations they were about to have.

Chris began to speak, but Jay cut him off. "Sorry for the interruption, Chris," he said, "but before we share *any* information, we need to sign some important documents. They're for your protection and, well, security. It will keep both of us safe from any international legal issues that might arise in the future. Even more to the point, it will allow me to make some key resources available to you, important assets that will help us solve these horrible war crimes and get you and your friends out of the dangerous predicament you've stumbled into."

As Jay was speaking, he retrieved a stack of forms and official documents from his backpack. "This first form is the most important. You need to agree and sign here," he said, pointing at the space for Chris's signature. "It's an employment form. You will again be working for me, back on the CIA payroll. You'll be given the same security clearance that you had before you retired." As Chris signed the form, Jay underscored his key point. "Chris, I'm sure you know, I'm sticking my neck out for you. It's not exactly normal to reinstate retired agents, especially in the midst of a complicated case. Thankfully, it's not entirely unprecedented, either. In this case, we're reinstating you—I'm reinstating you—because of your sterling record with us. The things you've already discovered, the leads you've generated, are very pertinent to the agency's ongoing work. Coincidentally, I was asked to investigate the same illegal scheme you were, but we had no idea how deep and how far the tentacles reached. This agreement makes it easy for me to defend my position in the unlikely event I must."

Jay folded the form neatly and slipped it into a special compartment deep in his backpack. "The caveat, of course, is we—the agency—must be given full access to everything you've discovered. They won't know it came from you, but I will also need to share it with our partners at Interpol and the French secret police. I just attended several meetings in Berlin on the subject of black-market sales of stolen war artifacts. Unfortunately, the United States was pulled into this web of underground criminals because so many pieces are showing up in private collections and museums across our country.

"Chris, this thing you're involved with? It not only caught my attention, but many other countries' security agencies, too. People want justice. Europe is crawling with secret police from all over the world. Some of what they're doing is entirely legitimate, but some of it is quite shady. Huge amounts of money are needed to identify these underground rings and put them jail.

"In 1940, an organization known as ERR was formed by Alfred Rosenberg. He remained as a figurehead, but Hermann Goering took control, with the singular mission to seize Jewish art collections from all Nazi-occupied countries.

"During the *blitzkrieg* of Poland in 1939, special Nazi units were given the specific task of stealing the country's most valuable art. They seized the Veit Stoss altarpiece, a Polish national treasure. They stole Leonardo da Vinci's *Lady with an Ermine*, as well as masterpieces by Raphael and Rembrandt. These works were the lifeblood of the country's art history. The Polish people held strong ties to these treasures. Even now, there are still undercurrents of hate and mistrust for what happened during that war.

"As the Nazis ramped up their system and turned it into a machine, all the loot was collected and inventoried at a central location in Paris. The Musée Jeu de Paume was the epicenter and Goering ruled it with an iron fist. Only his most loyal men knew the full extent of the scheme.

"There are official Nazi documents stating first Hitler, then Goering, were given the option to claim *anything that was seized* before it was considered property of Germany. This order was later amended by Hitler, directing *all confiscated artworks* to be made available directly to him for possible inclusion in his new, yet-to-be-constructed art museum; the infamous Führermuseum. It would be located in Linz and was to become the world's biggest, most magnificent museum, an incredible showcase for Hitler's *personal* art collection, a shining symbol of Nazi superiority and a monument to the so-called Aryan race.

"At the meetings I attended, I saw copies of numerous personal letters and documents written by Goering and Rosenberg to Hitler himself. There were manifests of entire trains, informing Hitler of the contents, all of it valuable art treasures. This loot was shipped from Paris directly to Germany. The amount of plunder found in Germany after the war was staggering and, Chris, I can assure you, there may be an equal amount that's never been located. They showed us list after list of unrecovered treasures from all over Europe. Hell, there are documents showing that Goering selected some 594 pieces from the Musée Jeu de Paume alone for his own personal collection. Where it all went, nobody knows.

"He personally owned four separate residences. As the war progressed and the outcome shifted in favor of the Allies, his collections were removed from his homes and sent to undisclosed locations. Some of his treasures were found and returned to their rightful owners after the war, but there are easily thousands of masterpieces, tapestries, and jewelry still out there somewhere. Countless people have been searching, following every lead, no matter how tenuous or circumstantial, waiting for the day when they can reclaim their property. It seems clear to me at this point, one way or another, they'll do whatever it takes to accomplish their goals.

"I'm not sure anyone actually knows how deep this goes, not even the criminals themselves. Whatever fraction you're tangled up in, it's just a tiny piece of a massive international problem. Either way, you and this art dealer Muller, you're tied to it in a very dangerous way."

Chris had long since stopped reading the employment document as he hung on every word Jay spoke. He flipped through it quickly and signed it, without question. He'd learned long ago to trust Jay for his insights and recommendations. He had no doubt Jay would make sure the agency held up their end of the bargain.

"I'm sure everything else is fine too," said Chris. "We can deal with them—"

"Chris, let me stop you right there," said Jay. "Before we can go any further, there is one stipulation you must know. If it's a deal breaker, we both need to walk away and pretend we never met here."

Chris silently nodded and Jay continued.

"Since you now work for the federal government of the United States, you cannot accept any future security contracts in the art industry, not for you *or your company*. If it even *looks* like it might lead to the realm of international art, you need to turn it down immediately. Any fees you've received to date, or any money you receive upon completion of your existing contract, will be yours. Beyond that, it's a no-fly zone. Do you have a problem with that?"

"None," Chris responded, definitively. "Now, I need to turn the table and ask a favor of you. As my boss and my friend, you told me more than once, 'Never share information or intelligence you don't need to share.' What I'm about to tell will put two people I care about very deeply in danger."

Jay raised his eyebrows and cocked his head slightly, as if to say, *I also told you never to get personally involved.* Chris could hear those very words somewhere in the back of his mind, but he also knew he was too far down the path to turn around now.

"The art dealer, Hans Muller, and his granddaughter, Alana . . . I need you and your agents to do anything possible to keep them safe. When I took this security contract, it was my understanding this would be a simple investigation. I had no idea it would blossom into a multiagency, international investigation with peoples' lives on the line. Hell, I didn't even know who I was when I met Alana. Had I known . . . I don't know . . . I might have done things differently. I might have made different . . . choices."

As Chris finished his thought, he noticed a pleasant smile bloom across Jay's face. "Is she the one?" he asked.

"Yes," Chris responded, without hesitation.

Jay seemed unsurprised. He nodded knowingly. "I don't have to tell you, the bonds we forge when we're under stress are truly unbelievable. *Unbreakable*, I should say." Jay raised his glass as if to toast. "I'm happy for you, Chris. I always thought you'd left the business because your fiancée pressured you. When I met her that one time I thought, *white picket fence, golden retriever, two kids, a boy and a girl, play set in the backyard* . . . You know, Chris, when I was your age, I met my future wife. I was also an active field agent who was often in harm's way. I know deep down she wished I had a different career, but she also knew how much it meant to me. Our love for one another was never influenced by family, religion, or my job. The bonds of true love rise above all other distractions.

"I think we're a lot alike. I didn't think you could walk away. I'm guessing the security business was your compromise, but it doesn't seem like your heart was in it. You've got a lot of good years left before you settle down and become a regular citizen."

They both shared a laugh. For a moment it was silent.

"I'm really happy for you, as your former boss and *friend*," said Jay. "I can see that the people who helped with your recovery are truly special, especially your dedicated nurse, Alana; the special person who made it all happen. I have to believe fate was looking out for you, putting you in a position to meet Alana and help her grandfather."

After that, the conversation shifted and Chris told Jay the incredible story of the Muller family, their expertise in the art restoration business, and how the three generations of men were coerced into working for Hermann Goering and other high-ranking members of the Nazi Party.

As Chris began to discuss the contents and importance of Hans's black ledger, Jay held up his hands and signaled for him to stop before he could say anything more.

"Please don't go any further," he said. "It's better for us both if I don't know any specifics about what's in that book. Not yet, anyway. If it is what I think it is, the fewer people who know its contents, the better. After this meeting, I'll need to debrief Interpol. They'll ask what I've learned from you and there's no reason to discuss something I have little or no knowledge about. I can only imagine the consequences it will have on the art world when the information gets out. Our agency shares a great working relationship with Interpol. We've agreed to partner on this investigation, but the dangers of misusing that book and leaking documented information to other less scrupulous actors is not worth the risk.

"Right now, we need to focus on the perpetrators of these crimes. Let's attack the problem at its roots and deal with that first. So, have you and this Hans Muller uncovered the key players behind these illicit sales? If not, are you getting close? What have you discovered to date? Where can the CIA and its resources be most helpful to you in your investigation?"

"Don't worry," said Chris with a chuckle, "I plan to be as thorough as you would be yourself."

Chris began to divulge everything he'd learned from Hans the previous night—everything except the book, that is, which would no doubt prove to be the cornerstone of the whole case. *Jay is right,* thought Chris, *I need to hold something back. In this business you never can tell when you might need a bargaining chip.*

CHAPTER 32

THE STRATEGY STARTS TO UNFOLD

"Not long after Hans arrived at Otto's shop following Kristallnacht," said Chris, "he was confronted by Reichsmarschall Hermann Goering, the second most powerful man in the Third Reich."

As Chris conveyed the heartbreaking details, a dark pall settled over the table. By then it was quite late, but Jay listened intently, hanging on every word. Chris could see Jay's mind fitting each new piece into the puzzle.

"Goering laid out a brutal proposal that put Hans in a double bind," Chris continued. "Goering would save the lives of Hans's mother and children and allow them to safe passage to Switzerland *only if* Hans and his wife were bound to Goering as indentured servants for the duration of the war. Their only job would be preserving and refurbishing all of the art Goering had selected for his personal collection.

"Naturally, for Hans it wasn't a question. Of course, he'd protect his family, even if he were bound to the devil himself. As time passed, however, and Hans was exposed to more of the horrible events taking place in the railyard, he fell into a deep depression. Often, he regretted his decision to work for such an evil person—a madman—who heartlessly sent thousands of Jews to their death.

"Hans was only able to keep his sanity with the help of his dear wife Elsa. They made a pact that if they survived, they would work to repatriate the stolen treasures and get them back to their rightful owners. Hans was in possession of documentary evidence to make that happen."

It was so quiet that the only sound was that of clanking dishes back in the kitchen as the servers put the clean dishes away.

"I believe Hans's work wasn't in vain. He will indeed have the opportunity to repatriate these stolen goods—if he isn't murdered first. There are only four people in the world with knowledge of this information: Hans and Alana and the two of us. Hans needs to be protected so the information he holds doesn't fall into the wrong hands. I can honestly say, without Hans and his granddaughter, I'd be wandering the streets of Paris with no earthly idea as to why I was there. I love the two of them dearly and I feel compelled to support Hans in his quest.

"In the course of our discussion," said Chris, "Hans also shared his most recent connection to the Louvre. The irony of the whole situation is unbelievable. Not long ago, the Louvre's director, Jean Pierre Rolland, asked him to authenticate an Old Master painting that was supposedly received from an anonymous source. The instructions were to put it on display in an exhibition and then put it up for auction. Precisely the same scheme and tactics I uncovered at the other museums I researched. The process, paperwork, procedures—all of it was identical."

Chris stopped for a moment so he could choose his words carefully. He knew if he wasn't measured, he might come across as some kind of conspiracy theorist, even to his friend Jay.

"Here is the point where truth is stranger than fiction. When Hans finally saw the painting that Jean Pierre had specifically asked him to authenticate, Hans recognized the piece as one he'd restored for Goering while he was held captive in that Berlin railyard. He remembered it vividly because when it was first brought to him by a Nazi Lieutenant for restoration, he was given a crystal-clear message. 'This piece is very special. It belongs to Reichsmarschall Hermann Goering. It's one of his most treasured paintings. It needs to be repaired and repacked with the utmost care for a long journey by train. If there's any damage, there will be a high price to pay.' The implication was obvious: handle this painting as though your life is at stake.

"In order for Hans to fully authenticate the piece and make sure it wasn't a forgery, however, he told Jean Pierre he needed more time in order to do a comprehensive evaluation.

"Hans has completed his work. He now knows without question who the original owner was and it definitely wasn't Goering. While he performed his analysis at the Louvre's restoration shop, he discovered the original packing materials that he'd used in Berlin, materials no longer used because they no longer meet the insurance requirements for safe shipping.

"After speaking with his contacts at many of the other top museums in Europe, Hans also discovered that dozens of other artworks have already been auctioned off or sold directly to private collectors. Hans believes someone has access to a previously unknown cache of paintings he restored in that railyard prison. He thinks dozens more are about to be *discovered* and put on the black market.

"Hans also thinks the Louvre is the source of all of these illegal operations. He can't prove it yet, but at his meeting with Jean Pierre, he hopes to somehow trick the man into giving away his secret. It's a dangerous move on his part.

"So far, I haven't had a chance to research Hans. It was only recently that he shared his story with me. He and I both believe Jean Pierre's cohort in this scheme is the man in charge of the Louvre's shipping and receiving departments, a man who happens to have an incredible memory. His name is Maurice Devenue. Essentially, he's worked at the museum all his life. As a young man he was forced to work for Goering there during the Nazi occupation of France. Without a doubt, he is the one individual who knows the entire inner workings of the Louvre and can control everything that comes in and everything that leaves from the shipping docks.

"Jay, both these men need to be investigated, and quickly. Jean Pierre travels all over Europe to high-profile museums and exhibitions. He is also well versed in international banking systems and money transfers. He and his cohort manipulate the paperwork to conceal the movement of these stolen goods to private individuals and museums."

"What a scheme they've hatched!"

"How long they've been at it, only the two of them know. As to the money they've already made, we can only guess, but surely its at least tens of millions.

"There are some other items that should also be investigated by the agency, such as what kind of construction took place at the Louvre during the Nazi occupation. We also need to research the key conspirators who were running the show and figure out what became of them. Are there any records that identify the shipments of stolen art to Goering and the personal residences of other Nazi commanders?"

Before Jay could answer, Chris continued. "I also need to find out who my anonymous client is. Who actually hired me? This individual is paying me a huge sum of money to identify the key people behind this scheme. I think my employer is likely a private collector or shady art dealer who is trying to muscle into this illegal operation."

"Recently, I learned from Hans there could be someone else, a third individual who must be tied to this entire affair, even if he doesn't know it. It's Maurice's son, Albert. He owns a private security firm that specializes in museum camera systems.

"Maurice told Hans that his son has installed these systems in all the major museums in Europe. The whole thing is powered by special identity software that his company developed. It can do facial recognition comparisons of individuals who attend art expositions all over Europe.

"I'm quite sure that's how they identified me. During my early investigations, I attended virtually every exhibition in Europe. My face must have showed up on dozens of feeds. Perhaps they thought I was an international art thief or maybe a spy from a little-known secret service organization trying to identify where all these previously lost artifacts were coming from.

"Either way, when you analyze this company's capabilities, it fits perfectly with their scheme. Aside from the forged paperwork, they can also hide anyone else who might be involved by editing the security footage. Various trucks show up at all hours of the day, building installations, performing maintenance or repair work—the possibilities are endless. And with Maurice as the gatekeeper of the entire security system, this outfit can hide even the smallest hint of their illegal activities, smuggling art pieces in and out via inconspicuous vans and deleting the evidence."

Chris took a deep breath as the magnitude of what he'd just said washed over him like a wave.

"Well, Chris, to say we have our work cut out for us is a bit of an understatement, don't you think?" Jay smiled reassuringly. As always, Chris could see that Jay was already several steps ahead. "Since you now work for me," he said with a welcoming tone, "I can share some additional information given to me by Interpol at the briefing I attended. Since the very day the war ended, Interpol and many other top security agencies from all over Europe have been actively tracking down and recovering the illicit sales of these stolen items. They've identified a number of unscrupulous art dealers in Europe and the US who thrive on this type of illegal activity. Interpol and others have been building legal cases against these criminals for years. It's a very painstaking process. Concrete evidence is rare, and these thieves can't be prosecuted on hearsay alone. Then there's also the issue of conflicting international tax laws and other regulations. Some of these cases have been buried in red tape for years.

"The evidence you've collected will no doubt help to close some of their open cases. Somehow, we need to uncover this entire affair without causing a panic. I'm sorry to say I can't share everything, but here's what I can tell you right now. Four shell companies that may been linked have been identified in the Paris metropolitan area. I'm willing to bet the client you're working for is one of them. If you can identify the key players responsible for these activities *and prove it*, well, you'll not only earn the rest of the money for your contract, you'll strengthen our agency's relationship with Interpol.

"From our standpoint, the timing of when you release your findings to your anonymous client is critical. You absolutely must coordinate that timing with me. The moment Interpol knows, they'll come down on those shell companies like a ton of bricks. There will be international lawsuits that may go on for years, but at least this scheme will be shut down.

"Chris, you have to act fast and I'm going to need you to access the Louvre *without* going through their security system. Inside, you'll need to gather any information you can to validate the theory you share with Hans. As to Jean Pierre and Maurice's complicity, during my time in Berlin I was told by one of the top security officials at Interpol—my counterpart in that organization—that undercover agents are working in the largest museum in Europe. It's time to activate them. I'll establish contact and strategize a way to get you in and out safely without showing up on their video detection system.

"As to the other information you're looking for, I'll make a call and immediately dedicate our resources to gathering intelligence on the people you've identified. I'll also put one of my top teams on protecting the Mullers. If Hans and Alana are that important to you, then they're my priority too."

It was dark and drizzly as they headed back to their bed-and-breakfast. Neither man wore the proper clothing to keep the chill out of their bodies. After all, they were just a pair of American tourists gawking at Normandy's most famous beaches.

Eventually, the silence of their walk was broken by Chris's remark. "Jay, you know we don't have much time to complete this mission. It will have to be as streamlined as possible."

"Yes, I know," he responded, "but I'm confident you'll make it happen. You now have unlimited resources at your disposal. It's great to have you back."

CHAPTER 33

THE NORMANDY EXPERIENCE

When Chris awoke the next morning, he felt like he hadn't slept at all. *Switching to that cognac last night after dinner was definitely not a good idea*, he thought. Still, its velvety, soothing effect had relaxed his mind and body—at least for a while—helping him release some of the tension that had been building up in him like a pressure cooker, ready to explode.

It was 6:45. His mind swirled with thoughts from the previous night's discussion, comingled with vivid images from his dreams. He needed to sort through it all and separate fact from fiction. As reality came into focus, Chris quickly realized, his next steps were the biggest priority.

Jay and Chris planned to meet for breakfast at 8:30. The LED numbers on the nightstand clock blurred in and out of focus. The two of them had nearly downed the entire bottle of that elixir last night.

Once he'd finally gotten to his room, Chris plunged into that deep, heavy sleep where a person somehow feels like he's still awake, watching himself dream, the weight of his own body pressing him heavily to the bed.

It had been quite a while since he'd been in this state, not since he was in his twenties, in fact. Why must he repeat the sins of the past? He knew full well that alcohol dulled and fogged the brain. He needed to right the ship and concentrate, to focus on the problem at hand.

The last thing Chris could remember, as he'd peeled off his clothes and fallen into bed, was Jay reminding him, "Don't be late in the morning. We're signed up for a four-hour tour of the Normandy beaches. We will have lunch at 2:00 and then take the train back to Paris at 3:15."

Thankfully, it was a short walk to the tour office. Chris wasn't sure why Jay had even gone to the trouble of setting up this tour. He was anxious to work on a strategy with Hans to trick Jean Pierre into revealing some scrap of information as to the whereabouts of Goering's hidden treasures.

Still, Chris knew Jay well enough that he trusted him completely. The man was always two steps ahead of everyone in his thinking and planning.

As the they turned off the main road, Rue Saint Jean, it was easy for them to see the tour company's all-white, eight-passenger vans with the brightly colored *OVERLORD TOUR* logos painted on the side.

One of the drivers signaled to them and they climbed into the van. Jay seemed a bit too chipper. Chris listened as well as he could.

"Chris, this whole thing is planned," said Jay. "We don't have to do a thing. Which, from the looks of it, is a good idea this morning." He laughed, then jumped right in. "There were five invasion beachheads on D-Day, June 6, 1944. We'll hit a lot of the highlights, but we're only scheduled to see the two American landing zones, Omaha and Utah, as well as some of the adjacent towns nearby.

"One of them, Sainte-Mère-Église, is the town and church where the men of the 82nd and 101st Airborne were slaughtered in the air, before they could even touch down. The tour will also take us to the American cemetery where 16,000 soldiers are buried. It's hard to comprehend, but the average age of those boys was twenty-four years. They fought and died on these beaches, liberating France. It was a crucial battle and a turning point in that war. If there was ever a place for us Americans to get down on our knees and thank God for our freedoms, that's the place. The cemetery is also the resting place for a great general and a medal of honor awardee from this invasion, General Theodore Roosevelt Jr.

"After that risky, hard-fought invasion, the Allies battled their way across France and into Germany. It was the beginning of the end for Hitler's Third Reich and ultimately led to Germany's unconditional surrender in June of 1945.

"I always wanted to come here, give thanks, pay my respects to all those fallen soldiers, and visit Roosevelt's grave. It's kind of funny, after all these years, here we are, caught up in some of the unfinished business of that tragic war. In a small way, Chris, by returning some of those personal treasures to families who were persecuted and killed during that war, we have the rare opportunity to help right an incredible wrong. I only hope we can succeed without panicking and disrupting the art market.

"If I know you, Chris, someday, you'll want to return here. We're only going to see a small portion of what happened during that fight. The defenses the Germans built along the coastline of France were thought to be impenetrable. The Utah Beach D-Day Museum is atop the ruins of one of the hundreds of bunkers the Germans built to defend the coast of France. We have the opportunity today to visit that site and other German fortifications and take note of their design and construction details. Who knows when it might come in handy. These structures were thought to be indestructible against our munitions at that time. The Germans had developed a special concrete mixture to stand up against our explosives. They passed this secret formula to the Japanese before Japan declared war on us December 1, 1941, with their bombing of Pearl Harbor. The Japanese used a similar design for the concrete in their underground bunkers which housed their soldiers and, in some cases, munitions."

As the two of them visited the historic sites where the tragic events had taken place, Chris tried to understand the magnitude of it all. The lives of so many taken. Chris felt a twinge of sadness and thought of home. He remembered the special memorial park dedicated to all the brave men and woman who'd died during that all-encompassing war. His grandfather's brother, who'd lived in Rockford, died in the Battle of the Bulge. Now, here was Chris, being pulled into a deeply emotional situation which would ultimately impact many lives, across a number of countries.

It was a four-hour tour. Their French guide spoke perfect English and knew many of the key battle scenes and events. He'd even spoken to some of the soldiers who had fought there. It was a heartbreaking, poignant experience for Chris and Jay, who felt deeply indebted to the young American heroes who'd died on this foreign shore.

"We don't have time now, Chris, but someday we need to visit the other invasion beaches of Normandy," said Jay. "They all have their own stories of bravery, sacrifice, and dedication—of men staunchly determined to defeat an enemy who tried to dominate the world.

"Incidentally, there's also a small museum here in Bayeux that houses one of the world's oldest tapestries. It's only about a foot-and-a-half high but measures an incredible 244 feet long. It shows seventy depictions of the events leading up to the Norman Invasion of England led by William the Conqueror, the Duke of Normandy. It dates back to sometime around 1070, a few short years after the battle took place. It is without equal anywhere in the world, a rare relic of the Medieval period that has survived to this day. It was coveted by the Nazis, Goering in particular, who had it sent to Louvre to be admired and studied before ultimately being sent to the Fatherland. Thankfully, they never succeeded in getting it to Germany and the tapestry remained safely in the Louvre's sub-basement for the duration of the war."

After a short lunch in Bayeux, they took a cab to the railroad station to catch the 3:15 train back to Paris. It was just a two-hour ride, but gave them plenty of time to finalize their plan to uncover the conspirators and find the location of the stolen art.

TRUST IS EARNED, NOT GIVEN

Unlike his father Maurice, Albert Devenue was a control freak with very few people skills. He hadn't inherited any of his father's photographic memory or mental recall abilities. He'd completed high school, however—unlike his father—and went on to attend technical college. There, he soon revealed a special aptitude for computer science and quickly became obsessed with what computers could do. At the Maurice's suggestion, Albert concentrated his efforts on becoming a computer technician, with a special emphasis in security.

As the technology developed, museum directors recognized the importance of cameras as a robust method for protecting their most valuable pieces. They also discovered numerous other uses and internal applications. As camera technology improved and the use of digital hard drives increased, the video security market exploded.

Having completed his studies, armed with all the latest skills and tech knowledge, Albert formed a private company that specialized in museum security. With the help of his father, Jean Pierre, and their many contacts in the industry, Albert was able to quickly build a successful business in Paris. Over time, he expanded into many other French cities.

In the beginning, he focused on protecting the museum's most valuable pieces and collections. Individual cameras were placed to observe attendees at various viewing areas, to help determine traffic patterns that would help museums manage resources more effectively. They also installed recorders at the entrances and exits of the museum and the shipping and receiving docks.

Albert's business flourished. He expanded and hired new people. Once facial recognition programs became commercially available, he directed his top engineers to integrate this game-changing software into all their security systems. Incredibly, this new capability allowed Albert and his team to target potential art thieves *before* any crime was committed. This unique feature gave his business a major competitive advantage, allowing him to charge higher prices and additional service fees.

Soon, Albert's company became the preeminent collection point for all the video footage, screen captures, and live streams of top museums all over Europe. The future of his business looked bright and highly profitable.

The one problem was potentially getting caught up in his father's highly illegal scheme, which was using Albert's technology for their own profit.

In order to protect his son as much as possible, Maurice was careful to never share the exact location deep beneath the Louvre where all the stolen treasures were hidden. Of course, Albert was fully aware of his father's so-called business partnership with Jean Pierre; a tenuous relationship, at present, that was very unstable. Albert sincerely hoped this shady business of theirs would soon end. The danger of them being caught jeopardized everything.

It was not to be, however. Albert's hopes were in vain.

The morning after Maurice and Jean Pierre met to settle their differences and forestall any problems, Maurice called to ask his son to come over immediately. The emotion Albert heard in his father's voice indicated the man's distress. The fact that it was caused by Jean Pierre was quite unexpected. Albert had never seen this kind of outrage coming from his father before, let alone related to Jean Pierre.

As soon as Albert entered his father's house, Maurice dragged him into the office and closed the door, as though the very house were crawling with spies.

"Our futures are in jeopardy," he said. "My business, your business, the money we've saved, possibly *my life*—everything we've worked for all of these years. It could all be lost, because of that greedy bastard, Jean Pierre. He must be stopped. He's made a sham of our partnership. It's hanging by a thread."

Maurice began to pace as a fountain of words came pouring out.

"I confronted him over the fact that he'd sold numerous artifacts from Goering's cache without telling me or sharing the profits! He thought I wouldn't know, because I once mentioned in passing that I felt like I was losing my recall abilities."

Maurice stopped and whirled to face Albert. His face was turning red.

"It was a ruse, of course. I was testing him! I still know *everything* that comes into and goes out of the Louvre. I know what's on display, in which gallery and for how long. I know where everything is stored. I still remember every detail. Jean Pierre is a fool. I thought he was my trusted partner, but clearly he's screwing me. I gave him the opportunity to make a fortune. I trusted him and shared the secret that made him wealthy. Now, he's putting our entire family in danger with his recklessness and greed.

"Even as we speak, I believe he's plotting our demise. When we spoke, I went after him with a vengeance. He offered to make amends by giving me a bigger cut, but it's not only about money. It's also about trust and respect. We had an agreement, a verbal contract. His deceit and greed has destroyed my respect for him. I can no longer trust him. I must sever our partnership, immediately. Nothing—no apology, no amount of money—can salvage our relationship. He is dead to me."

Maurice was in a frenzy. Albert saw no way to calm him down to the point where he could listen to logic. But he began to speak quietly, hoping his composure would be contagious and they could have a sensible conversation.

"Yes, Jean Pierre cheated you out of a small fortune," he said, "but you, Father, have already acquired more money than you could possibly spend in a lifetime. I know you trusted him with your secret—a secret that you'd kept hidden for *decades*. I know how much that must hurt. I agree with you. It is time to shut it all down and get out. But we also need to stay calm and keep our wits about us."

Maurice wasn't listening. His anger had made him deaf. For as long as Albert could remember, his father would come home from work and complain about how poorly he was treated, how much he was underpaid and pushed around like some kind of common servant. Especially Reichsmarschall Goering, the pompous, egotistical Nazi who'd controlled the flow of every valuable piece that came into the Louvre during the Nazi occupation of France. Maurice had complained about him endlessly and his hatred still burned. That man.

Albert tried once again to calm down his father.

"Jean Pierre is too greedy," he said. "He has an insatiable appetite to acquire more and more of those hidden treasures. Without question, yes, it's time to sever your relationship and walk away from this dangerous scheme. But we need to do it without drawing attention to you and jeopardizing my security business."

In the midst of his relentless tirade, however, eliminating Jean Pierre appeared to be the only solution Maurice would accept.

"Son, I've been taken advantage of *my entire career at that museum*," he snarled. "Time and time again I've been cheated. It's time for revenge. The only question is how to do it."

Albert thought back to the hit-and-run accident he'd staged to get rid of that nosy private detective. No one witnessed it—there were no leads and the truck went up in flames. The police had done a minimal investigation of the whole affair and nothing ever came of it. Now, however, he must leave some kind of false clue—incriminating evidence that would expose Jean Pierre and his illegal activities. The man's greed, without a doubt, had led him to his downfall. He had a secret stash of hidden treasures in Switzerland, and once discovered, they would end the question of where all these artifacts were coming from once and for all.

On his father's advice, Albert had secretly followed Jean Pierre on a number of his trips to Switzerland. Maurice had a hunch that Lucerne—with its stunningly preserved Medieval architecture—was where Jean Pierre was storing all his stashed pieces. Once there, it hadn't taken long for Albert to discover the precise location of Jean Pierre's plush apartment, located in an upscale Neustadt quarter of the city.

As the head of his own security firm, with all the latest systems and tools, Albert was able to investigate Jean Pierre in total secrecy. His father was right on the mark. Jean Pierre was a thief, robbing his partner blind. On more than one occasion, Albert had remained in the city after Jean Pierre left. With Jean Pierre out of the way, it was easy for Albert to use his company's sophisticated security equipment to bypass the alarm system, enter Jean Pierre's apartment, and film its contents.

The splendorous apartment was large and filled with plenty of sunlight, accentuating the dozens of smaller treasures the director had smuggled out of the Louvre. The rooms were like museum galleries, carefully arranged with valuable pictures, stunning tapestries, and gleaming silver objects. Aware of his father's mounting suspicion, Albert had been reluctant to show Maurice the tapes at the time, lest he overreact and do something foolish. Now, with a more-complete picture in his mind, Albert fully understood how and why their relationship had been destroyed. The mountain of irreplaceable pieces that Jean Pierre had personally smuggled from the Louvre was proof of the man's insatiable need to keep acquiring more. Like Reichsmarschall Goering, Jean Pierre would never be satisfied. His thirst would never be quenched; his hunger never sated. Without a doubt he was a scoundrel, a thief, and a liar, well deserving of Maurice's wrath.

Albert realized this danger could no longer be ignored. Right then and there he formulated a plan that would implicate only Jean Pierre.

All those treasures in his apartment, once discovered, would incriminate him as the mastermind behind the entire scheme. All Albert needed to do was to point the police in the right direction.

CHAPTER 35

GREED HAS AN ENDING POINT

It was well past midnight when Jean Pierre left his office at the Louvre. He'd spent the last two hours shredding documents, receipts, and invoices that could connect him to the shipping, receiving, and sale of the artifacts removed from the museum's secret underground chamber. He also destroyed all his anonymous correspondence to many museum directors outlining procedures for exhibiting each of the items to be displayed and sold, including the art hidden in his apartment in Switzerland.

Once he was finally finished, he knew there wasn't one piece of written evidence that tied him to the stolen artifacts. The carefully forged documentation that had made his plan work in the first place no longer existed. There were still some *human* issues that need to be resolved, but they could wait another day. *Or could they?* he wondered.

He and Maurice were now very wealthy men. All the money he'd earned was secure. There was no trail of evidence for anyone to follow. Both of them were clean. Virtually all of the cash had been deposited in four different Swiss banks, under false identities—two for himself and two for Maurice. The amount of money was staggering. He didn't understand why Maurice was bothered by a few paltry missing items.

He should be happy with the money I've made for him, thought Jean Pierre. *It's more than enough to fulfill his own needs—and Albert's—for their entire lifetimes. Instead of being indignant over a few measly trinkets removed without his knowledge, Maurice should be grateful. Wasn't I the brains behind the operation? Wasn't it me who possessed the financial knowledge and skills to implement their plan? That should be worth something! Perhaps Maurice will think about our conversation, consider my offer, and mellow out.*

Destroying the small mountain of incriminating documents had been his first priority. With that done, now he could focus on hiring someone in Switzerland to deal with the loose ends, namely Maurice and his son. In Jean Pierre's assessment, Albert was the bigger problem. The kid was a loose cannon. He was great with technology and did very well with his security business, but he didn't think things through. He was also quick to react and very low on patience. Above everything else, he was loyal to his father. He also knew too much. He'd been the delivery boy, picking up and dropping off various pieces to museums all over Europe. Both of them had to go. There was no other option. Father and son alike needed to be eliminated.

As Jean Pierre tidied up his office, he checked his file cabinets one last time to make sure nothing remained. Then he bagged all the shredded documents to burn in his fireplace later that night. Yes. He would open a good bottle of Bordeaux to celebrate his accomplishments as he watched the fire consume every scrap of evidence that could possibly incriminate him.

Jean Pierre left the building through his usual private entrance and proceeded to his car in his personal parking space. He popped the trunk on his old French Renault and placed the two bags inside. The car was not fancy at all, but it was economical and fit the low profile he tried to maintain. He didn't want to give anyone the impression that he was somehow making money from outside sources. After all, he was just a museum director with a modest income.

He chuckled as he closed the trunk. The fortune he'd quietly acquired through his illicit art scheme was safely hidden, ready to be used by a man with a new name. He had zero obligations to any institution or person. His lifestyle was about to change. Perhaps a brand-new car should be at the top of the list. He was exhilarated by the thought that he would no longer have to answer to anyone or anything. Nor would he need to deal with complaining, subordinate individuals like Maurice or his hot-headed son.

Jean Pierre was acutely aware that Maurice and Albert were the only people who could compromise his escape plan. Maurice was indeed clever, and that total recall mind of his had taken him quite far in the Louvre's organization. It was uncanny, unreal, how any one person could possibility know the whereabouts of all the Louvre's contents. *I misjudged him,* Jean Pierre thought to himself. *It is indeed a shame that he must be silenced.*

As he slid into the driver's seat, Jean Pierre noticed the time on the dashboard clock. It was early Friday morning. His scheduled lunch meeting with Hans was at 11:00 in his office. That man was still a mystery. He was extremely knowledgeable and quite talented. Jean Pierre had known him for years, but still had little knowledge of the man's background, other than the fact that he'd lived in Berlin and lost his wife during an Allied bombing raid. Somehow, despite being Jewish, Hans and his wife had avoided being sent to one of the Nazi concentration camps.

Jean Pierre's mind flashed back to the day when Hans viewed that Old Master painting on display for the exposition. The expression on his face was not one of excitement or exhilaration, as one might expect. Rather, the color had drained from his face, leaving him gray and ashen. As Hans had moved closer to the painting to examine it further, he had begun to shake uncontrollably.

Why should he be so disturbed by what he saw? What images from the past were conjured up in his mind to produce such fear and sadness? Without a doubt, thought Jean Pierre, *Hans must have restored that brilliant masterpiece.*

Yes, of course, Hans must have known the original owner. Perhaps it was near the time his wife was killed in the bombing raid. Hans had never spoken about that with him. Witnessing all the death and destruction during the height of the war would doubtlessly leave one wrestling with terrible, haunting memories, however. Very likely it would leave an indelible mark on a person's conscience for the rest of his life. One way or another, Jean Pierre knew he must get an answer from Hans today. He must find out if there was a link to him that could jeopardize his plan and safety. Exiting the business was his number-one priority and Hans could be yet another loose end, albeit of lesser consequence than his partner Maurice.

With all these thoughts running through his mind as he drove the familiar route home, Jean Pierre was not paying attention to the road conditions. It was a very dark and overcast night. A light rain fell. The glare from the streetlamps on the wet streets produced odd, shining shadows and reflections, making it difficult for him to pick out and identify familiar landmarks or read the street signs clearly.

Squinting to get a fix on his precise whereabouts, he suddenly noticed a large truck with only parking lights on. It seemed to be slowly moving toward the intersection a hundred meters ahead. Perhaps the truck driver was also confused, slowing to a crawl as he moved through the intersection.

Unfortunately for Jean Pierre, this wasn't the case at all.

After that, it all happened fast. Jean Pierre stomped down on his brakes, but because of the slippery conditions, his car slid straight into the intersection. With only a little additional acceleration, the truck driver had a perfect shot at a deadly T-bone on the driver's side door. The truck driver's maneuver was almost perfectly timed. The truck's high bumper impact almost bent Jean Pierre's much smaller car in half. The trunk crunched and broke open, revealing its contents. Meanwhile, the driver's door had been hit with so much force, Jean Pierre was pinned to the steering column, caught in a vice of death. There was no way to escape. The right side of Jean Pierre's body had taken a major hit, sustaining tremendous damage. The driver's side airbag had triggered but provided little protection for its occupant.

It's difficult to imagine the human body surviving such an impact, but so far Jean Pierre had. The massive injuries on his left side plunged him into a world of pain. The whiplash to his neck wasn't fatal—at least for the moment—but he couldn't move it or turn his head.

His chin slumped onto on his chest and his body went limp, going into shock from the excruciating pain and trauma. His eyes were out of focus. He heard the slam of a heavy door. *The truck driver,* he thought. *He is coming to help me. He will pull me from this wreck and save me.*

Suddenly, he wondered: *Wait, was this an accident?*

He frantically tried to patch the events together, but they didn't add up. The pain was severe. It clouded his thinking.

I must survive for my beautiful treasures, he thought. *I can't lose all of that money.*

Footsteps slapped on the cobblestones as the mystery man approached the passenger side door. He couldn't turn to look because of the pain and his fear of a broken neck. He slowly directed his eyes toward that side of the car. Straining the muscles to utilize as much of his peripheral vision as possible, he couldn't see anything higher than the man's waistline. In one hand the stranger held a large, ornate, golden jewelry box. In his other hand he held a small, but beautiful, Old Master painting.

Not one of mine, Jean Pierre thought.

He wasn't able to track the man's quick, purposeful movements, but he heard the rustling of the shredded paper in the trunk of his car. *What on earth is this man doing?* he thought. *Why isn't he helping me? Why isn't he calling for help?*

"I'm not sure if you can hear me, Jean Pierre," said a low, steady voice, "but my plan was to frame you with a couple of missing pieces from Goering's hidden chamber. All those shredded documents in your trunk sure pin you with the rose of guilt! I am much obliged," he snickered. "As you know, it's *all about trust.* In your case, I would probably also include greed. You sure riled up my father. I'm ashamed it has to come to this. After you admitted pilfering those additional objects, we decided we just couldn't trust you. You have put our lives *and my business* in jeopardy."

Time was running out for Jean Pierre. He'd suffered massive internal damage. His chest cavity was filling up with blood. He still couldn't see the man, but he thought he recognized the voice. *Is it Maurice's son?* The man he'd always feared in his partnership with Maurice; a person who acted first, without so much as a passing thought to consequences.

Jean Pierre tried to talk, but he could hardly breathe, let alone speak. Quietly, the mysterious man slipped into the passenger seat. Jean Pierre could now see his face. It was indeed Maurice's son. In Albert's hand was an instrument, like a hypodermic needle.

He moved in close and spoke softly. "By the way, Jean Pierre, your apartment in Switzerland looks like a small museum. Too bad you won't live to enjoy it." With that, Albert plunged the long needle-like device into Jean Pierre's inner ear. For a split second, he felt a sharp pain as the needle penetrated the innermost part of his ear and the cortex of his brain. The *coup de grace*. In a way, it was a merciful act, though it wasn't intended to be. Only a specially trained forensic pathologist would be able to detect the true cause of death. Jean Pierre had been slowly dying by asphyxiation. The needle had ended things instantly, without a trace.

As the killer exited the vehicle, he thought to himself, *This time there won't be any survivors* and disappeared into the pitch black night.

The entire event had taken mere minutes to execute. The light rain continued to fall. During the short duration, nobody had passed by to witness what had happened. It wasn't until after daylight that the tragic event was even discovered. The local fire department was summoned to extract the driver with a special tool called the Jaws of Life. In this case, of course, the person had been dead for some time. Either way, it didn't take long for the police to make a positive identification.

The car's trunk was partially open. In it lay the driver's briefcase with his personal calling card, driver's license, bank account numbers, and other documents.

Jean Pierre Rolland, said the various papers, director of the Louvre Museum in Paris, France.

Also of major interest were a pair of museum-quality art pieces, along with two full bags of shredded documents. The two very valuable items found in the trunk would require additional investigation. A special police unit was called to analyze the scene. It looked like multiple crimes had been committed: a hit-and-run and possible museum theft, at the very least.

It all appeared highly suspicious.

Because of the delicacy of the situation, involving a high-ranking employee at France's most famous museum, the only information released to the public was that it had been a hit-and-run accident, resulting in the death of the driver. Everything beyond that was pure speculation. Or so reporters were told.

CHAPTER 36

THE PLAN IS IMPLEMENTED

Chris and Jay disembarked from separate railcars. They'd agreed to meet the following day at 6:00 p.m. at Hans's shop to flesh out the details of their plan. Chris glanced at his watch. His all-day debriefing with Jay, coupled with the tour, had left him exhausted. He could sure use a shot of that cognac, but that wasn't going to happen. He needed to focus and clearly his stamina was not where it should be. Apparently the long period of recovery from his near-fatal accident had not been long enough.

He needed sleep, but that wouldn't happen either. If he hurried, he'd have just enough time to get back to his apartment to shower and shave before he met with Hans and Alana. He was sure they were already waiting at Hans's shop, discussing how they could get Jean Pierre to somehow slip and disclose his role in the illegal sale of the stolen art.

When he finally arrived, Hans and Alana were visibly tense. Other than a brief greeting, neither of them spoke, indicating to Chris that there was no solid plan. On the way over, Chris had wondered if Jean Pierre's meeting with Hans was a ruse, purely to lure Hans to the Louvre, where Jean Pierre could conveniently make the old conservator disappear. Surely, this was Alana's main concern too. Chris decided to break the tension by shifting their focus, bringing them up to date what he'd discussed with Jay earlier that morning.

"Before we get into the details about Hans's meeting, I need to share what I learned talking with my former boss. I was with him the past twenty-hour hours at a secure location. You see, before I quit my *day job* and started my own security business back in Minnesota, I was a CIA field agent.

"After I told my former boss about the security contract I'd made with the anonymous private party, he informed me that the CIA is actively working with France's secret police and Interpol to uncover a huge underground network of illicit dealers who sell art stolen during the war. He believes that my anonymous client is most likely an owner of a major gallery, art shop, or museum here in Paris. That entity is likely one of several underground dealers that have been selling master art painting and antiques all over Europe and the rest of the world.

"Hans, when I eventually identify this anonymous client of mine, it's likely we'll learn you unwittingly worked for him at some point in the past. Interestingly, the CIA was recently approached by Interpol to help identify potential black-market dealers in the United States. This illegal art scheme is a worldwide problem. For the first time they want the US to get involved. Interpol's sources indicate that many of these world-class antiques and Old Master paintings are being shipped to the Americas, much of it to the US. In fact, they've already identified a number of crooked dealers involved in the selling of artifacts that disappeared during the Nazi occupation of Europe.

"It appears the client I'm working for is one of at least eight art dealers here in Europe. Unscrupulous collectors and ruthless investors are willing to pay huge sums of money for rare antiques. It's a phenomenal investment for them and a hedge against world inflation. As you well know, such treasures never lose their value; they just keep appreciating. In fact, the value of some of these assets has already increased a hundred-fold since the war ended, especially in countries with the highest rates of inflation. As the world keeps churning out more millionaires and billionaires, the market keeps getting bigger and more lucrative. Interpol estimates that fifty to sixty countries are now involved in this underground racket.

"My small role in this work, the contract I have with my client, isn't technically illegal, but much of the information I give him is used to achieve nefarious goals. Like you," Chris looked at Hans, "I have inadvertently uncovered one small piece of a much larger puzzle. You, on the other hand, hold one of the most dangerous puzzle pieces there is. The information contained in your innocuous black ledger—especially the records you kept while you were imprisoned in Berlin—could potentially impact hundreds of transactions that have taken place over the years.

"The fact that I have made substantial progress toward unmasking one of these illicit art dealers has put me smack dab in the middle of these ongoing investigations. With my past experience working for the CIA, well, it's put me in position to be a lead investigator or undercover agent.

"Yesterday, my former boss officially asked me to rejoin the agency for the duration of this case. I've signed a legal document that reinstates me as a US government employee, working for the CIA. This gives me access to resources I wouldn't otherwise have and also gives me authority to arrange for your protection."

Chris softened his tone and pressed on.

"I'm sorry, Alana. I wanted to consult with you about my decision, but I had no choice. Based on what I learned yesterday, you and your grandfather are in imminent danger. You need security and you have it.

"Now, I'm also free—and legally protected—to pursue whatever plan we decide to execute. I believe we can control and mitigate the dangers that lie ahead for the three of us. Being an agent also gives me the authority to take certain risks that I couldn't as a civilian or private investigator. There's no doubt in my mind we can uncover and help break up this underground network.

"When this is all over, Alana, we can discuss if continuing to work for the agency is the right thing to do. For the moment, however, it's worth it to solve these crimes and bring the perpetrators to justice."

Chris slowly turned to Hans, a faint smile on his face.

"I'm also in a position, Hans, to help you in your quest to investigate *and return* many of these master artworks and antiques to their *rightful owners*. I know how important that is for you and I pledge to do everything I can to help make that happen."

Chris took a deep breath. It was silent for a moment as he searched for the right words.

"Unfortunately, I can't share much of what I learned from Jay. Discretion and secrecy are cornerstones of this job. It's the same reason I didn't tell Jay about your black ledger. I think he might suspect a book of provenance is out there, but he is required to share *any and all* information with Interpol and the French police. The less he knows about your detailed records, the safer you'll be. He also agrees that it's best to keep your family's involvement in the restoration of some of these pieces secret for now. He's sticking his neck out for us. We all need to remember that.

"Hans, I also shared our plan for your meeting with Jean Pierre tomorrow. As part of their investigation, Interpol has been collecting data on museum directors all over Europe. In Jean Pierre's case, it was tricky. He is shrewd and very cautious.

"Hans, you probably know more about Jean Pierre than everyone at Interpol and the CIA combined, but a lot of what they've uncovered fits our theory to a T. We've wondered how and why a museum director would have such sophisticated knowledge of international finance and banking systems. Well, Jean Pierre's first job was in a very different field. For years, he worked for a major French airline. There, he developed negotiating skills which enabled him to advance quickly through ranks of the company's finance department.

"Naturally, as he worked his way up the ladder, his financial skills were further refined. With his special abilities, he was soon making massive deals buying, selling, and leasing airplanes. He made his company millions of dollars and traveled constantly for his job. Through the years, he developed an affinity for European art and became a small collector. That affinity brought him to the Louvre.

"Hans, as you well know, after the war, the Louvre was in jeopardy of losing its world-class rating because so many of its treasures had been stolen and shipped to Germany. Today, Jean Pierre is credited as one of the key people who helped bring the Louvre back to its former glory as one of the biggest and best museums in the world.

"Here's where things get interesting. Over the past few years, he's traveled much more frequently to Switzerland, ostensibly for his employer. Recently, however, Interpol uncovered a long history of Jean Pierre working closely with Swiss banks and investment firms. On paper, the vast majority of these transactions appear to be nothing more than routine business for the Louvre. In reality, those payments work their way through a web of shell corporations to four separate personal accounts. In other words, Jean Pierre is savvy enough to know how to manipulate and launder money. His job, his credentials, and his status as one of the Louvre's star employees have put him in the perfect position to disguise or even bury any black-market transactions.

"The dots all seem to connect, but we need hard evidence to back it up.

"Hans, your meeting with him tomorrow should help us confirm our thinking. If he somehow comes out clean after this investigation, then we might be back to square one. I, for one, think he's the man behind some, if not all, of these illegal activities. Knowing international financing, wire transfers, and the key people in this industry makes him my number-one choice."

Having shared all this information, Chris seemed to relax.

"Tomorrow will be a big day for us all. Hans, you will receive a special package in the morning. It will contain an electronic device for you to wear so we can track your every move, from the time you leave this shop until you go to every location in the Louvre.

"We will also use three state-of-the-art phones to keep in touch with each other *and* for you to record your conversations with Jean Pierre. Importantly, for this recorded information to be admissible in court as part of a criminal investigation, you will need to be very careful about what you say. Jean Pierre can't appear to be pressured or enticed into a confession. It needs to be of his own volition.

"Alana, under *no circumstances* are you to go with your grandfather into the Louvre."

Chris was having a hard time keeping things purely professional. He loved Alana and how much she'd transformed his life. Their eyes locked for a moment, communicating the true depth of their feelings in a way that words couldn't.

He regained his composure and pressed on. "We need you to monitor your grandfather's movements while he's inside," he said. "We want you to keep a close watch on his location within that sprawling complex of buildings since you're familiar with the Louvre's layout and you won't raise any suspicions. You'll simply be a doting grand-daughter waiting for her grandfather.

"Your role will be of utmost value to me because I will also be inside the Louvre at that time. The French police have an undercover agent there, working on the security team. They've arranged for me to enter the building as an electronic technician doing some routine repair work. My objective is to find the secret storage location.

"Hans, you'll need to bait Jean Pierre into revealing the secret location where these objects are stored. If I can get close enough to you while you're in there, maybe I can be of assistance. The trick for me will be not losing your location in the maze of stone and concrete halls, rooms, and sub-basements."

After Chris detailed the plan and double-checked very step, they all agreed to meet very early the following morning in Hans's shop. There, they would prepare for their entry into the Louvre.

Once the meeting concluded, Hans needed to stay to finalize two documents for his briefing with Jean Pierre. Alana and Chris agreed to meet at a local bistro to share some final thoughts. Using the shop's back entrance and departing separately, they took two different routes to the bistro. After Chris was confident they hadn't been followed, he finally spoke.

"You've been very quiet tonight," he said. "Do you have a problem with our plan?"

"No, Chris, it's not that," said Alana, looking down at the table. "My grandfather is the most important person in my life. His protection must come first. I don't want to lose him and I don't want to lose *you*. I realize we've been dragged into this web of crime. The more we learn about what's happening, the stronger the web becomes, pulling us further and further into its grasp. I can feel it tightening around us, drawing us in with no way to escape. We're just minor players in this huge underground world of illicit art sales. For what? Who cares about all these objects? Not me, I assure you!

"My grandfather has been trying to drag me into his business since I was a little girl. Yes, I love beautiful art, but it's not going to control my life or decisions about my career path. I wish we could burn my grandfather's black ledger and every other scrap of information he has. Then, we'd all finally be safe. I beg you to tell me everything and stop this foolishness now."

With that, a flood of tears came down. They could no longer be restrained. Chris held her tenderly in his arms, not knowing what to say. He could only wish what she proposed was that easy to do.

They departed the restaurant. Neither food nor drink, or personal reassurance, could appease her or calm her. It was a short taxi ride to Chris's apartment. Inside, Alana collapsed, sinking into Chris's arms as she fell asleep.

Tomorrow, Chris thought. *Get to tomorrow. Then we'll have clear heads and I can address her concerns.*

CHAPTER 37

THE MEETING THAT DOESN'T HAPPEN

The special package of surveillance equipment from Chris's boss arrived right on time at Han's shop early Friday morning. As Hans prepared to put it on, Hans, Chris, and Alana were confronted with the reality of their situation.

Somehow Chris managed to keep Alana calm. It had been a fitful night and neither had gotten much sleep. Alana's thoughts kept returning to the potential dangers that lay ahead for her grandfather and Chris kept rehashing the plan, even as his head swirled with its own *what-if* scenarios.

Regardless, it was time for Hans and Alana to drive to the Louvre. The plan was for Alana to drop off Hans at the VIP gate. There, he would procure the pass Jean Pierre's secretary had prearranged for him to pick up. Alana was then to park in the specially designated area for VIPs, as close to the Louvre as possible to optimize the signal from the tracking device.

Having parked the car, Alana moved to the back seat. She locked the doors and began to monitor her grandfather's movements as he entered the Louvre. The tracking worked perfectly. She could see his exact, real-time location on the monitor in front of her as he walked to Jean Pierre's office. Amazed by the device's performance, she breathed a deep sigh of relief.

At the other end of the Louvre, at the service entrance, Chris was getting a work pass. He was dressed in gray coveralls and carrying an old, gray, metal toolbox surreptitiously outfitted with electronic equipment.

The procedure worked perfectly. No one batted an eye as Chris presented his work order, signed with a fictitious name, and entered the Louvre, undistinctive in the morning parade of other technicians.

Inside, a man he'd never met discreetly approached. They quietly exchanged code names and Chris was whisked away to a small, private workshop with an array of technical equipment and high-tech surveillance tools. Without a word, the anonymous contact gave Chris a detailed map of the entire Louvre campus, as well as technical drawings of the supposed work areas where Chris was scheduled to perform his "repairs." Before Chris could even react, the man slipped away.

When he worked for the CIA, Chris had been involved in a number of these drops. This was one of the boldest and riskiest exchanges he'd ever taken part in, for both the informer and himself. They risked being discovered at any point in the process.

Chris checked his watch. Twenty minutes had passed since Hans had entered the building. If everything went as planned, he was in Jean Pierre's office by now. Chris hurried to get his powerful tracking system set up in order to confirm this. Just as he tried to text Hans, he was distracted by the vibrating phone in his custom-designed service jacket. It was the phone Jay had provided, with an array of special features and a secure private phone number.

Normally, with very rare exceptions, active agents were not interrupted lest it put them in a life-threatening situation. He hesitated, only but for a moment, before activating the phone.

"He's dead!" said the voice on the other end of the phone.

"What?"

The voice was Jay's. He clarified. "Jean Pierre is dead. It happened sometime this morning. Allegedly—get this—it was a hit-and-run car accident, reported to the police at 6:05. A little too convenient, don't you think?"

Chris was completely stunned. He'd been down this ugly path himself. He wanted to cry out, *No! No, it can't possibly be!*

Horrible memories of pain and fear flooded his brain. Then his thoughts switched to Hans. He, too, must be in danger.

"Chris? Chris? Are you there?" barked Jay at the other end of the line.

"Yes," he muttered quietly. "Are they sure?"

"The accident scene has been entirely sealed off. I can't get one of my agents within a hundred yards of it. At least two special investigative units were called. Thankfully, I was briefed about an hour ago by my counterpart with the French secret police."

Jay's tone shifted, showing a clear undercurrent of fear.

"You're not going to believe what they've seen. The accident was so violent, it bent Jean Pierre's car in half and pinned him so tightly to the steering wheel that it took them nearly two and a half hours to remove his body.

"The car's trunk had popped open, and you're not going to believe this either. Hidden under a pile of shredded documents were two very valuable art pieces, a gold jeweled box about the size of a book, and what appears to be a missing painting by Monet.

"They're not releasing any information to the public yet. For now, they're treating it as two unrelated crimes: suspected vehicular homicide and the theft of extremely valuable art, likely taken from the Louvre.

"It's not only raising a lot of eyebrows, but also a lot of questions at the security office and Interpol. The Louvre's president is denying any involvement, stating that the items found in Jean Pierre's car do *not belong* to the museum.

"Either way, this event is going to shake the art community big time if the information gets out. They're holding off releasing any details about who the dead driver is and what they found in the vehicle's trunk. This is a game-changer in our investigations. You need to keep Hans Muller out of the museum."

"I'm afraid it's too late for that," Chris responded. "He entered the Louvre over thirty minutes ago. Because of all the procedures and the number of vendors lined up to get work passes, I was delayed in meeting my contact. You caught me just in the process of setting up my tracking equipment. At this point, I have no idea where he is. I've tried to text him from my present location. No response."

"I think it's best we get both of you out of the Louvre quickly," said Jay, "especially away from Jean Pierre's office. That place will be crawling with police and special investigators very soon. We can't take the chance of either of you getting detained in those buildings. We need to rethink our plan. It won't be difficult to get you back into the Louvre in a day or two once things settle down.

"One last bit of information: my agents in Switzerland have tracked down Jean Pierre's private residence in Lucerne. I authorized a stealth operation to search the place and document its contents with still photos and video. Hopefully we can get it done before Interpol gets involved. We'll talk again soon. Get yourself out of that building. Fast." Both parties hung up.

Chris dialed Hans's phone number. It rang several times, but there was still no answer. Chris texted the news about Jean Pierre. The rush of adrenaline from what Jay had just told him crashed upon him like waves upon a shore. He fought to regain his composure and focus on what to do next. Their entire plan was in jeopardy and it needed to be scrapped. He called Alana.

"Are you tracking your grandfather's movements?" he asked.

"Up until several minutes ago, the device worked perfectly," she said. "Then suddenly, the screen went blank and I haven't seen him since. Did I do something wrong? Chris, I'm getting worried."

Not wanting to alarm her, he didn't mention Jean Pierre's grisly death. "I'm sure you didn't do anything wrong," he said. "Your grandfather is probably in an elevator deep into the Louvre's sub-basement or something like that." Chris tried to sound upbeat, while still communicating a sense of urgency.

"Alana, there's been a change in plans," he said. "I just spoke to Jay. We think you should leave the Louvre's parking lot. We need you to reestablish surveillance at your grandfather's shop."

"Shouldn't I wait until he shows up on my tracking monitor first?" she asked.

"No, that's not necessary," he said. "I'm in the museum now. I'll track him with my portable device." Chris didn't want to lie to her, but in the interest of her safety, he had no choice. It was far better to get her back safely to Hans's shop. They agreed to meet there later.

Alana started her car and prepared to leave. She noticed a middle-aged, uniformed man running toward her, waving his arms. As she stopped and rolled down the window, he yelled, "Are you Hans Muller's granddaughter?"

"Yes. I am. Is something wrong?" she said, worriedly.

"No, no, no," the man reassured her. "Quite the opposite, actually. He sent me out here to tell you that his meeting with Jean Pierre is going very well. There's something he'd like to show you. He asked me to escort you to Jean Pierre's office."

Alana turned off the car, got out, and followed her escort through the security gate. As she entered the Louvre, her concern for her grandfather's safety largely evaporated. She wanted to call Chris to give him the good news but decided to wait until she was with her grandfather.

She gradually noticed they were not going to the administrative offices, but down two flights of stairs into the sub-basement. "We'll be there shortly," said the man. "We're going to one of the work shops where art restoration is done. That's where they're meeting."

CHAPTER 38

THE TRAP IS SET

At the VIP entrance one hour earlier, before Hans had even completed his security check, Maurice had greeted him warmly.

"Hans, it's good to see you," he said. "Come. Follow me. You don't need to sign in. I've already got your pass." The two of them breezed past the guards' desk without hesitation. One of them barely glanced up; the other paid them no mind at all. Clearly, Maurice was able to come and go as he pleased.

"Jean Pierre sends his apologies," Maurice continued, swiftly leading Hans down the hall. "He phoned to say he'll be late and asked me to escort you to his private conference room."

Maurice had planned so there would be no record of Hans ever entering the building. He wanted to cover his tracks and distance himself from Hans as much as possible. He knew Hans mustn't be connected to Jean Pierre or his secretary on this particular day. In fact, he was quite surprised that news of Jean Pierre's death had yet become public. *You'd think the police would have alerted museum officials by now. You'd think there'd be investigators crawling all over the place.* His son had called very early that morning to give him a status report but was careful not to reveal any significant details about the accident.

What could be holding up the official announcement of Jean Pierre's death? he wondered. *It's been over eight hours since Albert called to confirm his success.*

Placing those missing art pieces in Jean Pierre's vehicle had been a master stroke, but it was also a double-edged sword. Undoubtedly, it would confuse and slow the police in their investigation. Once the body was identified, however, things were sure to ramp up. The obvious assumption would be that Jean Pierre had stolen the art pieces. His office at the Louvre would quickly become the investigation's focal point. After the police determined that neither of the items had been part of the Louvre's collection—therefore not stolen from its premises—it likely wouldn't be long before the investigators turned their attention to Jean Pierre's residences, especially the one in Lucerne. *But that's a red herring too,* Maurice reminded himself. No other living person knew about the *second residence.* That would take the police at least a day or two to uncover.

The biggest issue was Hans. If he seemed to be involved in any way, even tangentially, Maurice might be implicated in the mystery of where the art came from. *I must keep him isolated,* thought Maurice, *as far from the police as possible. I don't intend to let him leave the Louvre any time soon.*

Maurice's previous encounters with Hans had been cordial. But now Hans was a threat to him. Maurice had to figure out what Hans knew and what he didn't. Clearly, his interest in that particular masterpiece extended well beyond mere professional evaluation. Maurice was sure of it. In fact, both he and Jean Pierre had sensed Hans's personal connection to it. Right then, Maurice made the decision Hans would live or die based on what he revealed and how much it might affect Maurice's chances of disappearing safely with his money.

During his escorted walk to the designated meeting place, Hans felt his phone vibrating in his pocket. Earlier, Chris had told him not to answer calls in an open setting, especially if the phone was vibrating instead of ringing. Hans knew the call could only be from his granddaughter or Chris. He decided not to reveal that he had a phone with him. They went deeper into the sub-basement. As they contin-ued to walk, Hans asserted that he needed to use the bathroom before his meeting with Jean Pierre.

"Yes, yes, of course. That is no problem at all," said Maurice. "We're getting close to where we're going and there are bathrooms nearby."

It was a small, single-stall water closet. Maurice indicated he would wait down the hall, a short distance. Hans entered the room and quickly locked the door. It only took him seconds to retrieve the phone from his pocket. He was only partially surprised when he read the text message from Chris: *Jean Pierre is dead! Get out of the Louvre as soon as you can!* Immediately, he tried to send a response, but he knew full well that they were so deep underground, no electronic signal could be sent or received.

From the time he'd met Maurice at the gate and entered the Lou-vre, he'd had an uncomfortable feeling in his stomach. Not signing in and going through the normal security protocol made him more suspicious. This long and circuitous walk through the maze of hall-ways must have been designed by Maurice to confuse and disorient him, limiting his ability to escape on his own. It all made sense now; it was a well-designed trap to lure him into the Louvre, where he would conveniently disappear.

As he exited the water closet, he realized it would gain him noth-ing to run from Maurice or to let him know he was aware the meeting with Jean Pierre was a ruse. He must let Maurice's charade play out and hope Chris would find his phone, left in the water closet. At least it would continue to send signals as to his approximate location. He hoped Chris would start looking for him once he discovered that he hadn't left the Louvre as instructed.

As Hans and Maurice continued their walk, Hans remarked, "This is a really funny area to view a masterpiece painting, no?"

"Not really," said Maurice, deflecting. "Since the painting is not sold yet, we thought it would be more exciting and educational to have the painting in front of us as you describe your findings. But it also was moved down here for security reasons. Oh, by the way, while you were indisposed, I received a call from Jean Pierre's secretary. Unfortunately, she told me that he won't be joining us. There will be others in attendance, however."

If there'd been the slightest doubt in Hans's mind about the danger of his present situation, it was immediately gone. Maurice's lies were piling up. Though his heart and mind were both racing, Hans maintained his composure and let Maurice think his charade was working. In truth, he really didn't have any other options.

After a few more twists and turns, the hallway led to a dead end. There were two doors in front of them: a double door on their left, marked as a utilities room where he could hear sounds of whirring fans and dehumidifiers, and a door further down the hall that was simply marked *Private*. Maurice retrieved a key, unlocked the door, and pushed it open.

Before Hans fully passed through the door, his granddaughter rushed into his arms. "There you are!" she exclaimed. "Are you all right, are you all right?"

"What is the meaning of this?" Hans demanded. "Why is my granddaughter here?" His voice was no longer calm. It was laced with contempt and hate. There was fire in his eyes. He slammed his briefcase on the table and pulled out some papers. "Whatever you people are doing, we want no part of it," he said, thrusting the report toward Maurice. "Here's the detailed report of my findings. I prepared it for Jean Pierre. Either way, the Louvre paid for it. Do what you will."

Maurice paused to consider this. Hans was right. He and his granddaughter had absolutely no knowledge or involvement in what he and Albert were up to. Letting them go right now would be the simplest way to remove them from this entire affair. He still had a gnawing feeling, however, that Hans was somehow connected to the painting on a deep, emotional level. Maurice had to find out why.

"Yes, Hans, you are right," he said. "There's no reason to keep you here. Frankly, that's not my intention. My son, whom you haven't met, saw your granddaughter waiting in her car. He'd seen her with you earlier. He's in the security business and happened to glance at the screen when you arrived. When my son saw her sitting alone, he felt bad for her and called to ask me what we could do. I suggested he bring her down here to this meeting so she could hear of your findings." He held up his hands reassuringly, as though pleading his case. "I have no intentions of harming either of you. I can escort both of you out of this building right now if you like." He spun and faced the painting, his arm gesturing grandly. "As you can see, we brought the painting to this room for you to tell us about your evaluation and any discoveries you've made. In fact, if you don't mind, I have some questions I'd like to ask you about this painting and your past connection to it."

The two men stared at each other. It was like a game of Liar's Poker. Hans was suddenly faced with calling Maurice's bluff. At this point, there was no proof that Maurice or his son had actually killed Jean Pierre. Nor was there any proof that Goering's treasures were still hidden there in the Louvre. The question burned in his mind as to whether he and Alana should stay or go. If they left right now, nothing would be gained. It was a dilemma that could imperil his precious granddaughter's life.

The choice seemed pretty clear to him.

Sensing the full gravity of the situation, Alana was quite sure she knew what her overprotective grandfather would do. "Grandfather," she began cheerfully, "you know, I've never really had the chance to see you in action. Presenting your assessment might get me more interested in learning the business. Besides, we have nothing else to do but go back to your dusty old art shop."

With those remarks, Hans decided to use this opportunity to stall for time and do the presentation. If Alana still had her cell phone, he thought, Chris would be able to track their location. That's if he was still in the Louvre somewhere and could figure what level they were on. It was a lot of *ifs*, but there weren't a lot of other options.

CHAPTER 39

DRASTIC ACTION REQUIRED

Unable to afford getting caught up in a police investigation, Chris decided to leave the Louvre immediately. He could only imagine the questions he'd be asked as a foreigner with a fake passport. An ex-CIA agent no less, who'd recently been reinstated. And he was the man who was at the center of a hit-and-run accident six months ago; the one who'd lost his memory and barely recovered.

In addition to blowing his cover, it would probably take weeks and weeks to unravel the political situation stirred up between the US and France if he were caught. No, getting out of the Louvre was by far the best solution for now. He was told many times in training to take the lowest profile in *all* situations, especially if you wanted to stay alive.

As he departed through the service exit, he noticed a number of police vehicles pulling up to the Louvre's main gate. There were no flashing lights or sirens, so they were most likely investigation units, coming to break the news to Jean Pierre's boss and interview people of interest.

He was anxious to call Jay for an update, but first, he needed to find Alana. He hurried off toward the VIP entrance where she'd parked. He'd told her to leave some time ago, but he wanted to make sure that she had. As he walked hurriedly toward the lot, he could see Hans's car parked in the front row.

He took a quick peek in the car's back seat to see if she was there, but she wasn't. Where had she gone? Into the Louvre? He could see her tracking equipment still on the seat, but he didn't want to linger since he knew he was probably being watched by multiple security cameras.

His stomach knotted up. He had to assume something happened. Since the car was still there and she wasn't in it, she must have left in a hurry. Very likely she'd gone into the Louvre and possibly harm's way.

He tried again to text both Hans and Alana but got no response. There was no way the signal could penetrate the Louvre's fortified concrete walls. He realized the chances that any signal could get through was close to zero. He slipped into a recess in the exterior wall and disappeared in the shadows. He decided to wait there until the police finally left.

It was much harder to remain calm in dangerous and dire situations if people you *loved* were involved. It would be almost impossible to make unemotional decisions. Chris was a seasoned undercover agent, but he'd never been in a situation where the stakes were this high. In the past, risk and critical decision-making came with the job; no second-guessing allowed. Now, with little time for planning and minimal resources, he knew he must act fast and do something drastic. He fought to regain control of his emotions and tap into the part of his brain that could make unambiguous decisions on the fly.

With Jean Pierre dead, Maurice must now be in charge—a man he knew little about. He needed to learn more about him and whoever was assisting him—this was definitely not a one-person operation.

The woman who'd saved his life was now in great danger, he was sure of it. He'd found a very special person to live the rest of his life with and he wasn't going to lose her.

Forget the consequences—he needed to get back inside the Louvre quickly, figure out where Hans and Alana were being held, and get them the hell out of there.

He called Jay. "They're both in the Louvre," said Chris with an unmistakable sense of urgency. "I believe they're both in danger, being held against their will."

"Wait, hold on. Take a moment to calm down," said Jay. "I know you're champing at the bit to get back in there, but I've got new information to share with you. Can I meet you at Hans's office? Yes, I'm well aware of the shop's back entrance."

Why does that not surprise me? thought Chris. *The man is always two steps of ahead of everyone else.*

Reluctantly, Chris traveled to Hans's shop. Jay and one of his tech boys were already inside, setting up surveillance equipment.

"We need a command center close to the Louvre to monitor your actions when you're back inside. Not our normal operational procedure, but time is of the essence. And I'm quite sure Mr. Muller wouldn't object, if his and Alana's lives are at stake.

"I've already arranged for you to return to the Louvre as soon as we get you wired up. Shortly, there will be a massive power outage and computer failure there. You and two other *technicians* will be called to evaluate and fix the breakdown. You'll receive a special pass giving you total access to all of the buildings. The two other servicemen will work to resolve the system failure. You, of course, will concentrate your efforts on locating Hans and Alana and removing them from the Louvre. Before you go, I'll bring you up to date on the police investigation and what our people discovered.

"The police have informed the authorities at the Louvre about Jean Pierre's highly suspicious hit-and-run death. At this point, they're still calling it an accident. There were no eyewitnesses to the collision and the truck was stolen early that morning, one or two hours before the accident occurred. They think the thief was in a hurry to hide the truck. The weather was bad and he made a driving error. No fingerprints, no leads. It's an open question whether they'll pursue this part of the investigation much further. It's very doubtful.

"Now, get ready for this! The shredded documents found in the trunk appear to be Jean Pierre's correspondence with the numerous museums and banks he used to move all manner of art through the black market. There are indications he was trying to shut down his operation, erasing all of the files that contained incriminating evidence on his computer at the Louvre. He was likely taking the shredded documents somewhere to be destroyed.

"From my vantage point, it seems highly unlikely this *accident* was a coincidence. I just don't buy it. If I were a betting man, I'd say this entire incident was a well-executed scheme by a very clever and dangerous person—very likely the same individual who did a number on you. You're very fortunate a passerby found you and saved your life.

"As we speak, the Paris police's special investigation unit is searching both the Louvre's and Jean Pierre's personal files. They're trying to determine if the stolen items belong to the Louvre before they release any information to the press. I don't think it will take them long to discover the stolen property *didn't* belong to the Louvre. The burning question, of course, is *where* Jean Pierre obtained these beautiful and very expensive treasures. It's a question we need to answer, and quickly.

"My agent in Lucerne is sending me a memory chip documenting all of his findings from Jean Pierre's apartment. I haven't seen anything yet, but he's assured me there are easily *millions of dollars* worth of art on display in this one apartment. In fact, he described it as *virtually a small museum*. Unsurprisingly, the apartment is in a wealthy apartment complex.

"Once the police discover his *second residence*, you can only imagine the issues that will quickly emerge. The biggest question will be, how did this man amass such a huge collection of valuable art and where did these treasures come from? Obviously, with his modest salary from the Louvre, he could never purchase such a valuable collection legally. How did he acquire these pieces? And what is their provenance? Now that the man is dead, we may never have satisfactory answers to these important questions.

"There are two other leads we need to follow up. The first is Maurice Devenue, the man in charge of shipping and receiving for everything coming into and going out of the Louvre. It's said the man is like a walking encyclopedia. Apparently, he's worked at the Louvre since he was thirteen years old—right in the thick of the World War I. Incredibly, Maurice is said to have *more* than just a photographic memory. He possesses recall capabilities ability only a handful people in the world have. It is called an eidetic memory, or colloquially, *total recall*. He knows where *everything* is in the entire complex.

"Our feeling is, he must be the inside man and possibly *the brains* behind this entire scheme. As you already know, the police have a sleeper agent working at the Louvre. He's constructed profiles on Maurice, Jean Pierre, and a number of other key players who work for the Louvre. All of this is tied to the massive investigation spearheaded by Interpol. When the time is right, they will fully expose, shut down, and convict the thieves, illegal dealers, and money launderers in the black-market art business.

"We have to assume the dangers that lie ahead are unlikely to come from Maurice himself. He is not a violent man. His son Albert, however, is a different story. He is a short-tempered bully who's quick to overreact and lash out. We believe he takes his orders directly from his father, who essentially controls him.

"With Maurice's help, Albert has built a successful and highly profitable security business specializing in museums. Presently, he has security operations in all the major museums and historical sites in France. One of his major selling points is his unrivalled identification software. It's able to compile and analyze video data from every museum they service. In fact, their equipment is able to track the frequency of a patron's visits to major museums, galleries, and high-profile exhibitions throughout Europe. This internally developed image recognition software can identify suspected art thieves before the crime even occurs.

"Once these individuals are identified, they can be tracked and apprehended if needed. They've been so successful with their facial recognition software that insurance companies have reduced their premiums on some of these museums' most valuable art treasures."

An alarm bell went off in Chris's head. For months he'd been wondering how in the world he'd been identified as a person "snooping around" the museums of Paris. It never dawned on him that museums had installed intelligent identification camera systems. Most security systems had a central location within the museum where trained professionals watched the various feeds looking for unusual events and potential thieves. This new smart system, by contrast, could identify and pinpoint specific individuals. *That's a game changer*, thought Chris, *and I am proof that the system works.* Without a doubt, that's how he'd been identified and subsequently tracked down by Maurice's son.

He wondered if Maurice and Albert were aware that he'd recovered from his memory loss. One of the last newspaper articles about him surmised there was very little chance of the accident victim regaining his full memory.

With a new understanding of Maurice's business and his connection to the security field, Chris also wondered if Albert had tried to continue keeping tabs on *Antone La Rue*, the private investigator who'd been getting dangerously close to discovering the methods they used to sell illegal art. Most likely not, he decided. As Chris knew from his own experience, Albert was a business owner with lots of important customers in the security field. People demanded his attention and the business required lots of high-touch customer service.

But what if the software captured my face once again, this morning? Chris wondered. *If so, was Albert merely biding his time, waiting for Antone La Rue to reenter the Louvre? What kind of trap might I be walking into? Albert has already shown no hesitation whatsoever in taking out someone who got to close to the truth . . .*

Jay interrupted his thoughts. "There are a few more things you need to see and be aware of before you return to the Louvre," he said, unfurling a large, detailed map. "The boys back at the home office sent me a set of architectural prints of the Louvre. Of course, we can't be sure how up to date these are, but it's better than going in blind.

"As you already know, it's a huge complex of buildings. Some date all the way back to the twelfth century. Below the newer structures are three basements with a labyrinth of rooms and corridors that continue under the older buildings.

"The first two lower levels are dedicated to exhibitions, displays, and visitor amenities. The third and sub-basement levels are storage facilities and maintenance equipment such as heat, furnaces, air conditioning, humidity controls, and air filtration systems. This sub-basement level contains most of the key functions that are the life blood of the Louvre's operation. Being deep underground, these were protected from bombing raids during the war. I believe once you enter the Louvre, this area is where you should begin your search.

"This second set of documents, dug up by the boys back at Langley, are articles written and pictures taken during the war. They show where structural improvements were made to protect the Louvre from potential collateral bomb damage. Notice the location of the two large construction cranes. Also take note of the supply barges and the location of the mooring docks used to unload all the building materials.

"The German engineers used the Seine to deliver and off-load their construction equipment and materials. They were very efficient and able to make improvements, changes, and maybe even additions without attracting much public attention. There's no specific mention in any of these articles regarding where the actual construction sites were. If you note the dates of all these newspaper clippings, you'll see that they were all published during the German occupation of France, from June 1940 to October 1944. They had plenty of time to implement Herr Goering's construction plans. Paris was declared an open city during this time, so the Nazis could build whatever they wanted without fear of bombing raids.

"It was also during this time that Reichsmarschall Hermann Goering used the Louvre as a central location to process the massive amounts of treasure stolen from the western European nations the Nazis invaded and occupied. If you think about the situation, it was the perfect opportunity for Goering to build bomb shelters to protect the Louvre and his valuable treasures. Or maybe even build a special hidden facility to house his growing, personal collection of stolen Jewish art.

"Goering had four separate residences, all located in Germany. It is a well-known fact that these were repositories for his huge art collection. Literal trainloads of the seized treasuries he'd obtained via his Nazi looting were sent to his and Hitler's residences. One of his most prolific looting groups was the ERR, run by a man named Alfred Rosenberg; a man who, after the war, was found guilty of numerous war crimes and hanged.

"The dates of these articles and the adjoining pictures suggest it took the German engineers less than twelve months to complete their construction. This further suggests to me they must have used standard, off-the-shelf architectural plans and construction techniques. With experienced German engineers doing all the work, our people couldn't find any records of specifications, drawings, or building permits for these improvements anywhere. Yet we know these improvements took place.

"How convenient that they were all planned and completed by the same German engineers who constructed hundreds of bunkers and underground structures along France's Atlantic coast during the war. You have to wonder if Goering—with his insatiable desire for more and more treasures—built a special repository for himself at the Louvre. Was he hedging his bets as to who would win the war? Or was he merely looking for yet another safe place to house more of his collection of stolen property?

"Well, Chris, we'll probably never really know the motives behind Goering's actions. With everything that's already happened, though, it's abundantly clear to me that we need to solve this mystery quickly. This burden is now on your shoulders. You must locate these hidden rooms, if they exist. We could certainly flood the museum with police and special agents, but the publicity from this action would create havoc, especially when coupled with Jean Pierre's mysterious death. Every crooked art dealer would go deeper underground and we would never learn the whereabouts of the lost art and all the perpetrators.

"We don't have much time before our undercover agent in the Louvre initiates the security system failure. You need to get hooked up with a special microphone so we can communicate with you and monitor your position within the complex. You will also carry an enhanced phone with the latest tracking receivers. It should be sensitive enough for us to track your location regardless of what floor you're on. Hopefully it will also pick up Hans's or Alana's phone signal once you're inside, unless their phones' batteries have gone dead or their phones have been destroyed.

"Now listen carefully: if you run into a difficult or dangerous situation that requires our help, use the code word *bully*. It's not the best plan in the world, but the situation we're in calls for quick and drastic action."

CHAPTER 40

PROMISES MADE, PROMISES KEPT

While Chris was putting together the final stages of his plan to reenter the Louvre, Hans and Alana were being held against their will in a small room in one of the many sub-basements beneath the sprawling complex.

Hans found himself staring at the beautiful old masterpiece. He'd almost completed the oral evaluation and detailed analysis he'd prepared for Jean Pierre. His strategy had been to prolong the proceedings as much as possible in the hopes that Chris would come to their rescue.

In a fit of desperation, Hans decided to give his captors the answers about why he was so emotionally entangled in this particular painting. Maybe after hearing the story, he thought, Maurice and Albert might be touched by his grief and let them go. After all, his only involvement in any of this was performing meticulous restoration work. He'd never been involved in the sale or distribution of art or antiques and was blissfully ignorant as to what took place in the underground art market. Hans knew his move was desperate, but it was worth a try. At this point in time, his captors were still unaware that both he and his granddaughter had any specific knowledge about their illegal activities. He realized he must protect this secret if they were to survive.

"You see, Maurice, this painting means nothing to me. It's just paint on canvas. Yes, it's very old and very valuable. In fact, the artist is renowned painter Hans Holbein the Younger, a master of the Northern Renaissance style. He was the *King's Painter* to Henry the VIII. Without question, this painting is one of the greatest portraits created during the Tudor period, completed in 1533. In today's art market it's worth a fortune. To me it is worth nothing, however, for it represents sorrow, heartbreak, and death.

"My family was involved in the restoration of Old Master paintings for at least three generations. My grandfather, who survived the Great War, worked on this painting. At the time, it belonged to one of the most famous museums in Berlin. After the war he was hired to clean it and make repairs. Years later, he died of pneumonia in his early sixties. They blamed his death on exposure to the poisonous mustard gas used during that war. My father did additional cleaning and restorative work on this piece years later. He was killed protecting our shop in Berlin on November 9, 1938. The Night of Broken Glass. Kristallnacht. That night there was a *pogrom* against the Jews. State terrorism, looting, arson, mass murder.

"Not long after that, my wife Elsa and I were prisoners of Hermann Goering, locked up on the second floor of a train warehouse in Berlin. I bartered to get my mother and children out of Germany and away from the death camps in return for working on Goering's stolen art, mostly taken from Jewish collectors.

"I worked on this evil man's stolen treasures *for years* to repay our debt to him. It was the worst period in our lives. The horrors and memories of our incarceration in that warehouse will haunt me until the day I die.

"This painting . . . Yes. I, too, invested my time and talent in its preservation. You see, over the years my entire family was plagued by its existence, but my pain goes well beyond those heartbreaks. Confined in that railroad warehouse, my wife and I were daily witnesses to the hundreds of train cars loaded with men, women, and children shipped to work camps and detention centers. This racial persecution of the Jewish population in Europe became an epidemic, leading to the death of millions of innocent Jews and anyone who didn't support the National Socialist Movement. The death camps that rose up out of this hatred and the inhumane acts that took place go beyond human comprehension.

"Elsa and I spent years working on Goering's stolen treasures. From our second-floor prison, we could hear the cries of children and see them being torn from their parents, as we had been torn from ours. Men were shot trying to resist what was happening to their families. Those horrific memories have consumed my thoughts and feelings for years, compounded by my guilt of being associated with this maniac and his bidding. I still carry that guilt to this day. I think about it constantly. *How does one erase, purge their brain and conscience of these horrors?*

"Day after day, week after week, year after year. It was endless. I learned to hate the screeching of train wheels and the high-pitched piercing sound of the whistle. You cannot erase such things from your mind.

"And then there was the constant shipping to Germany, if not to one of Goering's residences, then to Hitler's treasure room, to be housed eventually in the Führer's grand museum, which would be constructed in Austria as an edifice to the Angel of Death and his ethnic cleansing.

"This painting in front of me now . . . I still remember when the Nazi lieutenant handed it to me for restoration. 'This is one of Reichsmarschall Hermann Goering's favorite paintings,' he said. 'Make sure it's properly repaired and packaged for a long journey.' That order will never be erased from my mind, nor my family's role in its preservation amidst all these inhumane acts.

"At times when I was working on that portrait by Hans Holbein the Younger, I wanted to destroy it. My hate for Goering had no bounds. But that action would have meant immediate execution for my wife and me. Then I realized, *Who am I to destroy this remarkable piece of art?* This is no ordinary painting, but the work of an artist with unique abilities to capture life like images on an inanimate piece of oak wood. Holbein was a man with talents that few in the world possess. No, I set aside my hate for the narcissistic and greedy Goering and proceeded to complete my restoration of *The Ambassador*, as it's known. My focus was now to make sure this beautiful masterpiece—a symbol of art perfection—survived to be seen by future generations; to someday claim its rightful position in a museum for all to admire and marvel at.

"One day, I tried to escape and board one of those death trains. Elsa stopped me, pleaded with me. She made me promise that when this madness was all over, we would try to repatriate as many of those stolen treasures as we could. My promise to her was the only thing that prevented me from giving up on life.

"After that, Elsa made drapes out of packaging materials so we'd no longer have to look out the windows and see the trains being loaded up. But you could never shut out the sounds of desperate people. The crying of children and mothers. The gunshots we heard, knowing full well that another innocent person had just been *executed* for disobeying the commands of German soldiers.

"As the war progressed and the Allies started to win battles and gain the upper hand, the tempo of the activity and the frequency of the trains leaving the railyards only increased. It became unbearable. To this day, train engines spewing their hot vapor into the air brings back horrible, nightmarish visions.

"Our respite came when the bombs started to fall. We prayed they would hit the railyard and demolish us with it. The Nazis started using prisoners to repair damage to the rail lines. Madness was all around. There was no trace of compassion, only fear, sadness, and destruction.

"When the fatal bombing finally happened, I was one of the few survivors. My wife and two young carpenters were killed. I was upstairs in our small apartment at the furthest end of the warehouse when the bombs struck. It was a direct hit on the workshop they'd built for me to do my work. The paints, the solvents, the packing materials quickly became a blazing inferno. There entire railyard was mayhem. How I lived through that massive Allied bombing raid is a mystery to me.

"It was the promise I'd made to Elsa that willed me to escape in the aftermath. I knew there was nothing I could do to save my Elsa. God spared me to fulfill my promise.

"Elsa and I had prepared to escape. We were just waiting for the right opportunity. She had put together special homemade backpacks with hidden pockets to hold forged passports, travel documents, and money. There were small amounts of gold and precious gems hidden behind buttons and other special pockets designed for storing small amounts of food. Elsa was a genius when it came to sewing. Unfortunately, I had to destroy her things when I escaped, for fear they might be found. Her forged passport and documents, if discovered, would give away my escape route. It was a very difficult and emotional moment for me to throw her backpack into the infernal fire that had already consumed her. It was my last tangible connection to my Elsa, my life companion. I've carried the weight of these heartbreaking moments all my life. I want to be free from these rusted chains of memory and horror.

"You know, when I was a young boy growing up, I spent a great deal of time with my grandfather. He was a huge influence on my religious beliefs and my values. There was a time in my early teens when he asked me to do something important to him. I promised him that I would. 'Are you sure?' he asked. 'Yes! Yes!' I said. 'I promise with all of my heart.'

"Days went by and I never fulfilled the commitment I'd made to him. Not long after, he took me aside. He didn't yell or scold me, but he told me this: 'When you make a promise to someone, you're asking that person to trust you'll fulfill his request. If you do what is requested, you'll have completed your obligation and built trust. If you fail to fulfill your promise, however, you not only lose trust, but you define yourself as an unreliable person. In life, these values define you as a person. Cherish them. You know, my grandson, I have never, ever broken a promise that I made to someone else."

Hans took a deep breath, knowing what he was about to do may put him in danger, but that he must follow through to live up to his grandfather's words. "So, Maurice, this painting in front of me, I know the identity of the original owner. You and Jean Pierre have said that you don't even know who the present owner is. I beg you to inform the authorities, so it can be returned to the museum."

Hans removed the small black ledger from his vest pocket. He saw Maurice's eyes widen and heard a faint gasp.

"This ledger I hold shows the painting's original, legal owner. There are 565 more such notations detailing the provenance of other Old Master paintings. It's the sum total of three generations' worth of Muller family restorations, dating all the way back to the beginning of the twentieth century. This book identifies when the art was brought in for repairs or restoration, the name and address of its owner, what kinds of repairs were performed, which restorer did the work, and an estimated value of the painting at that time.

"With this book we can repatriate hundreds of art pieces back to their original owners. Yes, there are sure to be many legal problems, but I believe we can solve them by using the reward money for turning them over to one of the commissions for lost and stolen art. A number of these organizations were established after World War II to help people regain missing artifacts. I know this act will be just a small contribution to help make things right. There are millions of people who had their precious treasures stolen from them. Many have already died. But there are survivors and relatives of those who are no longer with us. Some of these injustices can still be reversed. I made a promise, not just to my wife, but also to my God and I will do whatever it takes to fulfill that sacred promise.

"I recommend—no, *I plead with you*—turn this painting in to the authorities. This beautiful painting doesn't belong in someone's private collection, never to be seen in public. It must be displayed and admired for its beauty and the talents this master artist possessed. This can only happen if it's returned to its rightful owner."

If Maurice felt any sympathy, his face didn't betray it. He stared at Hans with a steely gaze and said, "That's quite a story, Hans. You make a compelling case for turning this art over to the authorities. Personally, I couldn't care *less* about your promises. I'm also sure the process is not as simple as you describe. Where precious art is concerned, things are rarely straightforward."

Hans could see Maurice mulling over whether or not to share his secret. Certainly, it could be a quick and easy way to wash his hands of the whole affair. Perhaps he was going to crack.

"What do you mean, Maurice?" said Hans, pretending not to follow his logic, though he knew very well what Maurice was talking about.

"You can't possibly imagine the amount of the money we're talking about," said Maurice, sounding burdened by the weight of it all, "much less the full extent—the sheer number of artifacts—with undocumented provenance that have been showing up in museums and private collections all over the world. There is far more at stake here than your paltry promise of reparations. I think you are out of your depth."

Suddenly, the room went pitch dark and soundless.

Albert quickly moved toward the door, checking to see if the hall lights were on and, more importantly, whether the ventilation system and furnace had come back online. This was critical information because it would indicate the extent of the electrical failure. His well-founded fear was that the entire security system had lost power. His company's system was tied directly to the main electrical grid for the whole complex. Hundreds of video cameras—both inside and outside the museum—could have just been disabled. And if the entire system was down, then they might be in the midst of a security breach.

A coincidence? Albert wondered. *Is it somehow tied to the police investigation presently going on in the Louvre? Is this staged? Has someone entered the Louvre with the hope that he won't be detected?*

All were possible. He hoped the security functions were in the process of rebooting and would be back online shortly. Though the lights had only been off for a matter of seconds, the system's recordings would now be missing up to two minutes of security data. Even if the cameras had switched to their dedicated battery backup, there would be a gap. The whole system had to restart and it was far from instantaneous.

Slowly, it dawned on Albert. Somebody may have slipped through one of the exterior doors during this electrical failure. And if they did, now there would be no record nor any kind of image for the facial recognition software to flag.

If there was one unbending rule in the security business it was this: *there are no coincidences.* Someone knew what they were doing and whoever it was had breached the first line of defense.

He crossed the room quickly, pulled his father aside, and whispered in his ear, "I need to check on the power outage. This brief blackout has disrupted the entire security system. I think we might have an unwanted visitor inside the Louvre. You need to stall and prevent them from leaving this room until I return."

Albert disappeared through the door and hurried off to do his investigation. His first stop would be the security command center on the first floor.

Meanwhile, after listening to Hans's personal story, Maurice found himself considering the old man's proposition. If this painting was turned over to the authorities and the hidden chamber remained a secret, where would the police concentrate their investigations?

Of course! On Jean Pierre's art dealings. The man would be investigated for months, maybe even years, as authorities scrutinized every transaction that was even loosely connected to him. Then, once they discovered his treasure trove in Lucerne, the investigation would shift to Switzerland and their art dealers and museums.

From past discussions with Jean Pierre, Maurice was somewhat familiar with the methods art dealers used when buying, selling, trading, and even loaning out collectable pieces. It was quite complicated and a potentially dangerous business. Just between Paris and Lucerne, there would be hundreds of entities to investigate. Throw in the rest of Europe and the Americas and the amount of resources required would be staggering. It would be a time-consuming, almost impossible task. Even pursuing every lead, they'd never get to Maurice. Nothing tied him to any of it. He was merely in charge of shipping and receiving.

As Maurice's confidence rose, he was suddenly quite sure Jean Pierre's death would be viewed as an accident that inadvertently led to a stolen art ring. The authorities would assume Jean Pierre was adding newly acquired treasures to his valuable art collection. He'd obviously been in a hurry to get out of Paris, driving to his weekend apartment in Lucerne to stash away his steals. There were no connections to him stealing from the Louvre and there were no witnesses to the accident. The truck driver had vanished into thin air, and there were no other clues for the police to follow.

As he pondered all of this he wondered if *Hans* would be a loose end. If the old man revealed what he knew to the police, could that information jeopardize his life and Albert's? As far as he knew, Hans wasn't aware there might be a hidden storage chamber somewhere in the Louvre. But how could he be sure? If the real source of these treasures was identified, he and his son were finished. They'd spend the rest of their lives in jail. Everything they'd worked for would come to nothing. His name, the family name—they would be disgraced.

Maurice was confronted with a huge dilemma. He didn't want to kill Hans and his granddaughter, even though that would wipe out all possible connections between him and the illegal art. If he let them live and the painting were turned over to the authorities, he might be able to play innocent. This entire affair led back directly to Jean Pierre. Killing people was never part of the original plan. *How in the world has it come to this?* he wondered.

Maurice thought of his son's quick reaction in identifying the man he'd thought had discovered their secret. His facial recognition software had tipped him off; he'd reacted quickly and didn't consult with his father. That was a big mistake. Staging a hit-and-run accident on the man who had purportedly discovered their illegal system for the sale of stolen art, well, that should have never happened. Now there'd been another car accident, killing his partner Jean Pierre. Was that justified or just another hot-headed decision?

No, Maurice decided, *I will not be involved in any more loss of life. There has to be a safer, better way to defuse this entire affair.*

Alana spoke, interrupting his thinking. "This has been a long and emotional day for us. You have now been given my grandfather's professional assessment of the painting. You've even heard his story and know our family's connection to this artwork. I suggest you think about his recommendations. I also suggest *you share the information* you received here today with whomever owns this masterpiece. With the information my grandfather knows, you could use him to negotiate with the original owner for a fair reward for its return."

Maurice was overwhelmed by this woman's grasp of the situation and the clarity of her recommendation. It all made good sense to him. More importantly, no one else would get hurt.

"You're absolutely right, Alana," said Maurice. "All of this information needs to be shared with the present owner. And that's exactly what I'm going to do. I will escort you and your grandfather out of the Louvre. I sincerely apologize for the length of time it has taken for this review. However, in view of all that I learned, it was worth hearing Hans's analysis. I'm very glad he was consulted on this endeavor. It looks like a win-win for all involved."

As they left the meeting room, Hans made a request to use the bathroom facilities once again.

"Not a problem," he responded, and Hans was escorted back to the same water closet he'd used before, whereupon he took the opportunity to retrieve his cell phone and the note he'd planted for Chris to discover.

For Hans, the long, winding trip back to the visitor's entrance was fraught with thoughts of being stopped and mugged by some unknown assailant. He only relaxed when he saw the exit to the secure visitors' center ahead. There, Hans and Maurice exchanged niceties for a long, but productive meeting.

Alana sighed with relief as they walk out of the visitors' door. "I have to say, for some reason, I felt very uncomfortable in the presence of those two people, especially Maurice's son," she said.

"Yes, I agree," said her grandfather. "He is definitely *not* a very social person and appears to be a bit of a bully."

As they walked toward the exit gate that led to the parking area, a young docent called out, "I'm looking for Alana Muller. Is that you, *mademoiselle*? I have a message from Monsieur Antone La Rue. He requests you meet him at the entrance for vendors and service people. He says he has some good news. He asked me to escort the two of you there right now."

Hans glanced at Alana. He could see the concern on her face. They were both so relieved to almost be out of the Louvre and away from Maurice and his son. Now, they'd been asked to return. Alana removed her phone from her purse and initiated a call to Chris. There was no response.

"I am only delivering a message, *mademoiselle*," said the docent. "Monsieur La Rue is with my boss. Please, I am supposed to escort you to my boss's office."

With trepidation and fear, they both turned and followed the docent back through the visitor's gate.

CHAPTER 41

THE UNLIKELY PARTNERSHIP

With minor changes to his face created with makeup, Chris donned a gray serviceman's coverall with a conspicuous *Electronic Services* patch sewn on the front and reentered the Louvre moments after the power outage. His only objective was to get Alana and Hans out of the building. He could return later to hunt for the location of the stolen art. In fact, he still didn't have concrete proof that the art displayed and sold at the museums across Europe actually came from the Louvre. For all anyone knew, Jean Pierre's newly discovered apartment in Switzerland could well be the origin point. Now that man was dead, and the secret may be buried with him.

The same undercover agent met Chris at the service gate. After briefly exchanging new code words, the man slipped Chris a security pass bearing his name and likeness. "I cannot stay with you, monsieur," said the agent, his face briefly betraying his nervousness. "My cover may have been compromised." He handed Chris two master keys and detailed the most inconspicuous route to the Louvre's sprawling sub-basement. "You must avoid suspicion," he said. "These keys are copies. They will get you into many of the sub-basement's rooms, but not all of them. *Bonne chance, mon ami.*" With that, the man spun around and quickly walked away, dissolving into the crowd like an apparition.

Chris wondered at the man's peculiar remark about his cover being blown. Was the comment meant to alert him? Had his cover, too, been compromised? Was he walking into a trap?

This time, as Chris passed through the gates, he took careful notice of the security cameras' locations. He knew he should be safe from them due to the blackout, but he had worn his flimsy disguise just in case. If they did get a complete profile of his face, the information would undoubtedly trigger an alert, and if they were indeed using sophisticated facial recognition software, alarms would start blinking somewhere. His only hope was that his disguise would confuse and slow the recognition process, giving him additional precious time before the guards started looking for him. His facial disguise was minimal, but if they weren't yet using the newest, most advanced software, he might catch a break.

As Chris started advancing down the halls and descending further into the sub-basements, he checked his phone to see if its tracking device was picking up any signals from Alana or Hans's phones, but there was nothing. He knew the walls were too thick for any signals to penetrate. Besides, he was now probably thirty feet under the Louvre's main floor by now.

The Louvre was designed with two long wings running parallel to each other, separated in the middle by Tuileries Garden and its large, open-air sculpture garden representing different historical eras. He decided to investigate the west wing first. It was the closest set of buildings to the river Seine. After reviewing the pictures and newspaper records Jay had given him, it was a good place to begin his search.

As he moved through the corridor, he tried to open some of the doors. All of them were marked *Storage* and made of steel with heavy-duty locks. *There could be hundreds of these rooms*, he thought, *each with its own treasure trove of stolen art. It would take months to investigate each one.*

He glanced at the floor plan Jay had given him. It wasn't even close to what he was seeing. He continued walking the same direction, noting how the words on the doors changed subtly as he went. *Maintenance, Supplies, Heating, Ventilation.* Then, near the end of the hall, a lone door marked *Electrical.* It was the very last door before the hall became a dead-end. On the wall next to the door was a large, double-door steel cabinet. In faded paint it read *Janitorial Supplies.* It, too, was secured by a heavy-duty lock.

Before he tried the door marked *Electrical,* Chris decided to check his phone one more time for any missed calls or possible locational signals that might have come from Alana or Hans's phones. Nothing appeared on his screen except a compass reading and the time.

The door was locked. Chris quickly tried each of the keys he'd been given.

One fit!

He turned the knob slowly and cautiously entered the room. As his eyes adjusted to the darkness, he heard a deep, ominous voice. "Welcome, Monsieur Lu Rue," said a man he'd never seen before, "I've been expecting you."

The stranger held a taser that was pointed directly at Chris's chest. Chris opened his mouth to speak, but before any words came out, the man squeezed the trigger releasing two small, barbed darts. The darts struck Chris in the chest. He crumpled to the floor and began shaking violently. Maddeningly, as Chris felt waves of electricity pulsing through his body, he knew exactly what had happened—but there wasn't a damn thing he could do about it.

Neuromuscular incapacitation, he thought, trying to keep his wits as he fought back the pain. He knew it wouldn't last long. Not more than thirty seconds. When he trained for the CIA, he was subject to this physical test. He was also instructed on the effects a taser has on the body and how to minimize its downtime.

His gun was inside his coat pocket, underneath his coveralls, impossible to retrieve in his present condition. He felt the man searching through his exposed coverall pockets, removing his phone and the set of keys he'd been given.

Twenty seconds gone, he told himself.

He felt his muscles beginning to loosen from the electric shock but decided to continue his violent tremors and palsy-like body motions, hoping his deception would give him more time to recover.

He could hear the man pushing buttons on his phone, trying to call someone or maybe send a message? Unable to get reception in the bowels of the Louvre, the man grabbed Chris and tried to hold him steady in the midst of his violent shaking. He grabbed Chris's hand and tried to press his thumb against his phone's fingerprint sensor.

The man's trick must have worked, because after a moment he let go of Chris's hand and stepped away. As his arm fell to the floor, Chris sensed he had some control over his muscles. It had been at least fifty seconds and Chris knew he had to act fast.

The man was standing not more than two feet away, punching buttons on Chris's phone. Apparently, he found what he'd been looking for and it held his full attention. Chris unobtrusively pulled the two barbed prongs from his chest and initiated a massive leg whip with his right leg.

Chris felt his foot strike the back of both of the man's legs with a satisfying crack. The man toppled over backwards, his head crashing into a chair as he fell to the floor. With his body almost completely recovered, Chris rolled on top of the man, and he was now in full control of the situation. The man was semiconscious from banging his head. There was no need for further action.

Chris's first reaction was to search him, but he decided that could wait. The man would awaken shortly and he didn't need any more trouble. Instead, he quickly searched the room and found some wire cords, which he used to bind the man's arms and legs. As he did so, Chris wondered, *Why did this man choose this obscure location to lure and capture me? What was his intention? What's so important about this room or its contents?*

With the man bound and secured, Chris applied a wide piece of tape across his mouth to prevent him from yelling for help. Thankfully, the room was made of concrete and almost entirely soundproof.

The only sound was the steady, low-pitched humming of the electrical panels and myriad conduit wires. He surmised this to be the main electrical control center for the west wing of the Louvre.

The room was also filled with pressure switches and heavy-duty circuit breakers. Many were named and labeled with their specific zones of coverage. Chris remembered Hans's comments about the storage requirements for Old Master art—how they must be stored in a temperature- and humidity-controlled environment. Each separate display area and storage room required a special, dedicated HVAC system. The number of electrical motors to control and maintain airflow would be significant. Those systems, in turn, would require dedicated circuits for each exhibition room and gallery, as well as the storage rooms dedicated to the preservation of the art and antiques that weren't on display.

Chris couldn't help but wonder, *Does the room have some significance?* Perhaps the man had been merely checking on a specific bank of circuit breakers and panels after that power outage. *If so, why did he have a taser? Why did he say he'd been waiting for me? It was all very suspicious. Clearly, nothing had been a coincidence.*

Chris still had a few minutes before his assailant became fully conscious, so he continued his search. Reading each panel to determine its specific use was a daunting and time-consuming task. There were at least a hundred of these control boxes. He was almost to the end of one long row when he saw a panel box that was locked. There was no label indicating its use. Just then, his thoughts were interrupted by a muffled, moaning voice coming from the front of the room. His assailant was regaining consciousness, muttering indistinguishable words.

Chris yelled for him to shut up. "Sorry about that whack to your head, but in view of what you'd just done to me, I'd say we're even." The man muttered more muffled words. "I'll remove the tape on your mouth if you agree not to yell," said Chris. "Either way, you'll be kept tied until I learn who you are and why you assaulted me. Do you understand?"

The man nodded his head in agreement. Before the tape was fully removed, however, he shouted, "Release me, release me now!"

Chris resealed the tape and said firmly. "I promise you, I'm not playing games. If you cooperate, I'll release you in due time. First, you need to answer some questions."

Chris noticed a special Louvre vendors' entrance pass on the man's jacket lying on the floor. Unlike his own pass, which had been hand-printed by an office computer, this one was permanent and covered with a transparent laminate. He decided to check the man's credentials, which he retrieved from the inside pocket of the man's jacket.

After looking them over, Chris removed the tape once again. This time, the man didn't yell.

"It says here that your name is Leon Martelle," said Chris, "and you work for a company called Heating and Ventilation Engineering Services. With the permanent pass on your jacket, I'm guessing you must have access to this place quite frequently."

"Yes, yes. That's right," said Leon. "Please release me now!"

"But if you're just a vendor, here doing work for the Louvre, why did you shoot me with that stun gun, and how do you know my name? I can assure you, Monsieur Martelle, that you will remain where you are until I get some answers." And with that statement, Chris strode to the door and engaged the double-lock.

"Antone, you and I are on the same quest," the man began, in an almost collegial tone. "I was approached by the same man who has you under contract to investigate who is behind the emergence of these mysterious master art works that have been showing up around the world. You may or may not know this, but what we are dealing with is hundreds of millions of dollars' worth of stolen art and antiques.

"The person you and I work for simply wants a piece of the action. And he's willing to do what it takes to uncover whoever is behind this scheme. He does business worldwide, both legal and illegal. He's betting one of us is going to lead him to this huge pot of gold.

"Since I already had a service contract with complete access to the Louvre, I was the perfect person to snoop around for hidden treasures. That's all I have been doing, along with my maintenance work. I was specifically told not to interfere with a man called Antone La Rue. I was shown your picture and given some details of your history. I assure you, I have no intention of getting in your way or preventing you from completing your own contract. Once the mystery is solved, surely we'll both be paid, so there is no reason for us to be at odds with each other.

"Please, I suggest you release me, so we can partner up. If we share what we've learned, together we'll be able to solve this problem in no time."

Everything this man said made sense to Chris. As he began to untie the man's legs, he asked, "Why did you shoot me with that taser? Can I trust you?"

"Well, I know you're ex-CIA and you could kill me very quickly," he said. "I guess I wasn't sure that I would even live long enough to tell you my story."

"Trust is a two-way street," said Chris, with no hint of emotion. "Before I release your hands, what is the name of our client and what art company does he own?"

Chris could see Leon weighing the pros and cons of answering.

"If we don't trust each other, I'll lock you in this room and there won't be a partnership," Chris stated.

Leon's eyes grew wide as he nodded in agreement. "Yes, absolutely. You're absolutely right." Chris's threat had been enough. Clearly this maintenance worker wasn't a pro. Suddenly, a fount of information came pouring out of the man.

"Good ventilation systems are one of the keys to a healthy museum. Controlling temperature fluctuations, dust particles, and humidity are musts. I've worked on almost all the ventilation systems in the so-called new wing of the Louvre. This room we're in holds all of the electrical circuitry required to drive the lights and ventilation motors for the exhibition areas *just in this wing*. The Louvre's other wings have similar facilities. There is only a handful of circuits I have left to check out in this room. The two longer wings of the Louvre run almost due east, quite parallel to the river Seine. This last bank of electrical boxes, on the right side, still needs to be checked. We're looking for conduit wires coming from one of these boxes that run east by southeast to the Sully Wing, which is the original fortress. Obviously, that was built well before the advent of electricity. If we can locate the correct wires, it will help us in our search."

They needed to get up on a ladder to see which direction the conduits ran. Chris used his cell phone compass as he moved from one control panel to another, checking the wires' directions. He was almost to the end of the wall when he found a set of conduits that met on the exact compass coordinates they were searching for. The wires exited the panel going directly west of the Louvre toward the Denon Wing, which practically bordered the Seine.

The panel was marked *Not in Use*. Leon quickly unscrewed the panel cover, exposing all the circuits. Using his ohmmeter, he determined all the circuits *did* have active wires attached to them, even though the panel cover said otherwise. "As I should've known," he said, "all of these wires are live. The big question now is, where do they terminate?

The two of them moved to the *Electrical Services* door. If they turned and went east, back the way they came, it would take them to the Pont des Arts. On the other hand, if they went west, the hallway would be a dead-end about forty meters later. One would assume if there was an additional, hidden room, it would be at the edge of the Louvre's foundation. The Denon Wing was newer and likely easier to modify than the giant stones that formed the foundation of the original fortress.

Chris decided to pace off the distances from the door to the end of the hall, as well as from the *Electric Services* door to the back of the room. The distances varied by almost 2.5 meters! To make sure it wasn't his error or a miscalculation, Chris repeated his steps.

He got the same result.

It was quite apparent to both of them now that this variance in distance *could mean* there was some sort of hallway or small room *beyond* the outside wall of the electrical control center. There were no obvious entrances, though, to this potentially hidden area. Chris decided to check the architectural drawings of the Louvre he'd been given.

Nothing. There was no indication of modifications or additions above or below ground. Curiously, the electrical conduit pipes they just identified headed in the direction of the potential void.

The two of them decided to start searching for a hidden door. Chris was so engrossed in discovering the hidden art room that he completely forgot his original objective: to locate Hans and Alana. He decided to continue searching because he felt they must be getting close.

The two men returned to the electrical control center and checked each panel for clues. As Chris approached the last two banks of panels, he noticed a series of faint, circular scratches on the cement floor. Whatever caused the scratches appeared to have been swung in an arc, away from the back wall.

Curiously, all of the electrical control boxes on the back wall were attached to four-by-eight wood panels, ten of them in total. There was a thin, dark gap separating one panel from another.

"Leon, do you have a cigarette?" Chris asked.

"Yes, I do," he responded.

"I would like one, please, along with your lighter."

Chris lit the cigarette. A serpentine wisp of smoke rose up to the ceiling. He watched it carefully.

"I want you to unlock the door," said Chris, "and open it very slowly."

Leon opened the door and Chris began to walk slowly across the back of the room from left to right. The smoke from his cigarette continued to rise straight up toward the ceiling. Just before he got to the last panel, though, the smoke from the cigarette noticeably changed direction. The closer he got to the gap between the last two panels, the more the smoke angled sideways, toward a particular gap in the wall. It flowed toward that gap as though it were pulled, disappearing behind the wall. Leon stood spellbound as he watched this entire sequence of events.

Chris smiled, satisfied with his experiment. "Now all we have to do is determine how that panel is attached to the wall."

The two of them could barely contain their excitement. Each began to scrutinize every inch of the wall, from top to bottom. Before long, they'd pinpointed the mechanism that held the panel to the wall.

Leon handed Chris a long screwdriver. Chris slid it through the gap, activating the mechanism that kept the door latched. "A very clever design," he said, as the panel swung free. It was hinged on one side, revealing a threshold and entryway slightly smaller than the four-by-eight panel.

"Now, let's see what's in there," said Chris.

There was a light switch near the entrance. Chris switched it on to find a small staging area, strewn with various open crates. On the far end of the room was a faded swastika. Both Chris and Leon were startled. It was stenciled on a large steel door, secured with two deadbolt locks. Printed in German and French was a succinct warning: *Property of the Third Reich by Order of Reichsmarschall Hermann Goering.*

Chris had taken classes on the history of World War II at the University of Minnesota. His professor, Dr. Harold C. Deutsch, had served as head of research for the Office of Strategic Services. Deutsch had also been an interpreter for the Allies at the Nuremberg Trials after the war. He'd seen many of the incriminating documents as he witnessed the trials, interpreting testimonies given by Nazi generals, including the notorious Hermann Goering.

Dr. Deutsch's classes were grounded in facts about the horrors the Nazis had inflicted on the Jewish people. He showed the class copies of pictures and source documents—unequivocal proof that the Holocaust happened, and that millions of people were killed under Nazi rule.

Seeing this emblem before him sent a chill through Chris's body. Images documenting the Nazi reign of terror flashed through his mind. He felt a wave of nausea as his brain tried to process the atrocities that had taken place during that evil regime. When Chris had taken that course in college, the dates, events, and brutality had remained abstract. Horrific as it may be, it was someone else's story; a historical event.

Now, as he faced this evil sign of hate, suffering, greed, and death, Chris thought of Hans and his poor wife Elsa. They'd been imprisoned by Goering himself and made to bear witness to trainloads of innocent victims sent to the death camps every day.

He flipped the dead bolts open and entered a huge domed room filled with thousands of art objects. There were racks and racks of shelves, some almost touching the ceiling. Masterpiece paintings covered the walls, and every shelf was packed with treasures: antique furniture, mounds of family silverware and china, magnificent Persian rugs, stunning statuary, gorgeous tapestries, exquisite crystal chandeliers . . .

Chris shook his head in amazement as he tried to drink it all in. He felt as though he were floating on the crest of dazzling wave.

"My God! There's a fortune in here," Leon exclaimed, abruptly snapping Chris out of his reverie.

The voice echoed through the cavernous room, followed by absolute quiet as a weighty, oppressive stillness descended onto the room.

Suddenly, behind them, Chris and Leon heard the hasty, metallic *clunk-clunk* of two metal levers being bolted into place. Both men realized too late they were now trapped in a hidden, underground chamber with only one exit. Their excitement to confirm their discovery had caused them to make what could be a fatal error.

CHAPTER 42

A CALL FOR DRASTIC ACTION

Albert bolted from the conference room where the Mullers were being held, driven to determine why the Louvre's electrical system had momentarily failed. He'd never seen this happen before. The systems were supposed to be fail-safe.

He wasn't concerned about the millions of irreplaceable art objects that needed to be protected by his company's surveillance system. Somebody who wanted to avoid detection may have entered the Louvre in the brief moment his cameras were not online. *That* was his concern.

The coincidence of this failure coming on the heels of Jean Pierre's death was highly suspect, especially with Hans and his granddaughter presently in the Louvre. His suspicions were awakening, as was his growing paranoia of being caught by the police.

Whether he was being paranoid or merely cautious, it was imperative that he return to the security command center to check the tapes. There, he could assess what effect the downtime had on the Louvre's security operations.

As he approached the central commend station, one of the technicians informed him that their facial recognition software had flagged one individual moments before the power failure occurred.

"We believe he's now in the museum," said the technician. "Previously, this man was recognized by our security system as potentially dangerous. Sir, if anything, that likelihood has increased."

The process of reviewing the security tapes was very straightforward. Focusing in on footage from the entrances and exits in the hours before the power failure, it didn't take long for the technicians to isolate the images of the intruder on the computer monitor. At first, Albert drew a blank. He didn't recognize the man at all. As he studied the images in more detail, however, he realized the face *was* familiar. He asked the technician to search the facial recognition history files over the last twelve months. The high-capacity computer program kicked out an image match in a matter of moments.

Well, well, well, Albert thought to himself, *either this man is a twin or the most recent intel from my informant at the police department was incorrect. I wonder what could have possibly drawn Monsieur Antone La Rue back to the Louvre? After almost losing his life, why would he dare come back?*

Albert was baffled. Was he there purely for the money? What about his supposed *unrecoverable* memory loss? Even more confusing, La Rue had entered and exited in less than one hour—both occurring *before* the power outage. *What did he accomplish during that short time?* Albert wondered. His feeling was even stronger that all of the day's events were tied together.

What's the connection? he asked himself. *The painting! Of course, that must be it. Had La Rue been hired by Hans to do the investigation? No doubt there are many illegal art dealers just aching to get their hands on all these treasures.*

As all of these questions cascaded through Albert's mind, the high-tech security system sounded an alert. A breach was taking place in the west wing on the third-floor basement. Albert quickly asked a technician to switch to the camera that had picked up the breach.

The hidden video camera in this particular hallway had a specific purpose; a purpose only known to Maurice and Albert. Even Jean Pierre had been unaware such a camera existed. It had proved to be very beneficial because it had caught Jean Pierre repeatedly removing items from Hermann Goering's chamber. The tapes were tangible evidence of his activities, logged specifically when Jean Pierre was taking things without consulting Maurice—small but valuable pieces that had ruined Maurice's trust.

On the monitor Albert watched a video of someone in the maintenance hall. The person had a key and entered the electrical control center, the very room that concealed the secret entrance to the hidden chamber. As the tape continued, a second man also appeared. He also had a key to the room.

How could this be happening? Albert asked himself.

As he continued watching, one of the men looked out the doorway, directly into the hidden camera. His facial images were immediately captured and identified by the software. A flashing light acknowledged he was an intruder. The footage was automatically entered into the data bank by the system and compared to archived images of other suspicious visitors. As the computer screen showed two images side by side, the match was obvious. Once again, it was Antone La Rue!

But the last time he'd been on camera he was *exiting* the Louvre. *How did he avoid detection by the security system* the second time *he entered the Louvre? Of course,* Albert thought, *it was during that massive electrical outage. Though it was only brief, it allowed La Rue to enter without a trace. Either that, or he'd worn a disguise. The power outage was obviously staged to sneak La Rue back into the Louvre. The timing must have been coordinated to Hans Muller's meeting with Jean Pierre.*

Albert realized this guy La Rue was shrewd and wouldn't be deterred from accomplishing his objective—an objective Albert suddenly realized was finding the source of all the lost art. *Has La Rue found the entrance to the secret chamber?* he wondered. *How on earth has this man managed to do that?* That room was filled with rows and rows of electrical panels and conduit pipes going in every direction. It should've taken days to make that discovery.

There was no time to waste.

Albert told his technician to relay this information to his father and hurried off to catch the intruders before they had time to search the entire room. On the way there, he stopped briefly in his office, unlocked his desk drawer, and retrieved his revolver. He double-checked to confirm the gun was locked and loaded, then continued downstairs.

With his revolver in one hand and a master key in the other, Albert unlocked the door and slowly entered the room where the two intruders were last seen. He was surprised to find no one in the entrance area, so he started searching each aisle with his gun positioned to shoot. No one was found, but as he approached the last aisle, where he knew there was a secret door, he immediately saw that the back wall panel was partially open.

He couldn't believe his eyes. *How did they figure out the secret entrance so quickly?* With his gun in a steady position, he slowly opened the door and moved into the small hall that led to the large steel door with an emblem of a Nazi swastika.

He moved slowly and stealthily toward the door, listening for any activity from inside. As he approached the main entrance to the hidden chamber, he heard movement and a quiet conversation. Two people were saying something about "a treasure in here."

He paused to contemplate his next move. Bursting into the room and confronting these two men didn't appear smart. If both were armed, he would be outgunned. The outcome of that possibility was definitely not appealing. There had to be a better way. Upstairs, the Mullers were detained in his father's office. *What's their connection?* he wondered. With Jean Pierre now silenced, the exit strategy of this illegal art scheme looked simple, but now there were four other people to deal with.

Albert pulled the steel door shut and engaged both of the dead bolts, locking the men inside, with no way to escape—he was quite sure of that.

He returned to the main room and closed the four-by-eight door panel, returning it to its original position. Satisfied the room looked normal, he headed back to his security control center. He'd made the trip many times and knew every inch of the ten-minute walk. It was all a blur this time, however, as Albert began to fall into despair. *How are each of these people connected to this affair?* he wondered. He knew he must hurry back to confront this Hans Muller and his granddaughter. Their involvement was one of the biggest question marks.

The Mullers had been lured back into the Louvre under the false pretense that Antone was waiting for them in Maurice's office. When they arrived, however, his office was empty.

CHAPTER 43

TRACKING DEVICES HAVE THEIR LIMITS

The last information Jay had passed to Chris was that his agents were setting up their surveillance equipment and tracking system in Hans's shop. This decision was made to prevent both the local police and Interpol agents from interfering with their plan. In essence, it was to be a covert operation. They could maintain a low profile and keep the number of people involved to an absolute minimum.

Jay's agents had downloaded the Louvre's floor plan into their computer. Now they were able to track Chris as he proceeded from building to building and hallway to hallway, as they had earlier planned to do with Hans and Alana, carrying the same tracking phones. His location and progress would be tracked by the surveillance system as long as he carried his phone. The thought was they could initiate a pinpoint rescue operation if necessary.

Their electronic tracking system was working perfectly. The signals from Chris's phone showed up on the monitor as a red dot. Signal strength was key to the whole operation. Their set-up was less than ten miles from the Louvre, but whether they would be able to continue tracking Chris would ultimately depend on how deep into the sub-basements he descended.

At precisely 12:00, the staged blackout of the entire Louvre complex was initiated. The duration of the shutdown was short but long enough to interrupt all electric operations, including all their security taping equipment.

By the time the clock read 12:02, Chris's red dot was passing through the services security control station and proceeding into the building. Exactly according to plan, Chris had successfully reentered into the Louvre without being detected. Unfortunately, a short time after his entry, he disappeared from their video monitoring screen. It was a weird and scary event to watch that happen on the computer screen. Jay knew it was way too early to plan any action for recovery. He must be careful and patient. His concern for Chris's safety might force him to react prematurely.

As time continued to pass with no indication that they might be able to reestablish a signal, Jay decided it was best to move their operation to one of the many parking areas on the Right Bank of the Seine. With closer proximity to the Louvre, Jay hoped they would be able to quickly implement a recovery plan if they were called to do so. There was also a better chance for a stronger signal by moving closer to the action.

As Jay's men were packing up the surveillance equipment, Jay received a call from the head of the French secret police. There was nothing much new to report; it was merely a scheduled update they'd agreed to. As the police chief reiterated a lot of what he already knew, Jay was preoccupied with what was happening inside the Louvre. In fact, he wasn't much paying attention when the chief revealed some interesting details about Jean Pierre's accident.

" . . . but before he left his office that morning," the police chief was saying, "Jean Pierre collected and shredded all his personal documents. In his apartment, however, we also found a whole new set of files and a fairly large safe. The safe was wide open and contained a fake passport, the address of his new residence in Lucerne, and two previously un-known saving accounts containing large sums of money.

"As we continue to search his apartment, I'm not sure it makes much sense for us to keep investigating his office, or indeed the Lou-vre. This is really good news, Jay. You must do everything possible to confine your operation to internal people only. The media and the public must be kept out of the loop. Discretion is paramount. None of this can get out."

As the conversation wound down, one of the agents in the mobile security van called Jay's attention to the monitoring screen. Two in-dividuals, identified by their small red dots, were moving toward the VIP entrance. They were walking in the direction of Han's car. Sud-denly, there was a pause in their movement and they reversed course, going back inside the Louvre.

"What the *hell* is going on?" Jay said to the agent. "Why would they return and put themselves in danger again? Are we sure that this equipment is working properly?"

Jay felt his pulse quicken. Things were starting to escalate.

CHAPTER 44

EXPECTATIONS WITHOUT RESULTS

With the steel door double-locked, trapping both Chris and his companion in Goering's hidden chamber, Albert rushed off to the security office to interrogate the Mullers. As he entered, they confronted him. Before he even got a chance to speak, Hans was up in his face, staring at him with contempt.

Suddenly, Alana yelled out, "Where is Chris—I mean Antone?" She realized her mistake and pressed forward, hoping to cover her error. "We were told Antone La Rue was waiting for us here in your office," she blurted. "I don't see him. Where is he?"

But Albert had already detected Alana's error. *Chris who?* he wondered. *An alias for the man I know as Antone La Rue? Or is that the name of the other person who appears to be performing an investigation?* Whoever this guy was, he was trapped. *What's his connection to the Mullers?* he wondered.

"Where is Maurice?" Albert asked. "Why is he not here with you two?"

"He was called to his office for some sort of questioning," said Hans. "We were told to stay here in *your office* at the security center. As my granddaughter said, we were told somebody would be bringing Antone here. Where is he? We need to leave now."

"Why are you so interested in that man?" asked Albert. "What is he to you and your granddaughter?"

Albert slid into his chair and started punching code numbers into his computer. He spun the screen around so Hans and Alana could see the two side-by-side images his technician had shown him earlier. "Which one of these is Antone?" he asked, in a tone that demanded an answer. "Both men were taped entering the Louvre illegally."

Albert already knew the answer. He wanted to see if they would try to conceal the truth. Not waiting for a response, Albert called up a new set of pictures. It was the side-by-side image comparison of Antone, showing the first time he'd entered the Louvre next to the second time, with him in disguise.

Alana let out a small gasp. There was no doubt that they were both the same person, but she was surprised by Chris's feeble, almost laughable attempt to disguise himself.

"Our facial recognition software can't be fooled by a pair of sunglasses and a cheap fake mustache," he said. "I do think it might have improved his looks, however, if only slightly. Do you agree, Alana?" Albert's remark was meant to release some of the tension, but Alana didn't respond, so he tried a different approach.

"My business is security," he said, "and I'm very good at it. You people are not going to leave until I get some answers. I have other ways to find out who this Chris, or Antone is, whatever he's called." He looked directly at Alana, malevolence in his eyes. "Unfortunately, *that will take some time*, and I don't think you and your friend have very much to spare." The implied threat hit Alana hard. Albert turned back toward the computer and began punching keys, doing who knows what.

"Did you know the Louvre is over eight hundred years old?" he asked. "It was a fortress at one time with torture chambers and prison cells. There is an endless maze of rooms where people were taken to never be found." He slammed his hands on the desk. "I need answers now! Or you will never see this man again."

Alana was stunned. She feared for Chris's life, realizing she was in no position to bargain with this brute. Neither she nor her grandfather would be able to defend themselves in a physical confrontation with him. Her only recourse was to tell him what he wanted to know and hope he would let them leave. It had been a long, exhausting day. She and her grandfather were both at their breaking points.

"I was his trauma nurse," she said. "He was in a terrible car accident. I helped nurse him back to life and regain his lost memory."

Suddenly, the phone in her purse began to buzz and vibrate. *It must be Chris,* she thought, *he will come and help us.* She quickly opened her purse to answer the phone. Albert's hand shot out and snatched the phone away. Hans tried to intervene, but Albert flung him across the room. He crashed headfirst into a filing cabinet, as though he were a ragdoll, and collapsed to the floor. Seeing a small trickle of blood wind its way down her grandfather's face, Alana let go of her purse and rushed to his aid.

"You killed my grandfather!" she screamed, her voice full of rage. She turned to confront his assailant with fire in her eyes and hateful intentions. In nursing school she'd been schooled on how to handle situations like this, when patients got violent. Before she could lunge at him, though, she felt a dart-like needle hit her chest. She collapsed onto the floor next to her grandfather. Even though she was in great physical shape, her small, petite frame couldn't handle the massive jolt of electricity from the taser gun. The last thing she heard before she passed out was the man's comment: "This was not supposed to happen."

After he completed his interrogation with the Paris police, Maurice rushed off to his son's security offices, hoping to find him alone. As he stepped into Albert's office, however, what he saw startled him. It was Hans Muller, limp and lifeless in a heap on the floor, and next to him was his granddaughter, Alana, moaning and shaking violently.

"What the hell is going on here?" he screamed at his son. "The police are still moving throughout these buildings and here you have two people sprawled out on the floor. What kind of mess have you created?"

"I will explain it all later," said Albert. "Right now we must move them quickly down to the hidden chamber. We have been found out! They know too much. We must prevent them from being interviewed by the police. Our only chance of getting away is to keep them isolated until the police have left. Then, we should leave the country and be done with all of this. Help me bind their hands and blindfold them. We have to move them—*now*."

As they prepared to move the Mullers, Maurice retrieved Hans's black book and his cell phone from his pocket. There was a text message from Chris: *Get out! Jean Pierre is dead.* Without question, their scheme had been discovered. He thought of all those years working for the Louvre, putting up with their arrogant directors and being treated as an uneducated lowlife. He'd been preparing to leave for years, but now it was at the cost of even more human life. That was *never* part of his plan. Could he cope with this decision that confronted him? Horrible images of the things he'd be forced to do flashed rapidly before him. *How did it ever come to this?* he wondered, binding Hans's wrists together behind his back. *What have I become?*

CHAPTER 45

AN UNSCHEDULED RENDEZVOUS

Chris was very upset with himself. *I was trained to avoid precisely this kind of trap*, he thought, paralyzed by the deafening silence. His eyes scanned the room, desperately searching for any sign of an exit, but he only saw the massive array of treasures looted from all over Europe.

There are enough paintings, sculptures, antique furniture, and tapestries to furnish a hundred large homes, Chris realized. *The objects in this unknown underground bunker could fill an entire museum.*

It was indescribably opulent. There were stacks and stacks of crates containing paintings and sculptures—many of them still in their original shipping containers, stamped with that horrible symbol, the Nazi swastika.

Many years ago, Chris had read stories about Hermann Goering's insatiable desire to collect the world's most incredible treasures. After the war, the Allies had discovered hundreds of train cars loaded with looted property. In Germany, they removed thousands of pieces from his residences.

As Chris looked around the room, he noted this storage facility was designed and constructed exactly like the bomb-proof shelters built to protect and house soldiers. Similar bunkers had also held cannons, emplacements, and munitions. Hundreds of these structures were built all along France's Atlantic coastline to prevent an Allied invasion. The only difference between this structure and the ones he'd seen with Jay in Normandy was the absence of separate four-man bunkrooms with thick cement partisan walls for added protection.

It all made sense to him now. During the occupation of Paris in 1942 and 1943, the Nazis had constructed a supposed bomb shelter to protect some of the Louvre's most valuable treasures; it was built in record time with ruthless Nazi efficiency.

Of course! They'd been able to do it because they used the exact same plans and construction methods as the fortifications they'd built all along the coast. This room, however, had been impeccably designed to protect the art. With a high, domed ceiling and separate heating, cooling, and humidity systems, the bunker could maintain a perfectly controlled environment to house valuable treasures indefinitely.

Had the Reichsmarschall been secretly planning to live in Paris after the war?

Hell, Goering was no fool, he was simply hedging his bets as to who would emerge victorious. This was just another stash of stolen art that his troops had taken from the Jews. Thankfully, the Nazis lost the war, and Goering's war crimes cost him his life.

After that, these treasures remained hidden for generations. The only living person who knew Goering's precious secret was Maurice Devenue. He was the only one left who'd worked at the Louvre during the Nazi occupation.

He seemed like a loyal patriot to his country; perhaps he had been intensely afraid of exposing Goering's hoard in the fear he'd be implicated himself. In all likelihood, he would have been seen as an accomplice no matter what he said, accused of conspiring with and assisting the enemy during the occupation. It was a broadly publicized fact that so-called collaborators were hung in the streets—without a trial in most cases—if they were believed to have assisted the enemy in any way during the war. Not a pleasant thought for Maurice and his family.

But why did Maurice get involved in this illegal scheme? Chris wondered.

Maurice had preserved the secret of this indescribable room for decades, first under Director Louis Dequire. Dequire had wanted to be known for bringing glory back to the Louvre. Building, politicizing, and promoting special expositions at the museum enabled him to achieve his goals.

Dequire had become famous, but had he given Maurice any credit? Chris couldn't imagine he had. Then, along came Jean Pierre. Chris had read that Jean Pierre had wanted to be known for saving the Louvre from financial disaster. In the process of achieving this goal, perhaps Jean Pierre's innate greed had started to control him. After beguiling Maurice into revealing the existence and precise location Hermann Goering's secret bunker, he probably quickly ascertained the unbounded potential in all these hidden treasures. *Yes,* thought Chris, *with an astute understanding of financial systems and processes, Jean Pierre realized he could achieve all his financial ambitions: he could get the Louvre out of debt while making himself a fortune. There was also the huge ego boost, tremendous status, and recognition that came with personally owning world-class art, not to mention the prestige that came with it.*

Somehow, during his working relationship with Maurice, they had formed an unlikely partnership. This quiet, but bitter employee with an axe to grind—blessed with an unbelievable memory and flawless recall abilities—was the perfect person to help carry out Jean Pierre's scheme. Nobody had been more loyal to the Louvre—Maurice had basically given his entire life to the Louvre. When he saw his chance to profit from all those years of selfless service he'd given to the Louvre, a partnership was formed.

As Chris thought through what had happened and why things were taking such a dangerous course, Leon's deep baritone voice snapped him out of his reverie.

"So, how do we escape from this dungeon?" he asked.

"We don't," Chris replied mournfully. "I've walked all the way around this entire room. It's an impenetrable vault with only one way in and only one way out. There's a small office in the corner with a cot, a table, and some chairs. All we can do is wait. Hopefully someone will come and free us."

"No one is aware that we're even in the Louvre," said Leon, "let alone locked in this tomb."

Chris felt himself fall silent as the enormity of their situation washed over him, emotionally knocking him off balance.

"Each precious item in this room has a story to tell," he said. "History tells us there were many very evil men behind all the stolen goods in this room. Broken families, broken hearts—and in so many cases—death." As his mind raced forward, Chris laughed at the absurdity of it all. "Now, with you and me trapped in here, it could very well become a tomb for two men with questionable motives and character."

"And just what do you mean by *that*?" Leon snapped.

"Well, in my case, I was contracted to investigate and identify the source of these masterworks and how they were turning up in high-profile exhibitions. It was a simple, straightforward job, and I would make very good money in the process. Hell, a small fortune where I come from. I had no idea that I'd be dealing with plundered treasures that haven't been seen since the end of World War II.

"I almost lost my life in a major car accident. I lost my memory, and if it hadn't been for an amazing, dedicated trauma nurse, I wouldn't be here today. She not only saved my life, she was also instrumental in helping me to gain back my identity.

"Now, here I am, locked in a tomb with seemingly no chance of escape. I could possibly die with a man I don't know or trust who tells me he's a common worker in the heating and ventilation business. That he was hired to do a side job by an art company, to spy in the Louvre, to achieve the same objectives I was contracted to do.

"Leon, I look at your hands. There are no cuts or bruises, no calluses from hard work. Your clothes are not worn or tattered. The knees of your pants show no signs of wear. So, Leon Martelle, if that's even your real name, have I profiled you correctly? How and why could I trust *any* of the information that you've given me?"

Leon was startled by Chris's sudden, off-the-cuff analysis of him.

"Perhaps you're right in some of your comments, but by working together we *did* figure out entry into this hidden chamber. Leon Martelle is, in fact, my real name. My father is the owner of a large and very successful art gallery here in Paris. *He* is the anonymous person who hired the two Paris police officers to find you. Of course, he's also the one who paid half of your contract fee. He buys, sells, and exports art treasure all over the world—particularly to the United States.

"The market for treasures such as these—as private investments for wealthy people and for museums all over the world—is vast and very lucrative. Your country, with its millionaires and billionaires, is clamoring to get ahold of antiques and old master works. In most cases, buyers in the US don't care about the authentic provenance of the items they purchase. The prestige of owning these possessions far outweighs the risk of getting caught. Besides, 90 percent of the real owners and heirs are gone. Who is even left to make reparations to? It's an impossible task.

"It's very, very sad how all of this came about, but the original owners' love, appreciation, and joy were squeezed out of these inanimate objects a long time ago. I choose to believe these objects need new owners, so they can once again see the light of day. Only then can they be cherished and venerated for the beauty they possess. This is the thinking these days. Whether it's right or wrong, the path of provenance is no longer part of the equation. The world's demand has far outstripped the supply. Private collectors will pay and do whatever it takes to acquire these objects. The money to be made in commissions alone on could make you a millionaire. The objects in this room could make us multimillionaires on the transaction fees alone.

"Listen," Leon said, leaning in close to Chris. "If you can get us out of here alive, I will say—no, no, *I will promise*—that you'll share in all of the profits from the liquidation of these assets."

"That's an interesting proposition, Leon," said Chris with no hint of emotion. "The big question, though, is how will you remove all the treasures from this room without being caught?"

The room fell completely silent. After a moment, Chris nodded his head, as if to say, *That's what I thought.*

"In the meantime," Chris suggested, "let's check out that old safe at the far end of the room. Maybe it has some clues. If we can open it, it might help us figure out how to get out of here."

Both men walked to the safe. Chris looked at it carefully. "I don't think it's been opened since it was put here," he said. "One can only imagine what's inside it."

Nothing about the safe seemed special. In fact, it looked exactly like any other heavy-duty bank safe. The name *Fichet-Bauche* indicated it was indeed of French origin, likely manufactured locally. A real antique. Based on its size and weight, it was probably a commercial storage vault for customer assets.

"Give it a try, Leon," Chris quipped. "Maybe you'll get lucky and it'll open on your very first go. As for me, I assure you, I don't know a thing about safes."

"It would be a waste of my time," said Leon gruffly. "I'll continue my search for an exit."

There was a slight pause in their conversation as they detected the sound of scraping metal coming from the room's entrance. Moments later, a second set of scraping sounds. The two men quickly realized that someone was unlatching the two dead bolts.

A voice from the other side called out, "We're coming in! Do *not* rush the door, I'm armed!"

Chris and Leon froze. It would be fruitless to try and rush whoever it was from the far end of the room. Seconds later, Chris saw his friend Hans Muller enter. He looked gaunt and tired as he approached, seemingly on the verge of collapsing at any moment. As he came closer Chris noticed streaks of dried blood from a wound on the side of his face.

"Are you okay?" Chris asked, rushing to Hans's side.

"Yes, for the moment," said Hans as Chris steadied the old man with his arm. "I'm exhausted. They have Alana. By the entrance. They want you to send this other man in exchange for her." Hans's voice was broken and choppy, as though he were gasping for air from climbing or running. "Maurice's son. Albert. Wants to question him without any of us present. We are all to remain down here. Until they sort things out and they're satisfied, we aren't a threat."

Leon, who'd been listening carefully, blurted out, "I have no problem with that proposal. Come on! Let's do it now!"

Chris's first concern was Alana. He needed to see her face and know that she was okay *before* the exchange took place. As he slowly approached the secret entrance, Chris yelled out his terms, still partially hidden from Albert's view by the entryway.

"That's no problem," he said. "I'm just being cautious. There's an awful lot at stake for me here."

Albert pushed Alana into the room and Chris noticed the gun Albert was pointing at her. Even more alarming, the man's eyes were filled with fear and desperation. Chris had seen this before, a hallmark sign of a person who'd made a bargain with the devil.

For a moment, Chris wondered if Albert was trying to manipulate Leon, or if maybe it was the other way around. Leon's father, with his legitimate art business, might be able to offer Albert and Maurice a safe way out of this mess, maybe even a practical way to continue liquidating all of these hidden treasures worth untold millions. The only loose ends would be Chris and the two Mullers. Chris thought about Leon's earlier offer to share the profits from selling these objects. Only a fool would believe that agreement still stood.

Just then, he heard the sound of two dead bolts slamming into place. He felt his heart fall to his stomach.

I am responsible for this predicament, Chris thought to himself. *Neither Alana—the woman I love—nor her grandfather would be in this position if it weren't for me. I brought this on us all.*

Chris realized they had zero bargaining power with Maurice and Albert. Getting out of there and going to the police was their only recourse if they wanted to stay alive. No negotiation with this pair of desperate men would ever persuade them to let Chris and the Mullers go.

Besides, Chris thought, *I'm a CIA agent again. That's where my loyalty and responsibilities lie. The only real choice I have is to find a way out of this underground tomb.*

With the steel door slammed shut behind her, Alana rushed into Chris's arms. For the moment, she felt protected. "The way things are going today, I didn't think we'd ever see each other alive again," she said. "Now they've imprisoned us. We're totally at their mercy. What could they possibly want?"

"Your grandfather's silence," said Chris, "and now, mine as well. We've discovered their little secret. These people are so greedy, they assume your grandfather's information would be used to extort money from all those private owners they sold to. In today's criminal underworld, you and your grandfather, well, you're what they call *collateral damage.*

"We have nothing to negotiate or bargain with for these mad men. Maybe, just maybe, your grandfather's black ledger could still be used as a bargaining chip. We could also threaten to burn all the objects still in this room."

"You're right; that might've worked," said Alana, "but when they took our phones, they also took my grandfather's book. I fear we have no options. We might as well just give up . . . I need to attend to my grandfather. He may have a slight concussion from that short altercation with Albert. That bully threw him against the wall like he was a feather. That's when he banged his head. Then they blindfolded us and brought us here, stumbling through those damp and musty halls. That made grandfather even more unstable and dizzy. Look, you can see how he is about to collapse from the tension and fatigue.

"Chris," she said holding his arms and staring into his eyes, "I'm afraid he might not make it through the night. This has been a long, tedious, ugly day. Do we have any other options?"

"I don't know. But you're right that your grandfather needs rest, Alana," said Chris. "Take him to that small room next to the entrance. Oddly enough, it seems to have running water and a bunk. I'll help you move him there and then continue my search for another way to get out."

As Chris began to retrace the areas he and Leon had searched before, he realized there was something familiar about this underground bunker. He thought back to that little excursion he and Jay had gone on in Normandy. He'd seen the detailed maps of the German defensive line that had run all along the Atlantic coast, the entire length of France. Hundreds of gun emplacements complete with soldier barracks and bunkers.

He and Jay had walked through some of those underground bunkers. Many of them were buried ten or twenty feet underground. They all had the same profile when viewed from the outside. The German engineers had used the same fabrication techniques and forms to build the external parts of these structures. And why not! It was expedient and required a minimal number of skilled technicians to supervise construction. The interiors could be configured to accommodate whatever military function they needed—a barrack to house soldiers, a communications command center, or heavy gun emplacements. It was a proven design, and a perfect place to hide valuable treasures. All of it had been done with typical German efficiency, allowing them to accelerate their entire construction timetable for the inevitable Allied bombing raids of France.

One thing he and Jay had noticed was that every bunker had multiple ways in and out, strategically placed for entering and exiting depending on the bunker's use. The basic question for Chris as he surveyed the entire room: Where was the other exit? It must be here somewhere, but where? This bunker was a carbon copy of the soldiers' barracks he'd toured. The only thing missing, in this case, were bunks to house the soldiers.

This room, however, was filled with so much tiered shelving—all loaded with art—it was impossible to see if another door had been added. With no exit in plain sight, Chris decided to investigate the wall running parallel to the Seine. *The river,* he thought to himself, *would have been the fastest and most expedient way of getting all the building materials to the construction site. It's also a very fast, discreet way for someone to escape unnoticed from this underground complex.*

Chris remembered that when he'd looked at those French newspaper articles published during the time of Nazi occupation, he'd seen various pictures of two huge construction derricks located very close to the river. It all made sense to him now. He started working his way from the small room where Alana was attending to Hans, a distance of about 115 to 125 feet.

He had to move numerous objects away from the wall slowly to inspect it for marks made by the concrete forms; marks that would have been left behind once the cement had cured and the forms had been removed. He'd noticed these kinds of marks at all the military sites he'd visited. It was a very time-consuming endeavor, but he didn't have any other viable options.

As he continued, his mind drifted away from what he was doing. He was fearful that Albert would return before he'd had a chance to complete his search and he wouldn't be in position to protect Alana and her injured grandfather.

By himself, he might be able to overpower or lure Albert into a trap. With Alana and her grandfather so close to the entrance and Hans already in an unstable condition, though, the risks were far too high. Someone needed to guard the entrance door.

He remembered the comment Albert had made during their exchange of the Mullers for Leon. *There's an awful lot at stake for me here,* he'd said. It was strong evidence that he was plotting an outcome with only his future in mind. Of course, it made perfect sense. It would be a normal reaction for a criminal who was rapidly running out of options: tie up all the loose ends as quickly as possible by whatever means necessary. Chris had experienced this same kind of desperate thinking with career criminals when he'd worked for the CIA.

As Chris continued his search, he became increasingly convinced that Albert had been the man driving the truck that rammed into his car that night. Most likely, it was Albert who used the same hit-and-run technique to dispose of Jean Pierre. No wonder he was desperate and committed to disentangling himself and his father from their dangerous situation. Chris knew Albert would do whatever it took to prevent the police from uncovering their illegal scheme. The stakes were far too high.

Meanwhile, his beloved Alana was in great danger near the front entrance.

Having taken off the bulky and impractical technician's uniform, Chris had given himself better access to his revolver, carefully hidden in one of the special pockets sewn into his traveling jacket. For a moment, he thought maybe he should wait for his abductors by the entrance. If he couldn't negotiate Hans and Alana's release, at least he could cause some damage or maybe get someone's attention once the gun fired. With the door closed, however, there was no point. Also, it could be hours or maybe even days before Maurice and Albert returned. He realized instead he should continue his search for the escape door, which may or may not exist. *Solve the problem*, he told himself, *waiting for an answer isn't part of your DNA.*

Unable to watch the entrance and search at the same time, Chris decided to build a barrier behind the front door to prevent his abductors from making a quick, unannounced entrance into the room. This, he hoped, would allow him enough time to find a fortified area where he could position himself to protect the Mullers.

With the barrier of wooden pallets and packing materials in place, Chris returned to his search of the wall that ran parallel to the Seine. Tired from moving so many artifacts around, he paused for a moment in frustration.

He could see he was now less than twenty feet from the huge safe at the end of the room. He scanned the remaining distance. There were no telltale signs of a door that had been sealed. Chris was perplexed. He was almost positive German logic would dictate the inclusion of a second way out. Hell, no one would build an underground bunker with only one exit. It was a death trap.

As his eyes searched further down the remaining distance to the large safe, he noticed for the first time that the safe wasn't actually sitting on the concrete floor. Rather, it had been placed on large steel plates that were slightly larger than the safe's footprint.

That's odd, he thought, *why would they do that?*

Looking closer, he noticed there were two separate 3/8-inch steel plates, one on top of the other. Curiously, they were not welded together to form a single plate. In fact, their back ends were located inches away from the cement wall. There was just one metal strap. One end of the strap had been welded directly to the safe, while the other end had been bolted to the wall. *Why is there a small gap separating the safe from the wall?* Chris wondered. *Why would they bother to bolt a very heavy safe to anything in the first place? The safe is too heavy to move and it's in a bomb shelter. Few places on earth are anywhere near this secure.*

Chris decided to conduct his lighted match experiment to determine if there was a any air movement at the back end of the safe. The match lit, but he detected nothing. The smoke from the match rose straight up into his nose. The pungent smell of sulfur, however, didn't distract his thinking or quash his desire to continue.

Undeterred, he decided to remove the metal strap holding the safe to the wall. But where would he get the tools? He returned to the small room where Alana and her grandfather rested. He quickly brought them up to date on his progress and returned to the safe with some random tools used for unpacking crates.

In a matter of minutes, he'd broken loose the connecting bracket, freeing the safe from the wall. Jamming the tip of a large crowbar between the safe and the wall, he was able to gain a small toehold. As he applied stronger pressure, the heavy safe started to move *ever so slightly* away from the wall. At first it was only an eighth of an inch. Then, with tremendous effort, he opened a full one-inch gap. Eventually, the distance was big enough for him to wedge a large piece of wood in the gap he'd created.

He slipped his hand in behind the safe and discovered what felt like an opening, though he was unable to determine how large it was. Adrenaline was rushing through him at a feverish pace. He was determined to fully validate his discovery of an escape route and a way out of this mausoleum.

CHAPTER 46

THERE IS NO HONOR AMONG THIEVES

With the two steel doors to Goering's treasure chamber securely locked and the assurance that the Mullers and that snooping investigator were contained for the time being, Albert escorted Leon to the private room where the Mullers had been previously held.

Though his father had blindfolded the Mullers before escorting them to the secret room, Albert didn't even bother with Leon. Given that Leon and this Antone character had figured out where the room was located—not to mention that they'd found the hidden passageway to the entrance—what was there left to hide?

These facts, however, posed another major problem for Albert and his father. If they were going to escape the predicament they were in—and subsequent imprisonment—these four captives must be dealt with. Silenced, if necessary. The question was *how* and *where*?

"Where are you taking me?" Leon asked, as they proceeded through the underground maze of corridors.

"We have a lot to discuss about exactly *why* you were snooping around the Louvre disguised as a maintenance man," Albert responded.

Leon quickly realized Albert was in a desperate position. It would likely require extreme measures for Leon to get out of the equally desperate situation he found himself in. Albert and Maurice's entire scheme was about to unravel, with dire consequences for everyone.

Leon thought about the offer he'd made to Chris earlier. To survive this day, however, he knew he would need to make a much more compelling offer to the desperate father and son who still hoped to escape. *It's funny how quickly one's circumstances can change*, he thought. *There is no loyalty or honor among thieves when your life is at stake.*

Besides, why should he be loyal to people he didn't know? Business was business, and there were huge amounts of money at stake here. The Mullers and this Chris guy were expendable. Leon was quite sure that his father would've made the same decision. *It's the business we're in. With great risk comes great rewards.*

Once inside the room, Leon cut right to the chase: "Albert, Maurice," he said, acknowledging each man in turn, "let me explain to you who I am and how I can help. Soon you'll see for yourselves I am uniquely qualified to help the two of you escape your present situation.

"You see, my father is the owner of a very large art gallery here in Paris. We buy, sell, and trade antiques for customers all over the world. Our main office is located right here in Paris, but we have sales offices internationally, as well. We do business the *traditional way*, with museums and private parties. And also, occasionally, with what you might call *the black market*. As both of you already know, total anonymity is key to a great many of today's art transactions.

"The demand for the world's art far exceeds the supply. Today's collectors are exceedingly rich and don't care about current or original owners. Provenance is not a concern for any of them. They simply want these precious master works, whatever the cost. In almost every case, price is not a deal breaker. Since the war, investment in art has become one of the best hedges against inflation. The underground market is thriving, and we have the capability to sell all the goods you have in your hidden room. No questions will be asked, no provenance required, just a steady stream of money flowing into your bank accounts. It's nearly effortless, I tell you. My father's business has been involved in this kind of activity for many years and he is *highly successful*.

"What I saw when I was locked in that hidden chamber was the biggest fortune in the world." He laughed, amused with himself. "Believe me, I know I'm not telling you something you don't already know. The key is longevity. There is no possible way you could dump all of that art into the market at the same time.

"*Over* time, however, my father and his associates could sell every last item in that room, making the two of you multimillionaires ten times over. We have special relationships with many of the authorities and agencies who track lost and stolen art. It will take some time, and we will need to preserve the secrecy of that room and its contents, but I assure you we will maintain your privacy. We can protect you both from disgrace and going to jail.

"The investigator whom you've now imprisoned downstairs with the Mullers was hired by my father to investigate where the constant supply of lost and stolen art was coming from. My father paid the man a large sum of money to achieve this objective, which he's now accomplished. We can offer the man a sizable bonus to buy his silence. He has no vested interest and, as I have found, most Americans can be easily bought for the right price. In his case, I believe, it will be petty cash. Give him some pocket change and he will run back to that little hick town in Minnesota and no one will be the wiser.

"If that option isn't appealing, we can, of course, make him disappear. He's merely a small-town boy starting a new security business in the United States. Trust me, no one will miss him. He took a job in France, became a bohemian, and simply disappeared. It can be that simple.

"The Mullers, on the other hand, are likely a bigger problem. Hans is Jewish, as you well know, and he lived through horrible times under Nazi rule. He has seen his people persecuted, arrested, tortured, and murdered. You won't buy him off easily. Maybe not at all. He dreams of one day seeing reparations made to the original owners or their heirs. My father is acquainted with him. They were competitors, of a sort, at one time. They both made their living selling art internationally.

"Hans had a distinct advantage over all the other art dealers, however. He was—and remains—a master restorer, possessing unique talent in the refurbishment of Old Master paintings. When customers buy high art from him, they are always assured the art has been repaired and restored impeccably. The provenance of the art was *always* one of his concerns. My father actually used him extensively over the years. He's one of the few people left in the industry capable of doing the kind of delicate work true masterpieces require. He is the last of a dying breed and I fear he won't go quietly.

"Because of his age, Hans has largely retired from doing that kind of work. His health now prevents him from aggressively growing his business. His only heir is his granddaughter, whom he adores, but she shows little interest in taking over his business. Given his present health, I don't think it take much to eliminate him. During the exchange, I couldn't help but notice how fragile and exhausted he looked. He likely won't last long down in that hidden chamber.

"The only remaining problem, then, is what to do with the granddaughter. If her grandfather dies while confined in that chamber, she will hold the two of you accountable and her first stop will be the police. From what I can see, there isn't a clear-cut way to negotiate with her. She works as a nurse and dotes on her grandfather. I'm not sure there's any other leverage, so your options are limited.

"So," Leon said expectantly, "what is your decision: become multimillionaires or rot in jail? Lend me your phone and I can provide you with a document, signed by my father, outlining the proposal I've just offered you."

Desperate situations often require desperate actions. Without question, Leon's proposal gave both Albert and his father a rather quick, plausible solution, but it also meant disposing of two dead bodies.

Possibly three. The question for Albert became a matter of trust. Prior to today, this person had been totally unknown to him and his father. Incredibly, he had all the solutions to their problems. It all seemed a little convenient. Albert needed to take things slow. They'd come this far already—there was no sense in being reckless now.

"As much as I would like to believe and trust you, Leon," Albert said, "I will insist you remain with my father here in our secure office. There will be no outside communication with anyone until I return. Let's see if you hired an American investigator who is willing to negotiate his release, as you so confidently suggested. Then we can decide what further actions are required."

Albert departed, saying with an air of menace, "Wait here. I'll be back shortly."

CHAPTER 47

PREDICTABILITY

Having found a possible escape route, Chris looked for something long and strong enough to create a fulcrum lever. He needed to pry the safe farther away from the wall so he could get a better view of the void hidden behind it.

He glanced down to the base of the safe and noticed a black, gelatinous substance oozing out from between the two steel plates. Embedded in this gooey material were tiny, shimmering but barely visible flecks. He also detected a mild, acid-like odor wafting up from the area. It was a smell he knew very well, one that transported him back to his days on the farm.

"Ball-bearing grease," he mumbled. He'd used it all the time when he helped his father repair and maintain their farm equipment. He started to rub away some of the hardened material, exposing small ball bearings separating the two steel plates. *Of course*, he acknowledged to himself. *After all these years, it makes sense that the grease stiffened, almost to the point of being solid.*

This is brilliant, he thought. *The safe sits on a steel plate that floats on an array of ball bearings.* What an ingenious method of moving heavy objects, most likely the same technology—but on a larger scale—that the Germans had used to swivel their heavy cannons around in their bunkers. He imagined that at one time, a single person could have slid this massive safe away from the wall, revealing the exit with very little effort. After all these years, however, the grease was stiff and ineffective. All he needed to do now was break the slight bond between the large steel plates and the ball bearings.

Excited, Chris rushed back to the small room where the Mullers were waiting. He glanced down at his watch. It was midnight. They'd been in this stagnant bunker for so long. He knew Jay and his French secret police counterpart were not going to storm the Louvre to look for them. That would set off a massive search of the entire premises by a number of police organizations. This, in turn, would expose their secret operation to the media, and eventually the world. Without a doubt, this shocking news would create an international scandal that would rock the museum world, wreak havoc with private collectors, and create a tsunami of lawsuits.

Museums that had purchased or even exhibited artifacts from the Louvre would immediately distance themselves from doing any kind of business with the museum. No one would ever want to be connected to an organization that had worked with Nazi Reichsmarschall Hermann Goering or be associated with all of his stolen goods.

To think that these objects were now being sold illegally by someone who worked at the Louvre was deeply unsettling. There would be accusations of collaboration between French and German authorities. The individuals in charge of museum during the occupation would be branded as traitors and turncoats. The mysterious death of one of the Louvre's top directors, Jean Pierre, and his possible link to the illicit sale of these stolen treasures would cause a firestorm. The public would direct its rage at the Louvre and the French government.

Every international art recovery organization would be at their doorstep demanding justice. They wouldn't stop until they saw every record of what had been sold to whom. The entire world art market would be embroiled in chaos for years.

No, as much as Chris would like to think there might be a last-minute rescue mission for himself and the Mullers—by either the American or French police—it wouldn't happen. If they hoped to survive the night, they must find a way out. And time was running short.

Chris thought about his training with criminal minds. As a CIA agent, he had intimate knowledge about how criminals tended to react when cornered. They'd generally make quick decisions without thinking things through. He'd seen this kind of behavior many times before. Self-preservation overrode logic and rational thinking. Albert and his father were desperate, having amassed a fortune over all the years. They'd already come this far and they weren't about to jeopardize their future now. The way a criminal would see it, Chris and the Mullers were the only thing that stood in the way of successfully evading jail time.

Chris's mind raced to come up with a way to prevent his captors from making a quick entrance into the chamber. He didn't know how much time he had left to pry the safe away from the wall and escape. His eyes scanned the room with urgency. It was a race against time.

"Of course!" he said out loud. "Storage pallets!"

Storage pallets and empty crates made of sturdy hardwood were literally scattered all over the room after having been emptied of their treasures. Chris began to disassemble one to use as the main lever. The board was about three-and-a-half feet long. He hoped it would be long enough to use as a fulcrum arm to pry the heavy safe far enough from the wall.

Chris grabbed a long metal crowbar and began breaking open the other shipping crates in search of a can of lubricating oil.

As he was searching, his mind was preoccupied by *what-if* scenarios. What if Albert broke down his meager barricade and stormed the room with guns blazing? What if he decided to turn off the lights and the ventilation system?

If he were by himself, Chris was confident he could put up a good fight. With Hans and Alana, however, he'd be forced to capitulate quickly. At that point, they'd be done. That would be the end for them all.

Either way, Chris realized he couldn't leave the Mullers alone in the storage room. They'd be safer with him, in the back where he was working. Their proximity would also save precious time when they needed to escape. Besides, he may need to enlist Alana's help to finish prying the safe away from the concrete wall.

With his wood lever, the small can of oil, and the Mullers in tow, Chris hurried back to the safe. There was no time left for any more *what-if* thinking. He quickly ushered them back to the wall where the safe rested. He explained how he'd made a gap that was big enough to insert one end of his makeshift lever. As he began to initiate his plan and apply more pressure to the safe with his device, the safe started moving again. Alana squealed with excitement and joined him in his endeavor, adding whatever strength she could muster. As they pushed and pried together, the safe started breaking its bond between the two metal plates at a faster rate, exposing more and more of the ball bearings. Suddenly they were hit by the smell of stale, damp air flooding the room.

"That's a good sign," Chris said. "The entrance is partially visible, but still not accessible." Chris gestured toward the oil. "Alana, grab the oil and start squeezing it between the two steel plates. We need to lubricate the ball bearings." Chris hoped they had enough oil. A mechanism like this would surely require much more lubricant than a piece of farm machinery. "Try not to use too much," he cautioned. "We may need to use it for other purposes."

Before long, the opening was large enough to see the full, shadowy outline of a small archway with poured concrete form marks. The room's overhead light now cascaded down the wall as the opening got bigger and was fully exposed. Finally, the bunker's hidden secrets were revealed!

There was a short entrance tunnel that led to a small steel door. Surely, beyond that, the tunnel exited the bunker.

As Alana and Chris continued to apply more and more pressure to the fulcrum, the gap widened farther and farther away from the wall. It was now big enough for Alana to slip her shoulder between the safe and the wall. It was quite clear to both of them that this was indeed the special exit route designed by German engineers for a quick escape. Motivated by what they saw, though they were nearly in a state of complete exhaustion, Chris and Alana worked together to force the safe far enough that someone could enter the door's small threshold in a stooped position.

"What do you see, Alana?" Chris asked excitedly. "How far can you go into the tunnel?"

"Not far," she replied, in a frantic, somewhat disheartened voice. "There's another steel door that has a lock on it. It's definitely the way out of here. I think if we can somehow open this rusted steel door, we'll be home free."

As Alana turned to reenter the bunker, she noticed a leather pouch attached to the back of the safe. There was a swastika stenciled on it and a series of German words with Reichsmarschall Hermann Goering's signature below them.

She handed the pouch to Chris and said, "Listen. The room's gone completely silent. The hum of the ventilation system is gone."

She was right, and Chris hadn't noticed. It seemed she was becoming a bit of an agent in her own right. He liked the way she thought.

"That could mean one of two things," he said. "There was an equipment failure, which I highly doubt, or someone shut the system down. Either way, I'm sure we can expect undesirable company soon."

Chris removed the contents of the leather pouch. In his hand, he held a small book full of numbers and a set of keys. He handed the book and the pouch to Alana. "Your grandfather speaks German," he said. "We need him to interpret these two items immediately."

Hans had been resting nearby, watching his granddaughter and Chris endeavor to uncover this potential escape route. He was not yet fully recovered from the blow he'd received during his altercation with Albert earlier in the day. Thankfully, his dizziness had abated. Now, the excitement of finding a way out of the chamber energized him, helping him find the strength to stand.

Alana handed Hans the pouch and ledger. The sight of the swastika on the pouch unnerved him. That indelible symbol of hatred and death once again conjured up the horrible events he'd been forced to witness so long ago. He could never erase from his mind those sickening sights and sounds: train whistles, crying children, screams of desperation, murder—all of it rushed to the surface, flooding his mind.

"Are you okay, Grandfather?" Alana asked.

"Yes, it's okay," he said, his voice weighed down by sadness. "Give me a moment, please." Fighting to hold back his emotions, Hans slowly began to read, interpreting out loud for them in English.

"'By order of the Führer,'" Hans recited, "'the contents of this safe and this bunker are the sole property of Reichsmarschall Hermann Goering. Anyone caught tampering with or removing these items will be shot on sight.'"

Hans paused. They all stared at each other, contemplating the ominous words Hans had just read. Hans stared at the cover of the small black ledger. It also bore the swastika. He almost felt paralyzed, fearful that touching it would cause him pain. With his heart full of dread, he started to flip through the book's pages. He gasped loudly and sharply, as though his breath had been sucked away.

"You're not going to believe this," he said, "but this ledger appears to be a chronological listing of the money and safe deposit boxes Hermann Goering sent to various international banks. Dates, times, amounts . . . there are hundreds of entries!" Hans was aghast. "Look here," he said, pointing to one of the pages, "I think this series of numbers separated by dashes must be the combination to this very safe."

Chris and Alanna's mouths hung open in disbelief. It was a staggering discovery. All their work had paid off.

"Perhaps we can use this ledger as a bargaining chip," he said, "and trade it for our lives."

Chris glanced at Alana, his eyes a mixture of concern and confidence. "I studied the history of this in college," he said. "We were shown copies of documents from the Nuremberg Trials; specific documents that pertained to the looting of money, jewels, bonds, silver, and gold—you name it. Hermann Goering's notorious squads were known to strip banks of personal safety deposit boxes from every country they invaded. Much of this loot was thought to be recovered after the war, but there was no way of knowing for sure. Now we finally know the truth.

"What we just discovered will undoubtedly shake up the banks all over Europe. Because of their neutrality, I would guess Swiss banks were the main recipients of most of this wealth. Goering was no fool. He set himself up to be a rich man, regardless of who won the war. They say it was a fortune worth hundreds of millions of dollars, but it was forever tainted by the brutal methods he and his stooges used to acquire it. In the end, his involvement in war crimes destroyed any chance of his survival. Like Hitler, Goering ended up committing suicide. He went to his grave with the secret of his hidden personal fortune. *Until now*, that is."

Alana was the first to hear the sound of metal scraping on metal. First one dead bolt, then the other. With the two newly discovered keys in hand, Chris slipped behind the safe, into the escape entrance.

Thankfully, there was just enough light for him to locate the lock and try one of the keys. He vigorously tried to get it open, with no results. Frantic, he removed the first key and inserted the other. That key seemed to fit, but he was only able to turn the lock a short way. He decided to remove the key and squirt some of the lubricating oil into the lock and onto the key. Jiggling the key carefully, he heard the familiar sound of the locking latch disengaging.

Applying heavy force with his shoulder, the door began to open. As it swung out wide, Chris saw a long, dark tunnel. There was a light switch on the wall, so he flipped it on. To his astonishment, it worked. A series of lights glowed, naked bulbs ensconced in heavy-duty wire cages leading to what looked like stars off in the distance.

He chuckled to himself. *Those German bunker builders were certainly consistent*, he thought. *It's the exact same design we saw in Normandy at the German ramparts. There, German foot soldiers had been dispatched to guard the Third Reich's gun emplacements. Those tunnels were also lit with protected overhead lights.*

Chris knew he didn't have enough time to check out the rest of the tunnel. He was sure Albert was working to break down his flimsy barricade. If the three of them didn't make it all the way to the stairs, they'd be trapped in the tunnel, the perfect place for Albert to make them disappear for good. He must get Alana and Hans out, and quickly.

He returned to the main chamber and was immediately met by the sounds of someone trying to force his way through the barricade.

"Quickly," he said to Alana, motioning toward the tunnel's entrance. "You and Hans need to get out of here. I know this is the way. I've seen this design before. I'll hold off Albert. I'll shoot him if I must, but you two need to get going.

"You'll encounter another door or possibly a gate that should open quite near the river." He handed Alana the keys. "Here, you'll need to take these. The second key must open the lock at the other end of this tunnel. If that lock's like this one, you'll need to squirt some of this oil into the lock and onto the key. Be careful. The key is old and brittle. You don't want to break it off in the lock." He handed her his phone. "Please take this, as well. It won't do any good down here, but once you're on the stairs, near the outside, your movements will show up on Jay's tracking screen. Once he sees you, he'll be there with the cavalry."

"What is the *cavalry*?" Alana asked, confused.

"It means—never mind," said Chris. "I'll explain it to you later. It's an American expression, but it's a good thing. It means that you'll be rescued."

They held each other tightly and kissed. He hoped with all his heart that this wouldn't be the last time he'd feel Alana's warm, soft lips on his own. Alana and her grandfather disappeared into the tunnel. Chris watched them as long as he dared, then turned to face whatever fate lay in front of him.

Having doused all the ball bearings between the two steel plates with oil, Chris could now easily maneuver the safe back to its original position. It was purely a cautionary move, in case he would be unable to stop Albert from gunning him down. Alana and her grandfather needed to survive, whatever happened to Chris.

He closed his eyes and breathed deeply to slow his heart rate, contemplating his next move. A stalling tactic was warranted in this situation. He had to give Alana and Hans time to exit the tunnel and meet up with Jay. He also needed time to try to defuse the situation. Albert was excitable and unpredictable. Chris needed to stop him from doing something drastic. He knew the man was now desperate to salvage his life and his business. Undoubtedly, he was in survival mode, his attention laser-focused on eliminating any danger to himself and his father. It was all but certain that the two Mullers and Chris himself were his first priority.

CHAPTER 48

IS THERE TIME ENOUGH FOR A RESCUE?

"Sir! You need to see this," said the computer technician. "Something very strange just showed up on the tracking screen. It's your agent Chris's phone, and it looks like he's still in the Louvre."

Jay Ludicina had been with the agency since his graduation from the University of Notre Dame, top in his class with honors. He'd worked his way up through the ranks of the CIA with dedication to the job and a fierce sense of patriotism. Working as a field agent in his younger years, his adherence to these values had been quickly recognized by the top echelons of the agency. Before long, he'd become one of the youngest field directors in the organization's history.

Almost immediately, Jay was respected by the agents who worked both *with* and *for* him. They prized his thoroughness, attention to detail, and uncanny ability to analyze and assess critical situations. Every agent knew when Jay Ludicina led an operation, he would cover their backs. Jay had lost fewer agents than anyone else at the agency and he was driven to keep it that way.

The technician narrowed the field of view to the specific zone at the Louvre where the phone was signaling. On this signal he superimposed an outline of the Louvre's physical structure—its interior and exterior walls, as well as other architectural features, sidewalks, roads, and vegetation.

The technician gasped, his eyes open wide in amazement.

"What is it?" Jay asked.

"From what I'm seeing, whoever has that phone just slipped through one of the Louvre's exterior walls. One minute the signal was here," he said, pointing to a location within the Louvre. "The next minute it was outside," he said, pointing to the current position as it moved toward the river. "I know the system is working. I double-checked myself, but that's impossible. The map must be misaligned."

"On the contrary," said Jay. "Whoever has that phone just exited the Louvre through a hidden tunnel built by the Germans decades ago."

"What did you—how did you—*what*?" the technician stammered, completely dumfounded.

By then, Jay wasn't listening. He'd already picked up his phone and dialed his counterpart with the French secret service. Their conversation was quick and succinct.

"I need an armored boat," said Jay, calmly but with a sense of urgency. "No, it's just the two of us, but I'm confident we can handle it . . . Yes, I know where the boat pickup area is . . . Yes, of course, I agree, but we must hurry. They're somewhere in the middle of a long underground tunnel. I can't *confirm* it's my agent, but wherever he is, he's going to need our assistance. I fear someone may have unmasked him. I think he could well be in danger."

There was a lengthy pause. Jay listened to his colleague carefully before he finally spoke. "Yes, I understand," he said. "We'll be fine on our own. Your inside man, however, may need some assistance. I think we need to greenlight your backup plan and bottle them up discreetly. If we execute the protocol quickly, we can eliminate any local police involvement and prevent this operation from ever getting to the media and into the public eye."

Jay listened anxiously. His patience was now wearing thin. Every moment they didn't act exposed Chris to more danger. "Yes, yes, I consent," he said hurriedly. "You and your agency will have complete control. I'm sure you have procedures on how to handle these very delicate matters in order to protect your country's honor and reputation. But if we don't pull this off *now*, I guarantee your biggest problem *won't be* collateral damage."

A small but lethally armed and armored boat motored up alongside the Louvre's shoreline on the river Seine. Jay and Antonio, his colleague from the French secret police, scanned the area, looking for any sign of the place where this mysterious tunnel emerged out into the world.

Neither one of them needed to say it. Both men knew this was the same location where barges and heavy equipment had been located during the war. The newspaper articles Jay had given Chris confirmed it. Countless tons of construction materials had been unloaded on this very shore, allegedly to make improvements to the museum to reinforce it against bombardment. Very few people knew that during this same time, German engineers were busily constructing a maze of underground escape tunnels and bomb shelters that weren't designed to protect the Louvre. No, this underground maze was for an entirely different purpose.

With the sun still several hours from rising, the darkness was nearly impenetrable. The entire shoreline was covered with vegetation and bushes, making it very difficult to see any significant distance inland. Jay imagined there must be some vestigial signs of the heavy equipment that had torn up and reshaped this land, but in the darkness he couldn't see any such traces. The manmade disturbances had faded over the years, melting back into the landscape, forgotten by history.

After a few more minutes of searching in vain, Jay instructed the captain to find a spot on the shoreline where he and Antonio could land and go ashore. Earlier, before Jay had left the mobile tracking van, he'd instructed the technician to transfer all the GPS information on Chris's phone to his own.

Now that they were on land, his strategy was to lock onto Chris's phone coordinates and intercept whoever carried the device as they exited the tunnel. When he looked at his phone, however, Jay quickly noticed the tracking signal in question had hardly moved from its earlier position.

"This is not a good sign," he said with a twinge of concern. "They appear to have stopped. Something must have slowed them down. A physical barrier maybe, or a confrontation with someone who'd been following them? Quick, we need to hurry. According to the GPS coordinates, they're still at least thirty-five meters from the river."

Antonio interrupted. "Forget the phone location for now. There's nothing we can do about that. We need to start walking parallel to the river and find the tunnel's entrance."

The two changed direction and walked back the other way. It didn't take long before they found a drainage ditch that meandered back toward the Louvre. Moving quickly now, their feet wet and caked with mud, they came upon a large cement culvert. Without hesitation, Jay crouched down and began to enter. He activated the light on his phone and immediately saw, not ten meters in front of him, a large, heavy steel door.

He ran to it and banged with his fist. "Is there anyone in there?" he yelled, waiting for a response. "Hello . . .?"

Moments later, a woman's voice called out. "Yes! The door is stuck," she said. "We can't push it open. I think it's been rusted shut."

Jay removed his Swiss Army knife, the knife he'd carried with him since his days at Notre Dame. He quickly but carefully began to scrape the rust from between the door and the door jamb. Working with practiced precision, it didn't take long to remove the caked layers of rust.

"Apply pressure from the inside," he called to the woman. "Antonio, help me pull."

With the two of them pulling as hard as they could from the outside and Alana leaning her shoulder into the door with all her might, it reluctantly broke open with a mighty groan and a shower of reddish dust.

After they'd exchanged brief but excited greetings, Jay ushered Alana and Hans out into the open. In the cool night air, he debriefed the Mullers quickly and radioed to boat, telling the captain to expect two new passengers, one of whom required medical attention.

That part of their mission complete, Jay looked at Antonio and gave a brief, affirmative nod. Then he took a deep breath and plunged back into the dark tunnel with Antonio right on his heels. The cavalry was coming.

CHAPTER 49

THE ART OF NEGOTIATION

Albert was desperately trying to push back the door to enter Goering's hidden chamber. The door was clearly unlocked, but whatever his prisoners had piled up behind it as a barricade, Albert was unable to move by himself. He'd been shoving for quite some time, but all he achieved so far was a small opening that would measure less than eight inches.

"Hey, you! American boy! I've got a deal for you!" he yelled through the gap. "I had an interesting conversation with your friend and your *companion*. You know, that guy who helped you break into the Louvre? You both have committed a French federal crime. Both of you are wanted by the Sûreté Nationale, the French national police. If I were to turn you in, you'd get significant jail time, and I would become a hero."

Albert paused but didn't hear anything by way of response. He couldn't even be sure that the meddlesome American investigator was there to listen; all he could do was press on, putting his cards on the table.

"You're in luck!" Albert continued, confirming Chris's suspicions by connecting the dots. "It turns out that the man who *helped you* is the son of the man who's *paying you* a large sum of money to investigate the source of all the mysterious art turning up in museums throughout Europe.

"Hey, are you listening? It's awfully quiet in there. The temperature and humidity should be building up in that room, now that I've shut off the heating and cooling systems. How is *Mr. Muller*? I imagine it must be difficult for an elderly gentleman such as himself. It's going to get worse, you know. I still have some other options to make your stagnant environment even more miserable. I will smoke you out one way or another.

"How is Hans holding up? I must say, I'm a bit worried. If he *dies in there*, you know, his death will be on your hands. It's just a matter of time before I break through your flimsy barricade.

"I have to give you some credit, though. It was an interesting ploy to try to unnerve me. Too bad it won't work. It's ironic, don't you think? You've barricaded yourselves in, even as you barricaded me out. There's one crucial difference, however, a major flaw in your plan that you failed to consider. I have plenty of food and water, not to mention *fresh air* and *time*. You don't have these things and I'm the *only one* who can give them to you. I'm the gatekeeper and I can wait you out. I control *everything*.

"Think of the air that you're breathing. I know it seems stale and stuffy. Maybe I should pump in some toxic chemicals. Would that help you make up your mind a little more quickly? Let's talk. There's no harm in that, is there?"

As Chris listened to Albert, he was determined to keep himself grounded. If he'd learned anything in his time at the CIA it was the importance of keeping an even keel. Whoever managed to stay calm held the upper hand. If he refused to respond to Albert's threats, he could challenge the man's patience and stall for time. The longer he kept Albert's attention, the greater chance Alana and Hans had to find their way out.

Fifteen minutes had passed since they had entered the tunnel. He knew eventually they would encounter another door or barrier. Chris was confident the keys he'd given them would work, but would the two of them be able to get the door open? Would it also be rusted shut and virtually immobile from decades of disuse? For all Chris knew, that door had remained unopened since the very day the war ended, maybe even longer than that.

He decided to focus on the positives instead.

The room the Mullers had been in—where Chris was standing now—was at least twenty feet underground. It was signal-proof, both for sending and receiving. As Alana and Hans traveled through the tunnel, however, they'd continue to climb and get closer to ground level. At that point, Jay's surveillance team and their tracking equipment should be able to locate the Mullers' signal. The instant that happened, Chris knew, Jay would initiate extraction protocol without hesitation. Notably, if Jay and his team received that signal while it was still dark, the entire operation would remain unseen, hidden from the media as well as the public.

Calculating quickly, Chris concluded that not enough time had passed for the Mullers to reach the surface. He broke his silence and responded to Albert.

"What is it, exactly, that you want to talk about, Albert?" he asked loudly but calmly, seemingly unperturbed by the predicament he was in.

As Albert had spoken, Chris had moved within twenty feet of the door. He remained out of sight, but he had a clear view of the door's opening and the progress Albert had made in breaking down the barricade. Chris smiled to himself. He was surprised to see Albert had made very little progress. In fact, in his desperation to open the door, the man had managed to compact some of the barricade materials so tightly the wall had been strengthened; another data point that underscored how preparation is key. *By failing to prepare*, Chris thought, *you are preparing to fail. It's funny how much truth such axioms contain.*

"Well, for starters," Albert responded, "your client's son just informed me that you've *already met* the conditions of your contract with his father. He says you will get all the money you were promised . . ."

Albert had miscalculated. Since he was a greedy man, he'd assumed Chris was, too. Albert was confident that once Chris was free from his obligation, he would take the money and run. Albert didn't know that, for Chris, it had never been purely about the money, *especially* now with the future he envisioned with Alana.

Chris held his tongue. He could hear Albert's voice starting to crack. "I have much more good news to share," he said, "but only after you remove the barrier behind the door. We need to talk face to face. I'm sure we can work it all out. For the benefit of both parties. You can walk away and go back to America a very rich man!"

Chris let Albert's words hang for a minute before he finally responded. "And what about the Mullers?" he wanted to know.

"Yes, yes, of course. We will make them rich and happy too. I understand. You can trust me on this. I know how you feel."

Chris knew there was no way Hans could ever be bought off. The money was not important to him. He was a man of principle, with a good heart and strong values. His only objectives since the day his beloved Elsa was killed so senselessly were to help his granddaughter and to fulfill the promise he made to his wife as they'd watched thousands of people be put on railcars and shipped to the Nazis' horrific death camps. Reparations to the people who died—or at the very least, their heirs—for the countless treasures Hitler and Goering had stolen, *that* was his singular goal. No amount of money, *nothing*, would dissuade Hans from trying to achieve that until he'd breathed his last breath.

Chris knew Albert thought he controlled the situation, but Chris continued to string him along, giving the Mullers as much time as possible to make their escape. He waited silently as he imagined Albert squirming. Chris could almost see the feverish sweat forming, the anxiety taking control of Albert's thoughts.

Finally, he said, "Trust is *earned*, not given, Albert. We have a long way to go in our relationship before I'll give that trust. I'll remove the barrier on two conditions. One, no weapons of any kind, including that taser you love. It's just you and me in that small, private room adjacent to the door. Two, the Mullers remain where they are, out of sight and out of earshot, hidden in the back corner."

Chris hoped Albert had bought into the idea that the Mullers were still hidden somewhere in the room. *How could he ever imagine we moved the safe and found the tunnel?* Chris wondered. Hell, there was a decent chance Albert had no idea the tunnel even existed.

Albert was frustrated by the present situation and desperate to tie up these irksome loose ends. He didn't want to resort to other, more forceful tactics to gain entrance, nor did he wish to delay the confrontation he knew was coming. In his ignorance, he firmly believed he still had the upper hand. There wasn't a doubt in his mind he would win this bothersome battle; besides, he had another trick up his sleeve.

"All right," Albert responded. "I will take out the ammunition and slide my gun where you can see it. It's the only weapon I have, I promise."

Chris heard the metallic sound of the bullets dropping on the floor. Seconds later, the gun sild across the floor and came to rest halfway into a shaft of light.

"There," Albert called out.

"Slide your phone in, as well," Chris responded. "I can't let you have a way to call in reinforcements."

"The signal won't work down here," Albert countered.

"Do it now!" Chris insisted.

"Okay, okay," Albert muttered to himself. *There is no harm in giving up my phone*, Albert thought. *It won't work anyway.*

Chris methodically began to dismantle the barricade. Once it was taken down, Chris swung the door open further and let Albert come in. Their eyes stayed locked on each other's until they sat down on opposite sides of the table.

"Hands where I can see them," said Chris.

Albert put his hands on the table and spoke. "For somebody trapped in a very difficult situation, you seem quite calm," he said. "Have you already made your decision?"

"As a matter of fact, I have," Chris said. "Your proposal sounds like it's too good to be true. You and your father are in a heap of trouble. Quite frankly, I know that you're both in survival mode. The Mullers and myself are the only obstacles preventing the two of you from escaping cleanly and getting away with crimes against humanity."

Albert could feel Chris's eyes bearing down on him. He moved uncomfortably, unsure where things were going.

"As far as I'm concerned," said Chris, "the things that you and your father have done are just as bad as Hitler and Goering, and the entire Nazi regime. You're criminals of the lowest kind. Getting rich through illegal sales of treasures that were stolen from thousands of innocent people, not to mention other countries and famous museums. There are immeasurable stories of people, most of whom were Jewish, sent off to prison camps to starve to death or worse. You had a legitimate business. You didn't need to stoop so low; to profit off the backs of others."

Albert was stunned by Chris's accusations and the amount of blame Chris was laying at his feet. He felt his blood pressure skyrocket, and he was instantly overcome by a severe headache. Chris's words had cut so deep and triggered Albert so emotionally, he was speechless. In his typical hothead fashion, he reached down quickly and removed the small gun from his ankle holster. He looked straight into Chris's eyes.

"I should shoot you right here," he said, pointing the revolver at Chris's head, "but I don't want to clean up the mess. No, I have a better plan for you and the Mullers. You see, a long, long time ago, the Louvre started out as a castle. Castles, as you must know, have hidden rooms and *dungeons*. My father is the only living soul who knows where these places are. Where the three of you are going, no one will ever find you. You will all simply disappear without so much as a trace."

As Albert said this, Jay and Antonio continued to stealthily work their way through the tunnel to the hidden chamber. They could hear two men's voices at the far end of the room. Jay knew one of them must be Chris. In a flash, his intuitive reasoning suggested Chris was in danger and probably being held at gunpoint. From what Jay was hearing, it sounded like Chris was following his training, holding his antagonist's full attention by prolonging the conversation. Sometimes precious seconds are the difference between life and death.

Jay signaled for Antonio to remain completely silent and they methodically began to work their way across the chamber. Before long, they were hiding on either side of the door into where Albert held Chris. Jay signaled his colleague and they simultaneously burst into the room, yelling for Albert to drop his gun.

Shocked and stunned, Albert shouted, "How in the world did you people get into this hidden chamber?" He turned his gun toward the two intruders. This was the moment Chris had been waiting for. He immediately slid both of his hands under the metal table and swung it upward with amazing force and violence. The table slammed into Albert's chest, forcing his arm straight up toward the ceiling, discharging the bullet harmlessly. Albert's body catapulted backward, smashing his head against the concrete wall. In an instant Albert had been rendered unconscious with a severe head wound that was bleeding profusely.

It was 3:00 a.m. by the time Albert was silently and discreetly taken to the hospital in an emergency vehicle. His early diagnosis indicated that he had three broken ribs and a fractured ulna to go with his head wound. The swelling in his brain was already so severe he would have to be put into a coma in order to survive.

It had been a harrowing twenty-four hours for the Mullers and Chris. After emerging from the tunnel, the Mullers were taken by boat to the parking lot where they'd initially parked their car. Not wanting to take any chances with her grandfather's health, Alana immediately took Hans to the hospital where she worked. He was given a complete checkup, put on an IV to replace his bodily fluids, and told he could go home. Like everything else about the night's incident at the Louvre, there would be no record of Hans's hospital treatment or ambulance ride. Alana, having worked long hours and midnight shifts in the trauma unit for years, recovered from her own minor injuries very quickly.

Once the dust finally settled, Jay corralled Chris and Antonio and asked to be debriefed, top-level assessment only, with a full report to be filed after everyone had the chance to go home, get some rest, and recover from this ordeal.

Maurice and Leon were put under house arrest, fully isolated from the world and each other—no outside contact at all. They would also be debriefed and thoroughly interrogated by the French secret service. No doubt they would be embroiled in a long, grueling investigation.

Three days later, Alana was called into the hospital's trauma recovery unit. A recently admitted patient had undergone major surgery to relieve the life-threatening pressure on his brain. Because of her well-known success with a patient who'd suffered similar brain injuries recently, the surgeon in charge had requested Alana's assistance.

"Where am I?" the man asked, slowly emerging from his coma. "I can't remember anything. Wait, are you an angel? You sure look like one to me. Your voice is so soft and kind . . ."

"Shhh. Your name is Albert and you need to rest. My name is Alana. I'm your nurse. Don't worry about a thing. You're in good hands now. I will take care of you."

EPILOGUE

Several weeks had passed since the Louvre's hidden chamber was discovered. No news reports had been published about Hermann Goering's secret vault full of stolen masterpieces, much less anything about the perpetrators behind the illegal scheme that had been flooding ill-gotten art into European exhibitions. Only a handful people in the top levels of the French government were ever informed as to what took place at the Louvre. It was determined that this terrible injustice was to remain a secret until a plan and a process to return the stolen pieces was put in place. Unless the original owners or their heirs were properly identified—unless there was provenance—the authorities would be perpetuating the cycle, simply moving these treasures from one illegitimate owner to another.

The mysterious death of the Louvre's top director, Jean Pierre Rolland, was no longer a matter of national interest. The final police report concluded he'd been killed accidentally. No further evidence surfaced to refute this conclusion. Since the man had no heirs, as far as anyone could determine, the body was cremated and the case was closed.

The stolen art found in Jean Pierre's car and at his residencies was all recovered. A major investigation was underway to determine how this man had amassed such a prodigious collection of world-famous antiques.

A final, private meeting between the Mullers, Chris Da Vita, Jasper "Jay" Ludicina, and his French counterpart, Director Antonio Delacroix, took place in a small town outside Paris. Antonio was the first to speak.

"I asked Jay to set up this private gathering to share some of the official and *non-official* actions that have been undertaken, as well as those that will happen in the coming months. No doubt, this entire crime will take years to disentangle, resolve, and mend.

"The German ledgers found in the safe are providing my agents with very valuable information as to the ownership of much of the stolen property found in the Louvre's bunker. It's remarkable how the Nazis kept such accurate documents and highly detailed inventories of their heartless thievery. This documentation is proving to be of great assistance as we determine the true provenance of each item. All of that information, combined with Hans's family ledger and the documents he kept while imprisoned in the Berlin rail station, will enable us to track down many of the original owners."

Antonio turned toward Hans with a light in his eyes. "Hans, I have some really good news for you," he said. "The gold jeweled box found in Jean Pierre's car trunk was stolen from a Polish synagogue during the Nazi invasion in 1939. Even as we speak, negotiations are taking place to repatriate it back to that synagogue. The four-hundred-year-old Monet painting found in Jean Pierre's trunk was taken from a famous museum in Warsaw during that same invasion. It's already on its way home, where it belongs.

"Hans, after all these years, the promise you and your wife made to each other is being fulfilled. But this is only the beginning. The French government, with this discovery of Goering's personal treasure vault, can and will use this opportunity to heal some of these wounds and crimes against humanity.

"I am sorry to say, the three of you will never get the recognition you all deserve for helping the government and Interpol. The three of you cracked this case. I know it was not your intention to get involved in this dangerous affair; you all became entangled due to a strange set of events and circumstances.

"The French government is deeply indebted to all of you. The prime minister has been fully informed about everything that happened. We have his total support in resolving all the issues we face. He *personally* asked me to pass on his congratulations and thanks, including to you, Jay. Your efforts helped the Louvre avert national disgrace and worldwide condemnation. Our prime minister's authorized the formation of a special, dedicated art recovery team with Hans as one its key members.

"The goal of this team will be to repatriate the entire contents of Goering's bunker. A special group of art historians are being assembled to tackle this gargantuan problem. They have been charged not only with identifying each remaining piece's original owner, but also tracking down all the items previously sold to other museums and private collectors. If needed, we will leverage the full force of the French national courts and any relevant international bodies.

"A huge amount of money, gold, silver, jewelry, and other valuable items was stashed in the safe you moved to make your incredible escape. That, along with Rolland's private savings accounts in Switzerland, will be used to buy back all the items illegally sold and return them to the original owners. I gave my word to the prime minister that we will not rest until we've achieved this objective. It will take time, of course, but the task will be completed.

"Maurice and his son Albert may have avoided going to jail, but they're certainly not off the hook. Chris, I'm sorry to say, there is no definitive proof that they were the perpetrators of your accident, though we know they are almost certainly the villains behind this vicious act. Their freedom is tied to a number of conditions to which they must adhere, the most important being that they will never reveal any information about the existence of a hidden Nazi chamber full of stolen art deep below the Louvre. If either of them defies this condition, there will be an automatic prison sentence in solitary confinement *for both of them* for the rest of their natural lives. Maurice will retire from the Louvre with great fanfare and recognition for his many contributions during his lifetime of work there. During his career he played a major role in protecting and preserving national treasures.

"Due to Albert's irreparable mental impairment suffered as a result of the *accident* he suffered at the Louvre, he will become a ward of the state. At this point in his therapy, it appears he will never recover his memory. We have reason to believe Albert was the perpetrator of the hit-and-run that killed Jean Pierre, but no indisputable facts have been uncovered to substantiate this belief. And since Albert is incapable of standing trial, there is nothing to be gained by further investigating this unfortunate crime.

"Now, on the bright side, the French government have seen fit to compensate the three of you for your incredible efforts. Unlikely as it may seem, several long-standing rewards for information about the recovery of stolen goods from the war are still in effect. These reward moneys will go to each of you as these treasures are officially repatriated. It will take some time, of course, to sort out the numerous complex legal issues, but it will definitely be worth your wait.

"What you three have achieved here in taking down *one* illegal art scheme is just the beginning. We hope to use the testimony of those behind these sales to help us put an end to at least some of these black-market activities. What we've uncovered so far is the tip of a huge underground art market. These illegitimate businesses exist all over the world. Several are here in France. Because of your efforts, however, we have uncovered and compiled evidence, methods, and names to successfully pursue many other perpetrators. The major link you uncovered here gives us new impetus, as well as a road map, to break up this cabal of worldwide black marketers.

"Your black book, Hans, which shows provenance of so many master art pieces, well, it enables us to *legally prove* and *authenticate ownership* of numerous art treasures. We also believe the information in your book can be used as leverage to force other art dealers to stop their illicit activities.

"So, Hans, with your help, together we can fulfill the promise you made to your wife and to the thousands of Nazi theft victims."

Their celebration continued for some time. In one corner of the room, a discreet conversation took place between Chris and Jay. Jay congratulated Chris on a job well done. "There were some very tense moments while we tracked you, Chris. I fought the temptation to send in the cavalry and rescue the three of you. Had I done that, it would have blown this whole operation completely wide open. People all over the world would know about the shady operations that transpired at the Louvre. It would have become a public relations disaster for France and the world's art community.

"I want you to know that I was not being cavalier or jeopardizing your life at any point during this operation. Director Delacroix's people were inside and ready to intervene at any time if necessary. We always had a plan B, but I was confident things would never go that far. Chris, more than anyone else, I have total confidence in your ability to handle *any* situation. You're one of the best damn agents who's ever worked for me. You have an analytical mind; you're quick on your feet; and you make well thought-out decisions. You're also a quick learner. Case in point, I took you to Normandy for a number of reasons, not just to recruit you back to the agency. I wanted you to see and experience *firsthand* German construction techniques and their building designs.

"As you know, I was also a student of World War II history. I studied German leadership, with specific emphasis on Hitler and Goering. Goering was a mega-thief and a hoarder. Without question he was a *very evil* man. His many homes were filled with other people's treasures, but the more he acquired, the more he wanted. He ran out of space for all his possessions while the war's outcome was still in the balance. I am guessing, but it makes sense, he decided there was no better place than Paris, a city restricted from bombing, to hide his wealth and treasures.

"Win or lose the war, Goering was desperate to retain his wealth. The German underground bunker technology was proven to be successful—why not use it to protect his precious art? I know you've read plenty of Parisian news articles published during the time of Nazi occupation. You toured the German defensive structures in Normandy. I knew your analytical mind would solve the problem."

Jay paused for a moment as a wry smile grew across his face.

"I have an unexpected job offer for you, my friend: to remain with the agency and work with the French government in helping to repatriate Goering's stolen goods. You're the perfect man for it. You have contacts here, you speak the language, and you have personal access to one of the world's best master art advisers. As you heard, Antonio has already given the green light to hire Hans as a key member of the special recovery team in France. With you on that team, on behalf of the USA, I know we will be able to coordinate our efforts with Antonio's people and resolve the many issues we both have with the endless stream of illegal art that's being sent to the United States."

Jay smiled again and swirled the ice cubes in his glass.

"You don't have to make your decision now," he said. "I suspect you might want to discuss this with Alana and Hans first. By the way, when you signed those government documents in Bayeux reinstating you as a CIA agent, well, I think you know, as a government employee, you cannot accept rewards or special compensation for doing your job."

The two men looked at each other, grinning like schoolboys, and burst into unbridled laughter.

Alana appeared and took Chris's arm, pulling herself closer. "What's so funny?" she asked. "What did I just miss?"

How did I not see it? Chris asked himself. *During this whole crazy adventure, Jay was slowly luring me back. I should know by now he's always thinking of every possible angle, every contingency. He's thought through things a hundred times and he never makes a move unless his plan is foolproof.*

"Nothing, my love," Chris responded, wrapping his arm around her waist. "Jay was just reminding me how important it is to make sure you consider every possibility."

"Well, I need to get to the hospital," said Alana. "I have a new patient who's lost his memory. They say he'll never recover and I suspect they're right." She looked up at Chris with a gleam in her eye. "It takes a very special person to come back from something like that."

ACKNOWLEDGMENTS

IT WAS A DAUNTING TASK TO WRITE THIS BOOK.

Telling a story out loud is one thing, but sitting down, putting your thoughts and ideas on paper, and mapping out your plot is quite a challenge. When I was in my late forties, I put together a list of one hundred things I wanted to accomplish during my lifetime. Completing and publishing a book was high on the list at that time. However, family priorities came first so this endeavor got pushed off to a retirement project for me in my eighties.

What really reignited my desire to get moving was my wife's diagnosis of an advancing stage of Alzheimer's. My companion, my partner, and my soulmate was being stolen from me, little by little, through this insidious disease. We had talked about my project many times but with no action on my part. With her communication skills starting to degrade, but international travel still in our grasp, we decided to attempt two final trips. The places that had eluded us all these years, Jerusalem and Normandy, were foundational to getting my mind back on track to complete the book.

With our trips behind us, one of my first stops was to the Stillwater Public Library. With some computer help, advice, and a healthy dose of encouragement from Keri Goeltla, I started pounding out chapters.

My wife, a retired elementary-school teacher, with whom I raised five boys, became my encourager and sounding board for ideas. But most importantly, she also became my advisor and spell checker. At about five chapters in, I had the entire plot mapped out in my head, but only a few chapters in the computer. I began questioning, *Should I proceed?* My wife needed special attention, and no one in the family was aware of my endeavor (most still aren't). Writing time became a premium; my motivation to continue was waning and I wrote late in the evenings and very early mornings.

Then it was Christmastime and my son and his family were visiting us from Chicago. I was talking to my precocious ten-year-old granddaughter with high school reading skills about the types of books she enjoys. Mysteries were on her list, so I decided to let her in on my little project, if she would keep it a secret. She agreed. I gave her the first chapter to read and said, "Forget that I'm your grandfather. What do you think?" Her comments about the story were direct and encouraging. So, armed with some special thoughts from a very special person, I pressed on.

I continued to struggle with my minimal computer skills. About halfway into the book, however, I decided to enlist the help of two individuals: my wife's special longtime teacher friend, Lynn Koehler, who did some early proofreading and grammar checking, and my niece, Lesley Whitehouse, a retired nurse who did fact-checking on the medical statements and content. Both were so helpful and generous with their time and encouraging remarks. Their input not only motivated me but added substance to my story.

As the book's chapters built up, I turned to my Apple computer guru son Bradley. On one of his visits from New York City, I showed him my book draft, what I had banged out on my old Apple. After some amusing laughter at my expense, he taught me some of the basic rudiments on formatting for a book. Wow! That became a turning point for me: spell check, grammar, layout tools. I was now writing more aggressively and producing chapters weekly. At this point Bradley became only the fifth person aware that I was writing this book and only the second in our family.

With my manuscript almost complete, I decided to investigate how to publish—back to the library, my special gal. Armed with a list of publishers, I started to do my due diligence. Being a realist, I zeroed in on some smaller publishing houses in the Twin Cities area. I wanted to work with a team in person and have eye-to-eye discussions about my book's content and marketing strategies. This interaction with people charged my battery. It gave me more than a short-term energy boost—it reignited my goal and quest to get to the finish line.

I have been very pleased by the professionalism exemplified by the staff of the publisher I chose, and I'm thankful that they assigned John Schaidler to edit my manuscript. I am more a technical person. I look and describe things in a more concise and succinct manner due to my history as a technical writer in my early days with 3M. John's input was invaluable in helping me punch up and improve my book immensely.

There were others along the way, in this two-year quest, who contributed. If they buy the book, they'll know who they are. Open and free conversation leads the way to thoughts, ideas, and perspectives. Thank you all for your comments and input. I hope you enjoyed my story.

ABOUT THE AUTHOR

BERNARD RAPPA WAS BORN IN Rockford, Illinois, the son of second-generation Italian and Swedish immigrants. He grew up in an environment of love, Christian values, and strong work ethic. Rappa attended North Park College in Chicago, the University of Minnesota, and Cardinal Stritch University, but his schooling was briefly interrupted when called to serve his country with the United States Army. For almost forty years, Rappa worked for 3M in St. Paul, Minnesota, as a technical engineer, project manager, new business development manager, and an international corporate quality manager.

Rappa has traveled extensively throughout Europe, Latin America, and South America, often with his wife and soulmate of over sixty-one years, Diane. The two share five sons, twelve grandchildren, and one great-granddaughter. He drew on his travels and life experiences to write this story, his first novel.